PRAISE FOR KENT HARUF

'*Plainsong* is a well-crafted investigation into how disparate voices, each unique and interconnected, can come together in the most unlikely of circumstances . . . Haruf offers a fresh approach by creating layers which intensify and deepen as the novel progresses, alternating between each character's life at every chapter' *Observer*

'It's written in a flat, palms-on-the-table style, which effectively suppresses what could have been sentimental in the story. Plenty to gulp over still, though. A first-rate, old-fashioned read' *Time Out*

'Plainsong is the unisonous austere chant of a church service, and the hundreds of thousands of fans of this book have been nothing less than devotional in their praise of Kent Haruf' *Times Literary Supplement*

'Like all the best novels, *Plainsong* takes you into a world that is at once real and vividly imagined. Here is a poetry of landscape, a tender and passionate evocation of ordinary people in majestic country. It is a novel of the young and old, of the bonds that bind us to each other, and written with a kind of compassion that makes it ultimately powerfully uplifting' Niall Williams

'From simple strands of language and cuttings of talk, from the look of the high Colorado plains east of Denver almost to the place where Nebraska and Kansas meet, Haruf has made a novel so foursquare, so delicate and lovely, that it has the power to exalt the reader' *New York Times*

'The emotional register of *Plainsong*, though kept in check by understatement and a stoic approach to the vicissitudes of life, is powerful. And Haruf works a quiet magic in the way he fits his characters' lives in with the landscape and weather that surround them'   *Washington Post Book World*

'True to the country he writes about, Haruf builds his characters out of small gestures and daily rituals, not dialogue. Theirs is a deep language, like the rumble before an earthquake'
                    L.A. Times

'Satisfying and warm, *Plainsong* is as purehearted a novel as they come'   *Austin Chronicle*

'[Haruf] writes with a plainspoken, hardscrabble edge that saves his story from sentimentality. It's a noun-and-verb-only style that's part Russell Banks, part Raymond Carver, but altogether his own . . . Kent Haruf's splendid *Plainsong* succeeds beautifully. Elegant in its simplicity, elemental in its power, it arouses deep and hard-earned emotions'   *Newsday*

'A lovely read, illuminated by sparks of spare beauty'   *Time*

'With deftness and precision, *Plainsong* orchestrates the overlapping lives of these and other characters . . . Haruf's descriptions are sublime in their exacting simplicity . . . A beautiful, contemporary novel that reads very much like a story from another time'   *Philadelphia Enquirer*

Plainsong

KENT HARUF is the author of four novels (including, most recently, *Eventide*) and lives with his wife, Cathy, in the mountains in Colorado.

KENT HARUF

Plainsong

PICADOR

First published 1999 by Alfred A. Knopf Inc., New York

First published in Great Britain in paperback 1999 by Picador

This edition published 2001 by Picador
an imprint of Pan Macmillan Ltd
Pan Macmillan, 20 New Wharf Road, London N1 9RR
Basingstoke and Oxford
Associated companies throughout the world
www.panmacmillan.com

ISBN-13: 978-0-330-39314-0
ISBN-10: 0-330-39314-6

Sections of this book first appeared, in different form,
in *Crab Orchard Review* and *Grand Street*.

15 17 19 18 16 14

A CIP catalogue record for this book is available from
the British Library.

Printed and bound in Great Britain by
Mackays of Chatham plc, Chatham, Kent

For Cathy

And in memory of

Louis and Eleanor Haruf

The author wishes to acknowledge the generous support
and encouragement of:

Mark Haruf, Verne Haruf, Edith and Bryan Russell,
Sorel Haruf, Whitney Haruf, Chaney Haruf,
Rodney and Gloria Jones, Richard Peterson, Laura Hendrie,
John Walker, Jon Tribble, Ken Keith, Peter Matson,
Gary Fisketjon, Dr. Tom Parks, Dr. Douglas Gates,
Greg Schwipps, Alissa Cayton, Sue Howell,
Karen Greenberg, Southern Illinois University,
the Illinois Arts Council,
and most particularly, Cathy Haruf.

Plainsong—the unisonous vocal music used in the Christian church from the earliest times; any simple and unadorned melody or air

Plainsong

Guthrie.

Here was this man Tom Guthrie in Holt standing at the back window in the kitchen of his house smoking cigarettes and looking out over the back lot where the sun was just coming up. When the sun reached the top of the windmill, for a while he watched what it was doing, that increased reddening of sunrise along the steel blades and the tail vane above the wooden platform. After a time he put out the cigarette and went upstairs and walked past the closed door behind which she lay in bed in the darkened guest room sleeping or not and went down the hall to the glassy room over the kitchen where the two boys were.

The room was an old sleeping porch with uncurtained windows on three sides, airy-looking and open, with a pinewood floor. Across the way they were still asleep, together in the same bed under the north windows, cuddled up, although it was still early fall and not yet cold. They had been sleeping in the same bed for the past month and now the older boy had one hand stretched above his brother's head as if he hoped to shove something away and thereby save them both. They were nine and ten, with dark brown hair and unmarked faces, and cheeks that were still as pure and dear as a girl's.

Outside the house the wind came up suddenly out of the west and the tail vane turned with it and the blades of the windmill spun in a red whir, then the wind died down and the blades slowed and stopped.

You boys better come on, Guthrie said.

He watched their faces, standing at the foot of the bed in his bathrobe. A tall man with thinning black hair, wearing glasses. The older boy drew back his hand and they settled deeper under the cover. One of them sighed comfortably.

Ike.

What?

Come on now.

We are.

You too, Bobby.

He looked out the window. The sun was higher, the light beginning to slide down the ladder of the windmill, brightening it, making rungs of rose-gold.

When he turned again to the bed he saw by the change in their faces that they were awake now. He went out into the hall again past the closed door and on into the bathroom and shaved and rinsed his face and went back to the bedroom at the front of the house whose high windows overlooked Railroad Street and brought out shirt and pants from the closet and laid them out on the bed and took off his robe and got dressed. When he returned to the hallway he could hear them talking in their room, their voices thin and clear, already discussing something, first one then the other, intermittent, the early morning matter-of-fact voices of little boys out of the presence of adults. He went downstairs.

Ten minutes later when they entered the kitchen he was standing at the gas stove stirring eggs in a black cast-iron skillet. He turned to look at them. They sat down at the wood table by the window.

Didn't you boys hear the train this morning?

Yes, Ike said.

You should have gotten up then.

Well, Bobby said. We were tired.

That's because you don't go to bed at night.

We go to bed.

But you don't go to sleep. I can hear you back there talking and fooling around.

They watched their father out of identical blue eyes. Though there was a year between them they might have been twins. They'd put on blue jeans and flannel shirts and their dark hair was uncombed and fallen identically over their unmarked foreheads. They sat waiting for breakfast and appeared to be only half awake.

Guthrie brought two thick crockery plates of steaming eggs and buttered toast to the table and set them down and the boys spread jelly on the toast and began to eat at once, automatically, chewing, leaning forward over their plates. He carried two glasses of milk to the table.

He stood over the table watching them eat. I have to go to school early this morning, he said. I'll be leaving in a minute.

Aren't you going to eat breakfast with us? Ike said. He stopped chewing momentarily and looked up.

I can't this morning. He recrossed the room and set the skillet in the sink and ran water into it.

Why do you have to go to school so early?

I have to see Lloyd Crowder about somebody.

Who is it?

A boy in American history.

What'd he do? Bobby said. Look off somebody's paper?

Not yet. I don't doubt that'll be next, the way he's going.

Ike picked at something in his eggs and put it at the rim of his plate. He looked up again. But Dad, he said.

What.

Isn't Mother coming down today either?

I don't know, Guthrie said. I can't say what she'll do. But you shouldn't worry. Try not to. It'll be all right. It doesn't have anything to do with you.

He looked at them closely. They had stopped eating altogether and were staring out the window toward the barn and corral where the two horses were.

You better go on, he said. By the time you get done with your papers you'll be late for school.

He went upstairs once more. In the bedroom he removed a sweater from the chest of drawers and put it on and went down the hall and stopped in front of the closed door. He stood listening but there was no sound from inside. When he stepped into the room it was almost dark, with a feeling of being hushed and forbidding as in the sanctuary of an empty church after the funeral of a woman who had died too soon, a sudden impression of static air and unnatural quiet. The shades on the two windows were drawn down completely to the sill. He stood looking at her. Ella. Who lay in the bed with her eyes closed. He could just make out her face in the halflight, her face as pale as schoolhouse chalk and her fair hair massed and untended, fallen over her cheeks and thin neck, hiding that much of her. Looking at her, he couldn't say if she was asleep or not, but he believed she was not. He believed she was only waiting to hear what he had come in for, and then for him to leave.

Do you want anything? he said.

She didn't bother to open her eyes. He waited. He looked around the room. She had not yet changed the chrysanthemums in the vase on the chest of drawers and there was an odor rising from the stale water in the vase. He wondered that she didn't smell it. What was she thinking about.

Then I'll see you tonight, he said.

He waited. There was still no movement.

All right, he said. He stepped back into the hall and pulled the door shut and went on down the stairs.

As soon as he was gone she turned in the bed and looked

toward the door. Her eyes were intense, wide-awake, outsized. After a moment she turned again in the bed and studied the two thin pencils of light shining in at the edge of the window shade. There were fine dust motes swimming in the dimly lighted air like tiny creatures underwater, but in a moment she closed her eyes again. She folded her arm across her face and lay unmoving as though asleep.

Downstairs, passing through the house, Guthrie could hear the two boys talking in the kitchen, their voices clear, high-pitched, animated again. He stopped for a minute to listen. Something to do with school. Some boy saying this and this too and another one, the other boy, saying it wasn't any of that either because he knew better, on the gravel playground out back of school. He went outside across the porch and across the drive toward the pickup. A faded red Dodge with a deep dent in the left rear fender. The weather was clear, the day was bright and still early and the air felt fresh and sharp, and Guthrie had a brief feeling of uplift and hopefulness. He took a cigarette from his pocket and lit it and stood for a moment looking at the silver poplar tree. Then he got into the pickup and cranked it and drove out of the drive onto Railroad Street and headed up the five or six blocks toward Main. Behind him the pickup lifted a powdery plume from the road and the suspended dust shone like bright flecks of gold in the sun.

Victoria Roubideaux.

Even before she was awake she felt it rising in her chest and throat. Then she rose rapidly from bed in the white underpants and the outsized tee-shirt she wore at night and rushed into the bathroom where she crouched on the tile floor, holding her streaming hair away from her face and mouth with one hand and gripping the rim of the bowl with the other while she retched and gagged. Her body was wracked by spasms. Afterward a spit-string swung from her lip, stretched, elongated, then broke off. She felt weak and empty. Her throat burned, her chest hurt. Her brown face was unnaturally pale now, sallow and hollow beneath the high cheekbones. Her dark eyes looked larger and darker than ordinary, and on her forehead was a fine film of clammy sweat. She stayed kneeling, waiting for the gagging and paroxysms to pass.

A woman appeared in the doorway. She at once flipped the light on, filling the room with harsh yellow light. What's all this? Victoria, what's the matter with you?

Nothing, Mama.

Something is. You think I don't hear you in here?

Go back to bed, Mama.

Don't lie to me. You've been drinking, haven't you.

No.

Don't lie to me.

I'm not.

What is it then?

The girl rose from the floor. They looked at each other. The woman was thin, in her late forties, haggard of face, washed-out, still tired though she'd just risen from sleep, wearing a stained blue satin robe she clutched together over her sagging chest. Her hair had been dyed, but not recently; her hair was maroon, like no human natural color anywhere, the white roots showing at the temples and above her forehead.

The girl moved to the sink and ran water onto a washcloth and held the cloth to her face. The water dripped into the front of her thin shirt.

The woman watched her and removed cigarettes from her robe pocket and took out a lighter and lit the cigarette and stood in the door smoking. She scratched one naked ankle with the toes of the other foot.

Mama, do you have to smoke in here now?

I'm here, aren't I? This is my house.

Please, Mama.

Then she was sick again. She could feel it rising. She was kneeling again at the bowl, gagging, her shoulders and chest wrung by dry spasms. Her dark hair was caught as before in one hand, automatically.

The woman stood over her, smoking, surveying her. Finally the girl was finished. She stood up and returned to the sink.

You know what I think, little miss? the woman said.

The girl applied the wet washcloth to her face once more.

I think you got yourself knocked up. I think you got a baby in you and it's making you puking sick.

The girl held the cloth to her face and looked at her mother in the mirror.

Didn't you.

Mama.

That's it, isn't it.

Mama, don't.

Well you stupid little slut.

I'm not a slut. Don't call me that.

What do you want me to call it? That's the name for what you done. I told you before. And now look at you. Look here at what's happened. I told you, didn't I.

You told me a lot of things, Mama.

You better not get smart with me.

The girl's eyes filled. Help me, Mama. I need you to help me.

It's too late for that, the woman said. You got yourself into this, you can just get out of it. Your father wanted me to hold his head too. All them mornings when he'd come home feeling sick and sorry for himself. I won't hold yours too.

Mama, please.

And you can just leave this house. Like he did finally. You're so smart, you know everything. I won't have you in here like this.

You don't mean that.

See if I don't. You just try me, miss.

In the back bedroom she dressed for school in a short skirt and white tee-shirt and put on a jeans jacket, the same clothes she'd worn the day before, and looped a red shiny purse on a long strap over her shoulder. She left the house without eating anything.

She walked to school in a kind of dream, walking out of the meager street onto the pavement of Main, across the tracks and then up onto the wide vacant early-morning sidewalks past the display windows of the stores, watching her reflection, how she walked and carried her body, and as yet she could see no change. There was nothing she could discern outwardly. She went on in her skirt and jacket with the red purse swinging at her hip.

Ike and Bobby.

They mounted their bikes and rode out of the drive onto the loose gravel on Railroad Street and east toward town. The air was still cool, with the smells of horse manure and trees and dry weeds and dirt in the atmosphere and something else they couldn't name. Above them a pair of magpies swung on a cottonwood branch screaming, and then one of the birds flew off into the trees beyond Mrs. Frank's house and the other cried four times, harsh and rapid, before it too flapped away.

They rode along the gravel road and passed the old vacated light plant, its high windows boarded over, and turned onto the pavement at Main Street and then bounced over the railroad tracks onto the cobblestone platform at the depot. It was a single-story redbrick building with a green tile roof. Inside was a dim waiting room smelling of dust and being closed up, and three or four highbacked pewlike wood benches set in rows facing the train tracks and a ticket office with a single window set behind black grillwork. An old green milk wagon on iron wheels stood outside on the cobblestones beside the wall. The wagon was never used anymore. But Ralph Black, the depot agent, admired the way it looked on the platform and he left it there. He didn't have a lot to do. The passenger trains only stopped in Holt for five minutes, coming and going, long enough to allow the two or three passengers to board or get off and for the man in the baggage car to drop the *Denver News* onto the platform beside the tracks. The papers were there now, bound in twine in a single stack. The bottom papers had torn on the rough cobblestones.

The two boys leaned their bikes against the milk wagon, and with a jackknife Ike cut the twine. Then they knelt and counted the stack of papers into two piles and began to roll and rubber-band them.

When they were almost finished Ralph Black walked out of the ticket office and stood over the boys, his long shadow hanging across them, obscuring them while he watched them work. He was a gaunt old man with a paunch, he was chewing a cigar.

How come you little boys are late this morning? he said. The papers been there almost an hour.

We aren't little boys, Bobby said.

Ralph laughed. Maybe not, he said. But you're still late.

They didn't say anything.

Ain't you, Ralph said. I said, Ain't you still late.

What's it to you? Ike said.

What's that?

I said . . . He didn't finish but went on rolling papers, kneeling on the cobbles beside his brother.

That's right, Ralph Black said. You don't want to say something like that again. Or somebody might just paddle your little behind. How would you like me to do that for you? I will, by God.

He stared down at the tops of their heads. They refused to say anything or even to acknowledge him, so he looked out along the train tracks and spat brown tobacco over their heads toward the rails.

And stop leaning those bikes against that wagon there. I told you that before, he said. Next time I'll call your dad.

The boys finished rolling the papers and stood up to put them into the canvas bags on their bikes. Ralph Black watched them with satisfaction, then spat again onto the nearest track and returned to his office. When the door was shut Bobby said, He never told us that before.

He's just an old dogfart, Ike said. He never told us anything before. Let's go.

They separated and began their individual halves of the route. Between them they had the entire town. Bobby took the older, more established part of Holt, the south side where the wide flat streets were lined with elm trees and locust and hackberry and evergreen, where the comfortable two-story houses were set back in their own spaces of lawn and where behind them the car garages opened out onto the graveled alleys, while Ike, for his part, took the three blocks of Main Street on both sides, the stores and the dark apartments over the stores, and also the north side of town across the railroad tracks, where the houses were smaller with frequent vacant lots in between, where the houses were painted blue or yellow or pale green and might have chickens in the back lots in wire pens and here and there dogs on chains and also car bodies rusting among the cheetweed and redroot under the low-hanging mulberry trees.

To deliver the *Denver News* took about an hour. Then they met again at the corner of Main and Railroad and rode home, pedaling over the washboards in the gravel. They passed the line of lilac bushes in the side yard of Mrs. Frank's house, the fragrant blooms long dead now and dry and the heart-shaped leaves dusty with the traffic, and rode past the narrow pasture, the tree house in the silver poplar in the corner, and turned in onto the drive at home and left their bikes beside the house.

Upstairs in the bathroom they combed their hair wet, drawing it up into waves and fluffing it with their cupped hands so it stood up stiffly over their foreheads. Water trickled down their cheeks and dribbled behind their ears. They toweled off and went out into the hallway and stood hesitant before the door until Ike turned the knob and then they entered the hushed half-lit room.

She lay in the guest bed on her back now with her arm still folded across her face like someone in great distress. A thin woman, caught as though in some inescapable thought or attitude, motionless, almost as if she were not even breathing. They stopped inside the door. There were the brief lines of light at the edges of the drawn window shades and from across the room they could smell the dead flowers in the vase on the tall chest of drawers.

Yes? she said. She did not stir or move. Her voice was nearly a whisper.

Mother?

Yes.

Are you all right?

You can come over here, she said.

They approached the bed. She removed her arm from over her face and looked at them, one boy then the other. In the dim light their wet hair appeared very dark and their blue eyes were almost black. They stood beside the bed looking at her.

Do you feel any better? Ike said.

Do you feel like getting up? said Bobby.

Her eyes looked glassy, as if she were suffering from fever. Are you ready for school now? she said.

Yes.

What time is it?

They looked at the clock on the dresser. Quarter of eight, Ike said.

You better go. You don't want to be late. She smiled a little and reached a hand toward them. Will you each give me a kiss first?

They leaned forward and kissed her on the cheek, one after

the other, the quick embarrassed kisses of little boys. Her cheek felt cool and she smelled like herself. She took up their hands and held them for a moment against her cool cheeks while she looked at their faces and their dark wet hair. They could just bear to glance at her eyes. They stood waiting uncomfortably, leaning over the bed. At last she released their hands and they stood up. You'd better go on, she said.

Goodbye, Mother, Ike said.

I hope you get better, Bobby said.

They went out of the room and closed the door. Outside the house in the bright sunlight again they crossed the drive and went across Railroad Street and walked down in the path through the ditch weeds and across the railroad tracks and through the old park toward school. When they arrived at the playground they separated to join their own friends and stood talking with the other boys in their own grades until the first bell rang and called them into class.

Guthrie.

In the high school office Judy, the secretary, stood over a desk talking on the telephone and making notes on a pink pad of paper. The short skirt of her dress was stretched tight over her hips and she was wearing hose and spike-heeled shoes. Guthrie stood behind the front counter watching her. After a while she looked up at him and for his benefit rolled her eyes at what she was hearing.

I understand that, she said into the phone. No. I will too tell him. I know what you're saying. She put the phone back roughly in its cradle.

Who was that? Guthrie said.

That was a mother. She made another note on the pad of paper.

What'd she want?

About the school play last night.

What about it?

Didn't you see it?

No.

You ought to. It's pretty good.

What's the matter with it? Guthrie said.

Oh, there's this place where Lindy Rayburn walks out in a

black slip and sings a solo by herself. And this person on the telephone doesn't happen to think a seventeen-year-old girl ought to be doing that kind of thing in public. Not in a public high school.

Maybe I should go see it, Guthrie said.

Oh, she had everything covered. You couldn't see anything that counts.

What'd she want you to do about it?

Not me. She wanted to talk to Mr. Crowder. But he isn't available.

Where is he? I came in early to see him.

Oh, he's here. But he's across the hall. She nodded in the direction of the rest rooms.

I'll wait for him in his office, Guthrie said.

I would, she said.

He went into the office and sat down facing the principal's desk. Photographs of Lloyd Crowder's wife and his three children in hinged brass picture frames stood on the desk and on the wall behind it was a photograph of him kneeling in front of Douglas firs holding up the antlered head of a mule deer. Against the adjacent wall were gray filing cabinets. A large school-district calendar hung over them. Guthrie sat looking at the photograph of the deer. Its eyes were half-open, as though it were only sleepy.

After ten minutes Lloyd Crowder entered the office and sat down heavily in the swivel chair behind the desk. He was a big florid man with wisps of blond hair drawn in exact strands across his pink scalp. He set his hands out in front of him and looked across the desk. So, Tom, he said. What's this about?

You said you wanted to see me.

That's right. I did. He began to consult a list of names on a paper on his desktop. Under the light his scalp shone like water. How's the boys? he said.

They're fine.

And Ella?

Fine.

The principal raised the sheet of paper. Here it is. Russell Beckman. According to what I see here you're failing him this first quarter.

That's right.

How come?

Guthrie looked at the principal. Because, he said. He hasn't done the work he's supposed to.

That's not what I mean. I mean how come you're failing him.

Guthrie looked at him.

Because hell, Lloyd Crowder said. Everybody knows Mr. Beckman isn't any kind of student. Unless he gets struck by lightning he never will be. But he's got to have American history to graduate. It's what the state mandates.

Yes.

Plus he's a senior. He don't belong in there with all those juniors. He should of taken it last year. I wonder why he didn't.

I wouldn't have any idea about that.

Yes, well, the principal said.

The two men studied each other.

Maybe he ought to try for the GED, Guthrie said.

Now, Tom. Right there we got a problem. That kind of thinking, it makes me tired.

The principal leaned heavily forward onto the hams of his forearms.

Look here. I don't believe I'm asking too much. I'm just saying go a little easy on him. Think about what it means. We don't want him back next year. That wouldn't be good for anybody involved. Do you want him back next year?

I don't want him this year.

Nobody wants him this year. None of the teachers want him. But he's here. You see my point. Oh hell, give him a downslip if you want to. Scare the young son. But you don't want to fail him.

Guthrie looked at the framed pictures on the desktop. Did Wright put you up to this?

Wright? the principal said. How come? On account of basketball eligibility?

Guthrie nodded.

Why hell, he's not that good of a player. There's others can bring the ball down. Coach Wright never mentioned a thing about this to me. I'm just saying to you, as someone who has to consider the whole school. You think about it.

Guthrie stood up.

And Tom.

Guthrie waited.

I don't need somebody else to put me up to something. I can still do my own thinking. You try and remember that.

Then you better tell him to do the work he's supposed to do, Guthrie said.

He left the office. His classroom was at the far end of the building and he went down the wide hallway that was lined with student lockers that had sheets of colored paper taped to the metal doors with names and slogans written across them, and above the lockers attached to the walls were long paper banners bearing extravagant claims about the athletic teams. This early in the morning the tiled floors were still shiny.

He entered the classroom and sat down at his desk and took out the blue-backed lesson book, reading through the notes he'd made for the day. Then he removed an examination ditto from a desk drawer and went back out into the hallway, carrying the ditto.

When he entered the teacher's lounge Maggie Jones was using the copy machine. She turned and looked at him. He sat down at the table in the center of the room and lit a cigarette. She stood at the counter watching him.

I thought you quit that, she said.

I did.

How come you started again? You were doing okay.

He shrugged. Things change.

What's wrong? she said. You don't look good. You look like hell.

Thanks. You about done with that?

I mean it, she said. You look like you haven't even slept.

He pulled an ashtray closer, tapped the cigarette into it and looked at her. She turned back to the machine. He watched her working at the counter, her hand and arm turning rapidly with the crank of the machine, her hips moving at the same time and her skirt jumping and swaying. A tall healthy dark-haired woman, she was dressed in a black skirt and white blouse and wore considerable silver jewelry. Presently she stopped cranking the machine and put in another master.

What brings you here so early? she said.

Crowder wanted to talk to me.

What about?

Russell Beckman.

That little shit. What'd he do now?

Nothing. But he's going to if he wants to get out of American history.

Good luck, she said. She cranked the machine once and looked at the paper. Is that all that's bothering you?

Nothing's bothering me.

Like hell it isn't. I can see something is. She looked into his face, and he looked back without expression and sat smoking. Is it at home? she said.

He didn't answer but shrugged again and smoked.

Then the door opened and a muscular little man in a short-sleeve white shirt came in. Irving Curtis, who taught business. Morning one and all, he said.

He moved up beside Maggie Jones and put his arm around her waist. The top of his head came up to her eyes. He stood up on his toes and whispered something into her ear. Then he squeezed her hard, drawing her toward him. She removed his hand.

Don't be such an ass, she said. It's too early in the morning. It's only a joke.

And I'm just telling you.

Oh now, he said. He sat down at the table across from Guthrie and lit a cigarette with a silver lighter and snapped it shut and then played with the lighter on the tabletop. What's the good word? he said.

There isn't any, said Guthrie.

What's wrong with everybody? Irving Curtis said. Jesus. It's the middle of the week. I come in here feeling good and now look what you've done to me. I'm depressed already and it's not even eight o'clock in the morning.

You could shoot yourself, Guthrie said.

Ho, Curtis said. He laughed. That's better. That's funny.

They sat and smoked. Maggie Jones stopped the machine and gathered up her papers. Your turn, she said to Guthrie, and left the room.

Bye-bye, Irving Curtis said.

Guthrie rose and fed the ditto master into the slot on the drum and closed it and cranked the machine once and once more to see how the exam looked.

No shit, though, Curtis said. Just once I'd like to get her in a dark room.

You want to leave her alone, Guthrie said.

No. I mean, think about it.

Guthrie cranked the machine and turned the damp exams out into the tray. There was the sharp smell of spirits.

I told you what Gary Rawlson said about her.

You told me, Guthrie said.

Do you believe it?

No. And neither does Rawlson when he hasn't been drinking. When it's in the daylight.

Victoria Roubideaux.

At noon she came out of the noise and crush at school and walked over to the highway and then up a block to the Gas and Go. In her purse she had three dollars and some change and she wanted to think she could eat something now and keep it down. Thinking anyway she ought to try.

Approaching the store she passed two high school boys leaning together at the gas pumps, running fuel into an old blue Ford Mustang. They watched her walk across the blacktop in her short skirt. Once she glanced up at them. Hey, one of them called. Vicky. How you doing? She looked away and he said something she was unable to hear but it made the other boy laugh. She went on.

When she entered the store a group of high school kids was lined up at the counter, talking and waiting to pay for the cold meat sandwiches they'd taken from the refrigerated case and also the bags of chips and the plastic cups of pop. She walked back through the aisles, glancing at the labeled cans and the bright packages on the shelves. Nothing looked good now. She picked up a can of Vienna sausages and examined it and read the label and put it back thinking how slick they were, how they dripped and ran when you lifted them out. She moved

over to the popcorn case. At least that would be a salty taste.
She filled a bag of popcorn and then chose a can of pop from
the cooler. She carried these to the front and set them on the
counter next to the register.

Alice rang them up, a hard-looking thin woman with a
black mole on her cheek. Dollar twelve, she said. Her voice
sounded harsh. She watched the girl raise the purse on its strap
and open it.

You're looking kind of puny today. You okay, hon?

I'm just tired, the girl said, and set the money on the
counter.

You kids. You need to go to bed at night. She scooped the
money up and sorted it into the drawer. And I mean in your
own bed.

I do, the girl said.

Sure, Alice said. I know how that is.

The girl moved to the front window of the store past the
double glass doors and stood at the magazine rack, reading
about three girls her age who had trouble in California, while
she ate the popcorn one kernel at a time and sipped at the can
of pop. More kids came in and bought drinks during the noon
hour and went out, calling back and forth, and once a couple of
sophomores began to shove each other in the aisle stacked with
cans of motor oil and pork-and-beans until Alice said, You boys
can knock that off anytime.

A senior came in and paid for gas. He was a tall blond boy
with sunglasses pushed up on the top of his head. She knew
him from first-year biology. On his way out he stopped in the
doorway, leaning toward her, holding the door open with his
hip. Roubideaux, he said.

She looked at him.

Want a ride?

No.

Just back to school.

No thank you.

Why not?

I don't want to.

Hell then. You had your chance.

He stepped out and the door drew slowly shut behind him. She watched through the plate glass window over the top of the magazine rack as he got into his red car, revved it up and turned out onto the highway, making a little squeal when he shifted gears. Before the hour was up she went back to school.

After classes that day she departed the building with the other students, descending the front steps in that daily afternoon noise and exhilaration of release. She was alone again, taking the reverse of her morning's path to school. Turning north up Main, she walked by the boxy houses and under the tall legs of the old water tower, passed a few scattered businesses and along the three blocks of downtown where the stores were crowded together behind their false fronts, starting with the bank behind its tinted windows and the post office beneath its flag.

When she arrived at the Holt Café on the corner of Second and Main she stepped into the long fair-sized rectangular room. A pair of old men in adjustable caps sat talking and drinking black coffee from thick mugs at one of the tables, and there was a young woman in a print dress drinking tea in one of the booths along the wall. The girl went back to the kitchen and removed her jacket and hung it on a peg in the closet and draped the purse over it and then pulled on a long apron over her shirt and short skirt. The cook, standing at the grill looking at her, was a short heavy man with eyes hooded in his red face. The apron was stained over his thick middle and again at the skirts on both sides where he'd gathered up the apron to wipe his hands.

I'm going to want me some of them pots pretty quick, he told her. Quick's you can get em washed.

She immediately began to clear the two gray industrial

sinks, lifting out the stacked dirty pots and pans and setting them on the counters.

And that fry basket. I put that in there for you too. It needs cleaning.

You'll have it in a minute, she said.

She ran water in the sink and dipped in powdered soap from a box whose top was cut off. Steam began to rise from the swirling suds.

I didn't see Janine, the girl said.

Oh, she's here someplace. On the phone probably. Out in the office.

The girl stood over the sink working in the hot soapy water, her hands in rubber gloves. She began to scour the pots left over from the lunch trade. She came in every weekday after school and washed the pots the morning cook had used and also the plates and cups and silverware and platters from the noon hour. The old leather-faced man who came in to wash the breakfast dishes quit at nine. There were always high stacks waiting for her in the sinks and on the counters. She worked through the afternoon until seven, through supper, and had everything clean and finished to that point, when she'd take a plate of food out into the café and sit at the end of the counter talking to Janine or one of the waitresses and afterward she would go home.

Now, presently, Janine came into the kitchen in a brown pinafore and a white blouse and looked sharply all around and moved up beside the girl and put her arm around her waist.

Sugar honey. How's my girl today?

Okay.

The short blocky woman drew back to look at her. Well, you don't sound okay. What's wrong here?

Nothing.

She leaned close. Is it that time of month?

No.

Well, you're not sick, are you?

The girl shook her head.

You take it easy anyhow. You just sit and rest when you need to. Rodney can just wait. She looked at the cook. Is he been bothering you? Goddamn you, Rodney. You bothering this girl?

What are you talking about? the cook said.

No, the girl said. It's not him. It's not anything.

He better not. You better not, Janine said to him. Then she turned back to the girl. I'll can his fat ass. She pinched the girl's hip. And he knows it, she said.

Oh? he said. And where'd you get another cook in this piss-ant place?

Where I got the last one, the woman said and laughed in pleasure. She pinched the girl again. Would you look at his face, she said. I told him something that time.

Ike and Bobby.

When they entered their driveway his pickup wasn't parked in front of the house. They hadn't expected him to be there but sometimes he came home early. They crossed the porch and went inside the house. In the dining room they stopped next to the table and lifted their faces ceilingward, listening.

She's still in bed, Bobby said.

She might of come down and gone back, Ike said.

She might not of too.

She's going to hear you, Ike said.

She can't hear me. She can't hear anything from up there. She's asleep.

You don't know if she is. She could be awake.

Then how come she doesn't come downstairs? Bobby said.

Maybe she already did. Maybe she went back up. She has to eat sometime.

Together they looked at the ceiling as if they could see through it into the dark guest room where the shades were drawn down night and day blocking out the light and all the world, as if they could see her lying motionless in the bed as before, alone and withdrawn into her sad thoughts.

She should eat with us, Bobby said. If she wants to eat she can eat with us next time if she comes downstairs.

They went out to the kitchen and poured milk into two glasses and got down storebought glazed cookies from the cupboard and stood at the counter eating, standing close to each other, not talking but eating quietly, single-mindedly, until they were finished and then they drank off the remaining milk and set the glasses in the sink and went back outside again.

They crossed the drive toward the horse lot and opened the plank gate and passed through. In front of the barn the two horses Elko and Easter, one red, one a dark bay, stood dozing in the warm sun. When the horses heard the boys enter the corral they threw their heads up and watched them warily. Go on, Ike called. Get in the barn. The horses began to step sideways, sidling away. The boys spread out to head them. Here now, Ike said. No you don't. He ran forward.

The horses broke into a high-stepping trot, tossing their heads, and broke past the boys, flowing stiff-legged along the fence past the barn, and loped across the corral to the back fence where they wheeled again and eyed the boys, watching them with great interest. The boys stopped at the end of the barn.

I'll go get them, Ike said.

You want me to get them this time?

No. I will.

Bobby waited opposite where both halves of the door gaped open. Ike turned the horses back toward him, the horses trotting again now, their heads high up, watching the small boy standing wide-legged ahead of them in the corral dirt. Then he began to flap his arms and to shout. Hey! Hey! He looked very small in the open space of the corral. But at the last moment the two horses veered abruptly and clattered over the high doorsill into the barn, one after the other, and settled down immediately in the stalls. The boys followed them.

It was cool and dark inside, smelling of hay and manure. The horses stamped in the stalls, blowing into the empty grain boxes built into the corners of the mangers. The boys poured oats into each box and then brushed and saddled the horses while they ate. Then they buckled on the bridles and mounted up and rode out along the railroad tracks going to the west away from town.

Victoria Roubideaux.

The evening wasn't cold yet when the girl left the café. But the air was turning sharp, with a fall feeling of loneliness coming. Something unaccountable pending in the air.

She went out of the downtown, crossing the tracks and on toward home in the growing dark. The big globes had already shuddered on at the street corners, their blue lights shining now in flat pools on the sidewalks and pavement, and at the front of the houses the porch lights had come on, lifted above the closed doors. She turned into the meager street passing the low houses and arrived at her own. The house appeared unnaturally dark and silent.

She tried the door but it was locked. Mama? she said. She knocked once. Mama?

She stood up on her toes and peered inside through the narrow window set into the door. There was a faint light toward the back of the house. A single unshaded bulb burning in the little hall between the two bedrooms.

Mama. Let me in now. Do you hear me?

She clutched at the doorknob, pulling and twisting it, and she knocked on the window, rattling the hard little pane, but the door stayed locked. Then inside the house the dim hall light went out.

Mama. Don't. Please.

She clung to the door.

What are you doing? I'm sorry, Mama. Please. Can't you hear me?

She rattled the door. She leaned her head against it. The wood felt cold, hard, she felt tired now, all at once worn out. There was something like panic coming.

Mama. Don't do this.

She looked all around. Houses and bare trees. She slid down onto the porch in the cold, lapsing back against the chill boards of the housefront. She seemed to fade away, to drift and wander in a kind of daze of sorrow and disbelief. She sobbed a little. She stared out at the silent trees and the dark street and the houses across the street where people were moving about reasonably in the bright rooms beyond the windows, and she looked up at the movement in the trees when the wind sighed. She sat, staring out, not moving.

Later she came out of that.

Okay, Mama, she said. You don't have to worry. I'm gone.

Slowly a car went by in the street. The people inside looked at her, a man and a woman, their heads turned in her direction.

She pushed up from the porch and pulled her thin jacket tighter around her, over her thin body, her girl's chest, and walked away from the house toward town.

It was full dark now and it had turned off cold. The streets were almost empty. Once a dog came barking out at her from behind a house and she held out her hand to him. The dog stood back and barked, his mouth shutting and opening as though operated by a spring hinge. Here, she said. He came forward suspiciously and sniffed her hand, but as soon as she moved he began to bark again. Behind them in the house the front lights went on. A man appeared in the door and yelled Goddamn it, you get in here! and the dog turned and trotted toward the house and stopped and barked again and went inside.

She moved on. She crossed the tracks once more. Ahead at Second Street the traffic light blinked from red to green to yellow, unmindful of the hour, blinking over the black, almost empty pavement. She passed the shadowy stores and looked in the window of the café where the tables were arranged all quiet and neat in rows and the Pepsi light on the back wall shone on the orderly stacks of clean glasses set out ready on the counter. She walked up Main to the highway and crossed it and passed the Gas and Go, the untended fuel pumps and the bright lights overhead, the attendant inside reading a magazine at the counter, and turned at the corner and came to a frame house three blocks from school where she knew Maggie Jones lived.

She knocked at the door and stood blankly waiting. She was unconscious of any thoughts at all. After some time the yellow porch light came on over her head.

When Maggie Jones opened the door she was in her bathrobe and her black hair was already disheveled from sleep. Her face looked plainer than it had during the day, less dramatic without makeup, a little puffy. The robe she wore wasn't fastened or buttoned but had swung open in front when she had unlocked the door, revealing a soft yellow nightgown.

Victoria? Is that you?

Mrs. Jones. Could I talk to you? the girl said.

Well honey, yes. What's wrong?

The girl entered the house. They passed through the front room and Maggie took up a throw blanket from the couch and draped it around the girl's shoulders. Then for an hour they sat at the table in the kitchen in the silence of night, talking and drinking hot tea, while all around them the neighbors slept and breathed in and out and dreamed in their beds.

The girl sat at the table warming her hands on the tea cup. Gradually she had begun to tell about the boyfriend. About the nights in the backseat of his car parked out on a dirt road five miles north of town where the road stopped at an old fallen-in homestead house, where there was an old gray barn and broken windmill and the few low trees were dark against the dark sky and where the night wind came in through the open car windows smelling of sage and summer grass. And the love then. She told very briefly about that. The scent of him close up, his aftershave, the feel of his hands and the urgency of what they did, then the quiet talking for a little while afterward sometimes. And always afterward, the ride home.

Yes, Maggie said. But who was he?

A boy.

Of course, honey. But who exactly?

I don't want to say, the girl said. He's not going to want it anyhow. He won't claim it. He's not that kind.

What do you mean?

He's not the fathering kind.

But he ought to at least take some responsibility, Maggie said.

He's from another town, the girl said. I don't think you would know him, Mrs. Jones. He's older. He's a boy out of school.

How did you meet him?

The girl looked around the clean room. Dishes were set to dry in the draining rack on the counter, and there was an assemblage of white enameled cannisters ranged in a neat row under the shining cupboards. She drew up the blanket about her shoulders.

We met at a dance last summer, she said. I was sitting by the door and he came up and asked me to dance. He was good-looking too. When he came up to me I told him, I don't even know you. He said, What's there to know? Well, who are you? I said. What does that matter? he said. That don't matter. I'm just somebody that's requesting you to step out on the floor here and take a dance. He talked that way sometimes. So I told him, All right then. Let's see if you can dance, whoever you are since you won't tell me your name. I stood up and he took my hand and led me out on the floor. He was even taller than I thought he was. That's when it started. That's how.

Because he was a good dancer, Maggie said.

Yes. But you don't understand, the girl said. He was nice. He was nice to me. He would tell me things.

Would he?

Yes. He told me things.

Like what for instance?

Like once he said I had beautiful eyes. He said my eyes were like black diamonds lit up on a starry night.

They are, honey.

But nobody ever told me.

No, Maggie said. They never do. She looked out through the doorway into the other room. She lifted her tea cup and drank from it and set it down. Go on, she said. Do you want to tell the rest?

After that I began to meet him in the park, the girl said. That's where he'd pick me up. Across from the grain elevators. I'd get in his car and we'd go over to Shattuck's on the highway and get something to eat, a hamburger or something, and then we'd drive around out in the country for an hour with the windows rolled down and we'd talk and he'd say funny things and the radio would be tuned in to Denver, and all the time the night air would be coming in. And afterward, after a while, we'd always drive to that old homestead place and stop. He said it belonged to us.

But he never came to your house to pick you up?

No.

Didn't you want him to?

The girl shook her head. Not with Mama there. I told him not to.

I see, Maggie said. Go on.

There's not much more to tell, the girl said. After school started at the end of August we still went out a couple times more. But something happened. I don't know what. He didn't say anything. He didn't give me any warning. He just stopped picking me up. One day he didn't come for me anymore.

You don't know why?

No.

Do you know where he is now?

Not for sure, the girl said. He was talking about going to Denver. He knew somebody in Denver.

Maggie Jones studied her for a time. The girl looked tired and sad, the blanket wrapped about her shoulders as though she were some survivor of a train wreck or flood, the sad remnant from some disaster that had passed through and done its damage and gone on. Maggie stood up and collected their cups and emptied the remains of tea into the kitchen sink. She stood at the counter looking at the girl.

But honey, she said, talking a little heatedly now. For God's sake. Did you not know any better?

About what?

Well, did you not use any protection at all?

Yes, the girl said. He did. But it broke on him a couple of times. At least he said it did. He told me that. Afterward when I got home I used hot salt water. But it didn't do any good.

What do you mean you used hot salt water?

I squirted it inside myself.

Didn't that burn?

Yes.

I see. And now you want to keep it.

The girl looked at her quickly, startled.

Because you don't have to, Maggie said. I'll go with you and help you speak to a doctor. If that's what you want.

The girl turned away from the table and faced the window.

The glass reflected the room back on itself. Beyond were the neighbors' dark houses.

I want to keep it, she said, still facing out, speaking softly, steadily.

You're certain?

Yes, she said. She turned back. Her eyes appeared very large and dark, unblinking.

But if you change your mind.

I know.

All right, Maggie said. I think we better get you to bed.

The girl rose from the kitchen table. Thank you, Mrs. Jones, she said. I want to thank you for being so kind to me. I didn't know what else I was going to do.

Maggie Jones put her arms around the girl. Oh, honey, she said. I do feel sorry for you. You're going to have such a hard time. You just don't know it yet.

They stood hugging in the kitchen.

After a while Maggie said, But you know my father's here too. I don't know how he's going to understand this. He's an old man. But you're welcome to stay here. We'll just have to see.

They left the kitchen. She found the girl a long flannel nightgown and made up a bed in the living room on the couch. The girl lay down.

Good night, Mrs. Jones.

Good night, honey.

The girl settled deeper into the blankets. Maggie went back to her own bedroom and after a while the girl went to sleep.

Then in the night she woke when she heard someone coughing in the next room. She looked around in the unfamiliar darkness. The strange room, the things in it. A clock running somewhere. She sat up. But now she couldn't hear anything else. After a time she lay back down. She was almost asleep again when she heard him get up out of bed and enter the bathroom. She could hear him urinating. The toilet flushed. Afterward he came out and stood in the doorway looking at her. An old man with white hair, wearing baggy striped pajamas. He cleared his throat. He scratched himself along his skinny flank, his pajamas moving. He stood watching her. Then he shuffled back down the hall to bed. Only gradually did she fall back to sleep.

Ike and Bobby.

Saturdays they collected. They rose early and delivered the papers and came back home and went out to the barn where they fed the horses and afterward the mewling moiling cats and the dog and then returned to the house and washed up at the kitchen sink and ate breakfast with their father and then went out again. They made their collections together. It was better that way. They carried a book with tear-off tabs dated for the months and weeks and a canvas bag with a drawstring for the money.

They began on Main Street, collecting at the places of business before they became busy and crowded with the Saturday trade, before the townspeople would come downtown and the farm and ranch people would drive in from the country, buying things for the week and passing the time, neighborly. They started at Nexey's Lumberyard beside the railroad tracks and collected from Don Nexey himself, who was kind to them and had a bald head which shone like sculpted marble under the low tin-shaded lights above the front counter. Then they went next door to Schmidt's Barber Shop and stood their bikes against the brick storefront under the spiraling red and white barber pole.

When they entered the shop Harvey Schmidt was employing scissors on the hair of a man seated in the chair with a thin striped cloth pinned about his neck. There were black curls caught in the folds of the cloth like scraps of sewing. Sitting along the wall were another man and a boy, reading magazines and waiting. They looked up together when the two boys came in. The boys closed the door and stood just inside the room.

What do you two want? Harvey Schmidt said. He said this or something like it every Saturday.

Collecting for the paper, Ike said.

Collecting for the paper, he said. I don't think I'm even going to pay you. It's nothing, only bad news. What do you think of that?

They didn't say anything. The boy sitting against the wall was watching them from behind his magazine. He was an older boy from the grade school.

Pay them, Harvey, the man in the barber's chair said. You can afford to stop for a minute.

I'm considering, Harvey said, whether I'm even going to. He combed out the hair above the man's ear, drawing it away from his head, and cut it cleanly with the scissors and then combed it flat again. He looked at the two boys. Who cuts you boys' hair now?

What?

I said, Who cuts your hair?

Mother.

I thought your mother moved out. I heard she moved into that little house over on Chicago Street.

They didn't answer. They were not surprised that he knew. But they didn't want him talking about it in his barbershop on Main Street on Saturday morning.

Isn't that what I heard? he said.

They looked at him and then quickly at the boy sitting against the wall. He was still watching. They kept quiet and stared at the floor, at the clippings of men's hair under the raised leather-backed chair.

Leave them alone, Harvey.

I'm not bothering them. I'm asking them a question.

Leave them alone.

No, Harvey said to the boys again. Think about it. I buy your papers and you get your haircut from me. That's how it works. He pointed at them with the scissors. I buy from you and you buy from me. It's called commerce.

It's two dollars and fifty cents, Ike said.

The barber looked at him steadily for a moment and then turned back to the man's hair. They stayed at the door watching him. When he had finished with the scissors he folded a scrap of tissue paper over the man's collar, over the striped cloth at back, and dabbed rich soap on the man's neck, then he took the razor and shaved the back of his neck, scraping down exactly from the hairline, wiping the lather and hair on the back of his own hand each time, and finished that and removed the scrap of paper and wiped the razor on it and threw the dirty paper scrap away and cleaned his hand, then he wiped the man's neck and head all over with a towel. He shook out pink fragrant oil onto his palm and rubbed his hands together and massaged the oil into the man's scalp, then with a thin comb he parted the man's hair scrupulously on the side and formed a stiff wave of hair between his fingers over the man's high forehead. The man frowned at himself in the mirror and reached up out of the cloth and flattened the fussy wave with his hand.

I'm trying to give you some sex appeal, Harvey said.

I can't use any more, the man said. I've got too much already.

He stood up out of the chair and the barber unpinned the cloth and shook it out onto the tile floor and snapped the cloth, making it pop. The man paid and left a tip on the marble counter below the mirror. Pay these boys, Harvey, he said. They're waiting.

I reckon I'll have to. If I don't, they'll stand there all day. From the cash register he took out three one-dollar bills and held them forward. Well? he said.

Ike advanced and took the money and made change and gave Harvey Schmidt a tab from the collection book.

You're sure that's right, the barber said.

Yes.

What do you say then?

What?

What do you say when a man pays his bill?

Thank you, Ike said.

They went outside. From the sidewalk the two boys looked back into the barbershop through the wide plate glass window. Beyond the gold lettering arced over the window the man with the fresh haircut was putting his jacket on and the boy who had been waiting was climbing into the chair now.

Son of a bitch, Bobby said. Turdhead. But it didn't help. Ike didn't say anything.

They swung onto their bikes and pedaled south half a block to Duckwall's and entered and went back past the display of girls' underwear and folded brassieres without even speculating about them this time and walked past the combs and bobby pins and mirrors and plastic dishes and on past the pillows and curtains and bathtub hoses and knocked on the manager's door. He let them in and paid them quickly, indifferently, without fuss, and they went back outside and rode across Second and collected at Schulte's Department Store on the corner and went on to Bradbury's Bakery and stopped in front of the wedding cakes in the big window.

Ike said, You want to go in here first or upstairs first?

Upstairs, Bobby said. I want to get her over with.

They parked their bikes and opened a door that was set back into the building, and then entered into a small dark foyer. There were black mailboxes attached to the pasteboard inside the door and a brown pair of men's shoes stood on the floor.

They passed through and mounted the stairs and turned at the top down the long dim corridor which led back toward a fire escape above the alley. Behind one of the doors a dog was barking. They stopped at the last door where the morning's *Denver News* still lay on the mat. Ike picked it up and knocked and they stood before the door with their heads bowed, looking at the floorboards, listening. He knocked again. They could hear her now, coming.

Who is it? Her voice sounded as if she hadn't spoken in days. She was coughing.

We want to collect for the paper.

Who?

Paperboy.

She opened the door and peered at them.

You boys come in here.

It's two-fifty, Mrs. Stearns.

Come in here.

She shuffled back and they entered the apartment. The room was too hot. The heat was suffocating and the room crowded with all manner of things. Cardboard boxes. Papers. Piles of clothes. Yellowed stacks of newspaper. Flower pots. An oscillating fan. A box fan. A hat rack. A collection of Sears catalogs. An ironing board opened against one wall with a row of loaded grocery sacks spread across it. In the middle of the room was a television set built into a wood cabinet with another smaller portable television positioned atop the first like a head. Across from the television was a stuffed chair with hand towels laid over the worn arms, and off to the side a faded davenport shoved against the window.

Don't touch anything, she said. Sit over there.

They sat down together on the davenport and watched her limp with two metal canes across the room. There was a pathway between the boxes and the leaning stacks of paper and she followed that to the stuffed chair, then lowered herself painfully and stood the two silver canes between her knees.

She was an old woman in a thin flowered housedress with a long apron covering it. She was humpbacked and required a hearing aid, and her hair was yellow and pulled back into a knot, and her bare arms were spotted and freckled and the skin hung in folds above the elbows. On the back of one of her hands was a jagged purple bruise like a birthmark. When she was seated she took up a cigarette that was already lit and sucked on it and expelled smoke toward the ceiling in a gray stream. She was watching the two boys from behind her glasses. Her mouth was vivid red.

Well, she said. I'm waiting.

They looked at her.

Start talking, she said.

It's two dollars and fifty cents, Mrs. Stearns, Ike said. For the paper.

That's not talk. That's only business. What's the matter with you? What's the weather like?

They turned and looked through the gauzy curtain draped over the window behind them; the curtain smelled heavy of dust. The view was of the back alley. It's sunny, Bobby said.

The wind isn't blowing today, Ike said.

But the leaves are falling.

That's not weather, Ike said.

Bobby turned his head to look at his brother. It has something to do with it.

It isn't it, though.

Never mind, Mrs. Stearns said. She stetched a wrinkled arm along the wide armrest of the chair and tapped her cigarette. What are you doing at school? You go to school, don't you?

Yes.

Well.

They were silent.

You, she said. The oldest one. What's your name?

Ike.

What grade are you in?

Fifth.

Who's your teacher in school?

Miss Keene.

A big tall woman? With a long jaw?

I guess so, Ike said.

Is she a good teacher?

She lets us do seatwork at our own speed. She lets us do work at the board and do writing. Then she copies it and sends it to the other grades in school to look at.

So she is a good teacher, Mrs. Stearns said.

But she told a girl to shut up one time.

Did she? What for?

She didn't want to sit next to somebody.

Who didn't she want to sit next to?

Richard Peterson. She didn't like the way he was smelling.

Well, yes, Mrs. Stearns said. His people have a dairy. Don't they.

He smells like their cow parlor.

So would you if you lived on a dairy and you had to work on it, Mrs. Stearns said.

We have horses, Ike said.

Iva Stearns studied him for a moment. She appeared to be considering this remark. Then she drew on her cigarette and put it out. She turned to Bobby. What about you? she said. Who's your teacher?

Miss Carpenter, Bobby said.

Who?

Miss Carpenter.

I don't know her.

She's got long hair and . . .

And what? Mrs. Stearns said.

She always wears sweaters.

Does she.

Mostly, he said.

What do you know about sweaters?

I don't know, Bobby said. I like them, I guess.

Huh, she said. You're too young to be thinking about women in sweaters. She seemed to laugh a little. It was a strange sound, awkward and tentative, as if she didn't know how. Then suddenly she began to cough. She knew how to do that. Her head was thrown back and her face darkened while her sunken chest shook beneath the apron and housedress. The boys watched her out of the corners of their eyes, fascinated and afraid. She wrapped her hand over her mouth and shut her eyes and coughed. Thin tears squeezed out of her eyes. But at last she stopped, and then she took her glasses off and removed a clot of Kleenex from the pocket of her apron and dabbed her eyes and blew her nose. She put her glasses on once more and looked at the two brothers sitting on the sofa watching her. Don't you boys ever smoke, she said. Her voice was a rasping whisper now.

But you do, Bobby said.

What?

You smoke.

Why do you think I'm telling you? You want to end up like me? An old woman left all by herself staying in rooms that don't even belong to her. Living upstairs over a dirty back alley?

No.

Then don't, she said.

The boys looked at her and then around the room. But don't you have any family, Mrs. Stearns? Ike said. Somebody for you to live with?

No, she said. Not anymore.

What happened to them?

Speak up. I can't hear you.

What happened to your family? Ike said.

They're all gone, she said. Or they're all dead.

They stared at her, waiting for what else she would say. They could not think what she should do, how she might correct the way her life had turned out. But she said no more about it. Instead, she appeared to be looking past them toward the curtained window overlooking the alley. Behind her glasses her eyes were the pale blue of the finest paper and the whites too appeared bluish, with the finest squills of red. It was very quiet in the room. The vivid lipstick was smeared onto her chin from when she had covered her mouth, trying to stifle her cough. They watched her and waited. But she didn't speak.

At last Bobby said, Our mother moved out of the house.

The old woman's eyes turned slowly back now from where they'd been looking. What did you say?

She moved out a few weeks ago, Bobby said. He was speaking softly. She doesn't live with us anymore.

Doesn't she?

No.

Where does she live?

Shut up, Bobby, Ike said. That's nobody's business.

It's all right, Mrs. Stearns said. I'm not going to tell anyone. Who would I tell anyway?

She studied Bobby and then his brother for a long while. They sat on the davenport waiting for her to speak again.

I'm very sorry, she said finally. I'm very sorry to hear about your mother. Here I was, talking about myself. You must be lonely.

They didn't know how to say anything about that.

Well then, she said. You come and see me if you want to. Will you?

They watched her doubtfully, sitting on the sofa, the room silent and the air about them smelling of dust and her cigarette smoke.

Will you? she said again.

At last they nodded.

Very well, she said. Hand me my pocketbook so I can pay you. In there in the other room on the table. One of you can get it and bring it to me. Will you do that for me, please? I won't torment you any longer. Afterward you can go on if you want to.

Victoria Roubideaux.

She was certain of it. In herself, she was.

But Maggie Jones said, It happens. For all kinds of reasons, for reasons you can't anticipate or expect or know about. It could be something else. You just don't know always what's going on. You want to be sure.

Even though she felt in herself that she was sure because for one thing she had never missed before. Until the last months she'd always been as predictable as clockwork, and because for some time she'd been feeling different, not just the way she felt in the morning when she was still at home and could feel it rising even before she was all the way awake, or when her mother came in and made it worse smoking, standing over her in the bathroom watching her, but other times too when she had a private feeling that she didn't know how to talk about or to explain to anyone. And there were still other things, when she was feeling tired and about to cry, having to cry for no good reason. Or her breasts feeling too tender, she'd noticed that sometimes at night when she got into bed, and look at her nipples, how they were now, all swollen dark.

But Maggie Jones said, Still you want to be sure.

And so she, Maggie Jones, had brought the kit home from

the store one evening. They were out in the kitchen. Maggie Jones said, At least try it. Then we'll know for sure.

You think I should?

Yes, I think you should.

How do I? she said.

It says here, you hold the absorbent tip in the urine stream. Hold it under you while you go. Then you wait for five minutes and if both lines turn red in the viewing window, then you are. Here. Take it.

You mean now? the girl said.

Why not?

But Mrs. Jones, I don't know. It seems strange. Deciding about it this way, so definite and you here knowing what I'm doing.

Honey, Maggie Jones said. You've got to wake up. It's time for you to wake up now.

So she took the small flat box with the kit in it and the picture on top of the young honey-haired woman with the look of religious exaltation on her face and the sunshiny garden stretched out behind her, full of what could have been roses though that wasn't clear, took it into the bathroom and locked the door and opened the kit and did what it said, holding it in place under herself while she spread her knees, dribbling a little on her fingers, but she couldn't be bothered by that now, and afterward she set it out on the counter and waited thinking: What if I am? But I might not be, how would that feel after these weeks believing I was, that could be worse, the loss of that after already beginning to wonder about it and plan on it a little, thinking ahead. But what if I am? Then she knew it was time enough, more than the five minutes required, and she looked inside the window and both lines were colored, so she was. She stood up and looked in the mirror at her face. I knew I was anyway, she said to herself, I felt sure, so why should this be any different, that already it would show in my face, it wouldn't, it doesn't, not even in my eyes.

She unlocked the door and took the kit out to the kitchen and showed it to Maggie Jones who looked inside the little window. Well, honey, yes, she said. Now we know. Are you all right?

I think I am, the girl said.

Good. I'll make you an appointment.

You have to do that already?

It's better to go right away. You don't want to be careless. You should've gone before this. Do you have somebody you go to?

No.

When was the last time you saw anyone? For any reason.

I don't know, the girl said. Six or seven years ago. I was sick then.

Who was it?

It was an old man. I don't remember his name.

That would be Dr. Martin.

But Mrs. Jones, the girl said. Isn't there a woman doctor I could go to?

Not here. Not in Holt.

Maybe I could go to another town.

Honey, Maggie Jones said. Victoria. Listen to me. You're here now. This is where you are.

Ike and Bobby.

Midnight. He came back from the bathroom into the glassy room, where his brother slept undisturbed in the single bed against the north wall. Despite windows in three of the walls the room was dark. There was no moon. He looked once toward the west and then stood still, peering out. In the sunken vacant house to the west was a flicker of light. He could see it beyond the back wall of the old man's house next door. It was indistinct, as if seen through haze or fog, but it was there. A steady faint wavering light. Then he could see somebody was in the room too.

He shoved at Bobby.

What? Bobby turned over. Quit it.

Look at this.

Stop poking.

In that old house, Ike said.

What is it?

Bobby kneeled up in his pajamas and peered out the window. At the dead end of Railroad Street the light flickered and waltzed in the small square of the window in the old house.

What about it?

Somebody's over there.

Then somebody, whoever it was, passed by the window again, silhouetted against the dim light.

Ike turned away and began to haul on his clothes.

What are you doing?

I'm going over there. He hiked his pants on over his pajamas and bent to pull on his socks.

Can't you wait? Bobby said. He slid out of bed and dressed rapidly.

They carried their shoes down the hall and stopped at the top landing where they could see into their father's room, dark at the front of the house; through the open door they could hear him, it was like rattling, then a release then a pause, then like rattling again. They went downstairs one after the other, being quiet, and moved to the porch and sat on the steps to put on their shoes. Outside it was fresh, almost cold. The sky was clear and crowded with stars, the stars looked hard and pure. The last clinging leaves at the tops of the cottonwoods washed and fluttered in the soft nightwind.

They moved away from the house out across the drive onto Railroad Street and under the purple-shining streetlamp purring high on its pole and stayed along the edge of the dirt road, moving out of the pool of light into the increasing dark. The old man's house next door was silent and pale, like the gray houses of dreams. They went on along the road edge. Then they could see it. Parked at the side of the road one hundred feet ahead in the ragweed was a dark car.

They stopped abruptly. Ike motioned and they ducked into the railroad ditch and walked quiet in the dry weeds. When they came opposite the car they stopped again. They studied it, the faint starlit glint on its round hood and trunk, the silver hubcaps. They couldn't hear anything, even the wind had stopped. They came up out of the ditch toward the car, feeling exposed now in the open road, but when they rose up and looked past the car windows they found there was nobody and nothing inside, only empty beer cans on the floorboards and a jacket thrown over the backseat. They went on. They rounded to the locust trees in the front yard and stopped, then moved again, stepping into the wild overgrown lot of cheetweed and dead sunflowers, and moved across it and gained the side of the house. They slid along the cold clapboards until they came to the window where the flicker of light spilled out onto the side yard, where it flickered ever more faintly in a kind of illuminated echo on the dirt and the dry weeds.

Then they could hear talking coming from inside. There was no glass in the window since the panes had been smashed in by thrown rocks years ago. But there was still an old lacy yellowed crocheted curtain hanging over the void of the frame, and through the gauze of the curtain when they raised their heads they could see a blond girl lying on the floor on an old mattress. Two candles were set into beer bottles on the floor and in the flickering light they saw that the girl was one of the high school girls they often saw on Main Street, and she was completely naked. An army blanket was spread over the mattress and she was lying on the blanket with her knees raised up and they could see the damp hair glistening between her legs and her soft flattened breasts and her hips and thin arms, and she was the color of cream all over and pink-toned and they looked at her in surprise and something akin to religious astoundment and awe. Lying next to her there was a big hard-muscled red-haired boy who was as naked as she was, only he was wearing a gray tee-shirt that had its sleeves cut off. He was from the high school too. They'd also seen him before. And now he was saying, That's not it. Because it's only this once.

Why? the girl said.

I told you. Because he come along with us tonight. Because if he did I told him he could.

But I don't want to.

Do it for me then.

You don't love me, the girl said.

I told you I did.

Like hell. If you did you wouldn't make me do this.

I'm not making you, he said. I'm only saying for a favor.

But I don't want to.

Okay, Sharlene. Fuck it. You don't have to.

The high school boy got up from the mattress. The two boys watched him from outside the house. He stood in the candlelight in the sleeveless tee-shirt, bare-legged, muscular, tall. His was big. The hair was red too, but lighter, orange looking, above it; it had a purple head. He bent and picked up his jeans, stepped into them and hauled them up and buckled the belt.

Russ, the girl said. She was looking at him from the mattress, watching his face.

What?

Are you mad?

I already told him, he said. Now I don't know what I'm going to tell him.

All right, she said. I will, for you. I don't want him to, though.

He looked at her. I know, he said. I'll go tell him.

But you better appreciate this, goddamn it.

I appreciate it.

I mean you better appreciate it afterwards too, the girl said.

He went out through the open door and in the dark from outside the house they watched her by herself now. She turned on her side toward them and shook cigarettes from a red pack and lit one leaning forward toward the flame of the candle, her breasts swinging free, cone-shaped, her slender thigh and girl's flank sleek in the dancing candlelight, and lay back and smoked and blew the smoke straight up above her into the room and flicked the ashes onto the floor. She lifted her other arm and inspected the back of her hand and ran her hand through her blond hair and brushed it back away from her face. Then there was another boy standing in the doorway looking at her. He came into the room. He was a big boy too, from the high school.

The girl didn't even look at him. This isn't on account of you, she said. So don't get any idea that it is.

I know, he said.

Just so you do.

You going to let me set down?

Well I'm not going to stand up, she said.

He squatted on the army blanket and looked at her. After a moment he reached out and with the extended fingers of one hand touched one of her dark nipples.

What are you doing? the girl said.

He said it was all right.

It's not fucking all right. But I told him. So hurry up.

I'm going to, the boy said.

Take your clothes off, she said. For christsakes.

He kicked his shoes off and unbuckled his belt and dropped his pants and underwear, and from outside the house they watched him now, and they could see he had hair too. The one he had was bigger and it was swollen-looking, sticking straight up, and without saying any word at all to her he stretched out on her, lying between her legs while she had her knees up, spread again, adjusting under his weight. He started moving on her at once. They could see his pale ass cheeks rising and falling. Then quicker and then beginning to pound and after a brief time he shouted something wild and unintelligible as if he were in pain, crying some kind of words into her neck and he jerked and shivered and then he stopped, and all the time she lay wordlessly and still, looking at the ceiling with her arms flat at her sides as if she were in some other place and he was not in her life at all.

Get off, she said.

The big boy raised up and looked in her face and rolled from her body and lay on his back on the blanket. In a little while he said, Hey.

She took up her cigarette from the jar lid where she had placed it when he had come in and she puffed on the cigarette but it had gone out. She leaned toward the candle flame and lit it again.

Hey, he said again. Sharlene?

What?

You're good.

Well, you're not.

He lifted up onto his elbow on the mattress to look at her. Why is that?

She didn't look at him. She was lying back again, smoking, looking straight up toward the spot where the candlelight was flickering on the filthy ceiling. Why don't you get the hell out of here.

What'd I do that was so bad? he said.

Will you just get the hell out of here. She was almost shouting now.

He stood up and put his clothes on, looking down at her all the time. Then he went out of the room.

The first boy came back in, fully dressed. He was wearing a high school jacket now.

The girl looked at him from the mattress.

How was it? he said.

Don't be ridiculous. You could at least come here and kiss me.

He squatted down and kissed her on the mouth and fondled her breast and put his hand in the hair between her legs.

Quit, she said. Don't. Let's get out of here. It's starting to give me the creeps in here.

From beyond the window the two boys watched the big high school boy leave the room. Then they watched the girl step into her underpants and pull them up and fasten her white brassiere, her elbows pointed out from her body, her hands working behind her back, then she shook the brassiere, and then she stepped into her jeans and pulled a shirt over her head, and lastly she bent and blew out the two candles. Instantly the room went dark and they heard only her footsteps going out across the bare pinewood floor. Outside they slid forward toward the front of the house and hid in the dark against the cold clapboards and watched without a word when the girl and the two big boys came out into the overgrown lot and crossed under the trees and got into the car and then drove away in the dark on Railroad Street, leaving only the red eyes of the tail-lights diminishing in the faint dust above the road as the car rushed away toward Main Street and downtown.

That son of a bitch, Ike said.

That other one too, Bobby said. What about him.

They stepped out into the ragweed and dry sunflowers and started home.

McPherons.

They had the cattle in the corral already, the mother cows and the two-year-old heifers waiting in the bright cold late-fall afternoon. The cows were moiling and bawling and the dust rose in the cold air and hung above the corrals and chutes like brown clouds of gnats swimming in schools above the cold ground. The two old McPheron brothers stood at the far end of the corral surveying the cattle. They wore jeans and boots and canvas chore jackets and caps with flannel earflaps. At the tip of Harold's nose a watery drip quivered, then dropped off, while Raymond's eyes were bleary and red from the cow dust and the cold. They were almost ready now. They were waiting only for Tom Guthrie to come and help, so they could finish this work for the fall. They stood in the corral and looked past the cattle and examined the sky.

I reckon it's decided to hold off, Raymond said. It don't appear like it wants to snow anymore.

It's too cold to snow, Harold said. Too dry, too.

It might snow tonight, Raymond said. I've seen it happen.

It's not going to snow, Harold said. Look at the sky over there.

That's what I'm looking at, Raymond said.

They turned back to surveying the cattle. Then without saying anything more they left the corral and drove to the horse barn where they backed the pickup into the wide sliding door of the bay and began to load the vaccination guns, the Ivermec, the medicine vials and the cattle prods into the back end. They lifted the smudge pot in with the other gear and wired the tall blackened smokestack to the sideboards, and returned to the corral to the squeeze chute and set the equipment out on the upended wooden telephone spool they used for a table. The smudge pot they stood upright on the ground near the chute and Harold bent over stiffly and held a match to it. When it ignited he adjusted the flue so it gave off heat, and its smoke rose black and smelling of kerosene into the wintry air, mixing with the cattle dust.

They looked up at the sound of a truck out beyond the house: Guthrie's pickup just turning off the county road. It came on around the house and the few outbuildings past the stunted trees and pulled up where they stood waiting. Guthrie and the two boys climbed out in their winter coats and caps.

Now who's these hired men? Harold said. He looked at Ike and Bobby standing beside their father.

I brought them along, Guthrie said. They said they wanted to come.

Well I just hope they're not too costly, Harold said. We can't afford any city wages. Tom, you know that. He was speaking soberly, in a kind of mock quarrelsome voice. The two boys stared back at him.

I can't say what they'll charge, Guthrie said. You'll have to ask them.

Raymond stepped up. What say, you boys. What's this going to put us back today?

They turned toward this second old man, younger than the other one, his face raw looking and grizzled in the cold air and his dirty cap pulled down low above his dust-bleared eyes. How much you going to charge us to join this escapade? he said.

They didn't know what to say. They shrugged their shoulders and looked at their father.

Well, Raymond said. I reckon we'll have to negotiate it later. After we see how you manage.

He winked and turned away and then they understood it was all right. They walked over to the chute and stood at the makeshift table and looked at the vaccination guns and the boxes of medicine vials. They inspected it all and felt cautiously of the dehorner, its sharp cupped blood-encrusted ends, and they edged up to the smudge pot and held out their gloved hands to its gassy heat. Suddenly one of the cows bawled from inside the corral and they ducked to see through the boards to tell which one it was, and the cattle were milling around waiting for what was to come.

The men went to work. Guthrie climbed into the corral and immediately the cattle eyed him and began to shove back against the far side of the lot. He walked steadily toward them. The cattle started to herd and shift along the back fence, and he ran up swiftly, cutting off the last two animals, a black heifer and an old speckle-faced cow, and turned them back out across the trampled dirt. They tried to double back, but each time he flapped his arms and yelled at them, and finally they trotted suspiciously into the narrow alley that fed into the chute. From outside the alley, Raymond jammed a pole though the fence behind them so they couldn't back out and then he jabbed the heifer with the electric prod and it made a sizzling sound against her flank, and she snorted and leaped into the squeeze chute. He caught her head in the head-catch and she kicked and crashed until he squeezed the sidebars against her ribs. She lifted her black rubbery muzzle and bawled in terror.

Meanwhile Harold had taken off his canvas jacket and pulled on an old orange sweatshirt that had one of its sleeves scissored off, and he had greased his bare arm with lubricant jelly. Now he stepped up behind the chute and twisted the heifer's tail over her back. He fit his hand inside her and pawed out the loose green warm manure and shoved in deeper, feeling for a calf. His face was turned skyward against her flank, his eyes squinted shut in concentration. He could feel the round hard knot of the cervix, the larger swelling beyond. He rotated his hand over it. The bones were already forming.

Yeah. She's got one, he hollered to Raymond.

He withdrew his arm. It was red and slick, spotted with mucus and flecks of manure and little threads of blood. He held his arm away from his body and it steamed in the cold air, and while he waited for the next one to come in he stood near the smudge pot beside the two boys to warm himself. They looked at his arm in fascination and then looked up into his old reddened face and he nodded at them, and they turned to watch the heifer in the chute.

While his brother had felt inside her for a calf Raymond had checked her eyes and mouth, and now he shot her in the hip, high up with the two vaccination guns, injecting her with Ivermec against lice and worms, and lepto against aborting. When he was done he opened the chute and she jumped out crow-hopping, kicking up loose dirt and hard clods of manure, and she came to a stop in the middle of the holding pen where she swung her head around, bawling forlornly into the wintry afternoon, and slung a long silver rope of slaver across her shoulder.

Raymond jumped the next one, the old speckle-faced cow, into the chute and caught her head and tightened the sidebars, and Harold stepped forward and lifted her tail and cleaned out the green flop and went in with his hand and arm, feeling. But there was nothing to feel; she was empty. He wiggled his fingers, feeling for what was supposed to be there, but there wasn't anything.

She's open, he hollered. She must not of stuck. What you want to do with her?

She always had good calves before, Raymond said.

Yeah, but she's getting old. Look at her. Look at how gaunt she's taken in the flank there.

She might stick the next time.

I don't want to put any more feed in her, waiting to see if she's going to, Harold said. Pay for that all winter. Do you?

Leave her go then, Raymond said. But she was a good mother, you have to say that for her.

He swung the gate open ahead of her and released the chute, and the old cow trotted out into the empty loading pen from which she would be trucked away, and she raised her speckled face, sniffed the air and turned completely around and stood still. She looked nervous and displaced, jittery-looking. The black heifer in the holding pen on the other side of the fence bawled at her, and the old cow trotted over to the rails where they stood, separated by the fence, breathing at one another.

From the smudge pot the two boys watched it all. They stamped their feet and flapped their arms in their winter coats, warming themselves and watching their father and the old McPheron brothers in their efforts. Overhead the sky was as blue as just-washed café crockery and the sun was shining brilliantly. But the afternoon was turning even colder. There was something building up in the west. From far off over the mountains the clouds were stacking up. The boys stayed near the smudge pot, trying to keep warm.

Later, when there were only a few of the cows and heifers left to test, their father came over to the fence near the smudge pot. He blew his nose thoroughly on a blue handkerchief and folded it and put it back in his pocket. You boys want to come in here and help me? he said.

Yes.

I could use you.

They climbed the fence and dropped down into the corral. The remaining cattle shied back, eyeing them, nervous and jittery, their heads lifted alertly like antelope or deer. The air inside the pen was thick and made the boys want to cover their noses and mouths with something.

Now. Watch me, their father said. They're excited already. So don't do anything unnecessary.

The boys looked at the cattle.

Stay even with me. Spread out a little. But watch they don't kick you. That's the way they're going to hurt you. That tall red cow there particularly.

Which one is she? Ike said.

That old tall one, Guthrie said. Without any white on her front legs. See her? With that chewed-off tail.

What's wrong with her?

She's gotten spooky. You want to watch her is all.

The boys stayed even with their father. They moved fan-wise across the corral. The cattle began to shift and bunch, piling back on one another; they wheeled and massed against the back fence. Behind them a board cracked. Then the cattle began to string out, sliding along the rails, and at the last moment their father rushed forward and yelled at them and lashed out with a thin braided whip and popped an old frost-eared cow across the nose and she skidded in the dirt and snorted, then wheeled around. Behind her there was a young white-faced heifer that turned with her.

Guthrie and the boys headed these two across the corral. The boys kept spread out beside him, and the animals trotted ahead kicking up spurts of dirt and dust from the trampled ground, and then at the mouth of the alley the young heifer got frightened and turned back.

Head her, Guthrie shouted. Don't let her get past. Turn her.

Bobby flapped his arms and hollered, Hey! Hey!

The heifer glared at him, her eyes white-rimmed, and then she whirled around and her tail went up and she bucked once and kicked and then rushed on into the alley, crowding past the old cow that was already there in that narrow space. Raymond jammed the pole through behind them.

All right, their father said. You think you can do that?

What do you mean?

Just do that every time. Bring two in at a time. But be careful.

Where will you be? Ike said.

I need to help up front, Guthrie said. Raymond's getting tired. It's too much for one man to do. And that second cow there has a horn that needs to be taken off. He looked at the boys. Here, you can have this.

He handed the thin herding whip to Ike who took it and hefted it and swung it limberly back and forth over his shoulder. He snapped the end of it at a clod of manure. The clod jumped.

What do I get to use? Bobby said. I ought to have something too.

Their father looked around. All right, he said. He called at Raymond: Let me have one of those hot shots out there.

The old man brought one of the cattle prods and handed it over the fence. Guthrie took it and demonstrated it to them, how to rotate the handle and release the little button so it would give a charge. See how you do that? he said. He poked it against his boot toe and it sparked. He handed the cattle prod to Bobby, and Bobby examined it and touched it against his shoe. It sizzled and he jerked his foot back, then he glanced up at them and there was a surprised look on his face.

I get to use it too, Ike said.

Trade off with it, Guthrie said. You can swap the whip with him. But don't get carried away. It's just if you need it. And anyway you have to be close enough to even be able to use it.

Does it hurt them? Bobby said.

They don't like it, Guthrie said. It gets their attention for sure. He put his hands on their shoulders. So. All set?

I guess so.

I'll be right out here.

He climbed out of the corral and joined the McPheron brothers at the chute. They brought the heifer in and Harold tested her. She was carrying a calf and Raymond shot her twice in the hip and let her out into the holding pen with the others. Then they brought the cow in, and after she was tested and vaccinated Guthrie wrapped his arms around her head and pulled her head violently to one side, her neck stretching tight, her eyes wild and frantic, while Raymond fit the sharp ends of the dehorner over the malformed horn. It was a hard ugly thing, twisting out from where it had been cut off unsuccessfully once before. He clamped down with the dehorner, twisting it, applying pressure on the grips, and finally cut through. The horn dropped off like a piece of sawed wood and left a white dished-out tender-looking place at her skull. Immediately the blood spurted out in a thin spray, making a little puddle in the dirt. Guthrie held on to the cow's head and she bawled, rolling her eyes in panic, fighting him, while Raymond shook out powdered blood-stop into the cut, and the blood soaked it up and trickled down her face. He shook out more powder and pressed it in, mixing it with his finger, and they released her into the holding pen and she went out tossing her head, with a line of blood still dribbling along her eye.

In the corral the two boys worked hard with the remaining cattle amidst the dirt and swirling dust and they managed to line two more into the alley, and the men began to work on them. But one of the cows turned up open. They released her into the separate loading pen with the old speckle-faced cow, and the two animals nosed one another and stood facing the direction they'd come from.

That's another one never stuck, Harold said.

Maybe you ought to let old Doc Wycoff breed them, Guthrie said. With his A-I.

Sure. We could do that, Raymond said. Only he's kind of steep.

That makes me think, Harold said. Didn't we ever tell you about that time Raymond and me walked in on him?

If you did, Guthrie said, I don't recall it.

Well, yeah, Harold said. One time me and Raymond went in to see him about something. A cow sick or something. In his clinic there. When we got inside the front door we heard something that sounded kind of like scuffling or thrashing coming from in back of the front counter there. We couldn't tell what it was. So we looked over the top of the counter and old Doc had this gal on her back on the floor behind the counter, and she had her arms and legs wrapped around him about like he was a fifty-dollar bill. She looked up and seen us staring at them. She wasn't scared by that, she wasn't even took by surprise. She just stopped moving and released her clench on him. Then she tapped him on the head, still looking up at us over his shoulder, and stopped moving and working, and pretty soon Doc did too. What's a matter? he says. We got company, she says. Do we? Doc says. We do for a fact, she says. So he moves his head so he can look up at us. Boys, he says. Is it any emergency? It can wait, we tell him. All right then, he says. I'll be with you in a minute.

Guthrie laughed. That sounds like him, he said.

Don't it? Harold said.

It didn't take him long, Raymond said. I imagine he was about finished anyway.

Her too, I reckon, Harold said.

What was she doing, Guthrie said, paying a bill?

No, Harold said. I don't guess so. It was more like they both got excited by the same idea all of a sudden and couldn't help themselves.

That happens, Guthrie said.

Yeah, Harold said. I guess.

I guess it does, Raymond said. He looked out across the flat open treeless country toward the horizon where there were blue mounds of sandhill.

. . .

At last there was only the red-legged cow left to test, the one
their father had warned them about. She was worse now. She
regarded the two boys steadily with her head lifted as if she
were some wild range animal that had never seen a human on
foot before. The boys had stayed back from her in the corral.
They were afraid of her and didn't want to be kicked. But now
they walked toward her, and she eyed them steadily and began
to shift and trot along the fence. They cut her off. She was tall
and all four of her legs were red; her eyes were white-rimmed.
She dropped her head and whirled around, her stubby tail up,
stiffened, and galloped across to the other side. They followed
her again and came up behind her once more, where she was
trapped in a corner. She faced them, her eyes baleful-looking
and her sides heaving, and Ike moved closer and swung the
whip and snapped it across her face. This surprised her. She
jumped sideways, then she leaped forward. She galloped into
Bobby, knocking him back off his feet before he could jump out
of the way. He landed on his back and bounced once like a piece
of thrown stove wood. She kicked back at him and then leaped
and bucked across to the far side of the corral. Bobby lay spilled
out on the ground. His stocking cap was at his feet, the electric
cattle prod flung out to the side. He lay on the trampled dirt
looking up at the empty sky, trying to breathe. But his breath
wouldn't come and he began to gouge his feet in the loose
ground, while Ike bent over him in panic, talking to him.
Bobby's eyes looked big and scared. Then all at once his breath
came back in a rush and he choked and gave a kind of high sob.

His father had seen what happened and had leaped into the
corral and come running, and he was bent over now beside him,
kneeling at his head. Bobby. You okay? Son?

The boy's eyes looked all around. He looked scared and surprised. He peered up at the faces over him. I think so, he said.

Did you break anything, do you think? Guthrie said.

He felt of himself. He tried his arms and legs. No, he said. I
don't guess so.

Can you sit up?

The boy sat up and hunched his shoulders. He moved his head back and forth.

You took a bad one, Guthrie said. But you seem to be all right. I guess you are. Are you? He helped the boy stand up and he brushed the corral dirt off his shoulders and where it was stuck to the back of his head. Here, he said. You need to blow your nose, son. Bobby took the handkerchief and used it and wiped his nose and looked at the handkerchief for blood, but it was only dirt and cow dust, and gave it back. His brother pushed the stocking cap back onto his head.

You boys have been doing a good job, Guthrie said. I'm proud of you.

They looked up at his face, then out across the corral.

You did just fine. You did the best you could, he said.

But what about her? Ike said.

Let me have that whip back, Guthrie said. You can help if you want to. But stay clear of her.

They moved once more toward the red-legged cow. She waited at the far side of the corral standing sideways, watching them. She looked as wild as some alley cat, like she might try to scramble over the six-foot-high corral fence and get free that way. She began to step and shift, sliding away. Guthrie walked steadily toward her, the boys following. Then as she was turning he ran up quick behind her and struck her hard with the whip, and she kicked back at him viciously and missed his face and he followed, running, and slashed her again and then just as she was about to head into the alley she wheeled sharply and ran at the fence, gathered herself and jumped at it. She got only halfway across. She crashed through the top pole and was stuck there. Now she was scissored over the fence and she began to bawl, crazy with terror. She thrashed and kicked.

Goddamn it. Quit it, Harold yelled at her. He and Raymond had come running over. Here now. Stop that. You goddamn crazy old raw-boned bitch.

They gathered around, wanting to stop her, to quiet her, but she was kicking and thrashing in a crazy frenzy, and they couldn't get close. Finally Guthrie climbed over to face her, to shove her back, to see if she'd come that way, but she had thrashed and kicked so much, rocking, teetering on the corral board, that she managed to tip herself forward, and suddenly she went over headfirst into the holding pen, making a heavy crashing somersault, her old angular head down, her hindquarters following, flopping over with a great thump onto the ground. Then she lay still.

I want you to look at that, Harold said. Go ahead then. Stay there. Maybe that'll knock some goddamn sense into you.

They watched her. Her sides heaved but nothing else was moving. Her eyes stared. Climbing into the holding pen, Guthrie approached and lifted her head with his foot. That seemed to rouse her. She began to tremble and suddenly she rose up, Guthrie stepped back, and then she stood wobbly, glaring around. There was a gash along one flank where it had torn on the splintered corral board. The torn hide quivered and dripped blood in bright quick drops, and all along the back of her and over the top of her head she was covered with a mantle of dirt. She looked like some kind of beast from a medieval pageant, dirty and gory, threatening. She shook her dirty head sideways and took a couple of steps and then limped, trotting, over to the other cattle and heifers. They seemed leery of her and backed away.

Guthrie said, You want me to bring her back around?

No. Let her go, Harold said. We'd have to about kill her to get her in here now. She either stuck when she was with the bull or she didn't. She seems to think she did, since she wants over there so bad. He looked at her with the other cattle. Anyhow, she seems to of took a serious dislike to you, Tom.

I'll sort her out again, he said. If that's what you want.

No. Let her go. We'll keep an eye on her.

What about that cut?

She'll heal up. I reckon she's too disgusted with us to go off and die. She wouldn't want to give us the satisfaction.

The two boys helped push the tested cattle out into a nearby pasture. The wild red-legged cow limped along in the middle of them. The two open cows were left in the holding pen and they called after the other cattle, their heads lifted, bawling, and moved over to the fence where they stood looking out through the rails. At the chutes the boys helped collect the medicine and the vaccination guns and put them away in the back of the truck. Then they climbed into the Dodge pickup and sat beside their father with the heater pushing out hot air onto their knees while he talked a little more to Harold. Raymond came around to their side of the truck.

Roll your window down, their father said. He wants to say something to you.

The old man stood in the cold in the sandy gravel beside the pickup and took out a soft leather purse from an inner pocket of his canvas jacket and held the purse in his hands and unzipped it. He poked around and picked out two bills. He handed them in through the opened window to the two boys. I hope that'll be compensation, he said.

They took the money shyly and said thank you to him.

You boys can come back here any time, he said. You'd be welcome.

Wait now, their father said. That isn't necessary.

You stay out of this, Raymond said. This is between me and these boys here. This don't concern you, Tom. You boys, you come again any time.

He stepped back. The two boys looked at him. At his old weather-chafed face and reddened eyes under the winter cap. He looked quiet and kindly. They held the money in their closed fists, waiting, not looking at it until their father had finally said goodbye and not until he had put the pickup in motion and they were turned back away from the cattle chutes and had driven past the house and were rattling on the county road with the gravel banging up under the fenders and then were pointed toward the west where the sky was beginning now to fade. Then they looked at the money. They turned it over. He had given them each a ten-dollar bill.

That's too much, their father said.

Should we give it back?

No, he said. He took his hat off and scratched the back of his head and put the hat back on. I guess not. That would be an insult. They want you to keep it. They enjoyed having you out there.

But Dad, Ike said.

Yes?

Why didn't they ever get married? And have a family like everybody else?

I don't know, Guthrie said. People don't sometimes.

In the pickup it was warm now, driving along the county road. Beyond the ditch the fenceline passed by, thickened and snarled with tumbleweed and brush. Above, on the cross arm of a telephone pole perched a hawk the color of copper in the lowering sun, and they watched him but his head didn't turn at all when they passed under him.

I just guess they never found the right girl, their father said. I don't rightly know.

Bobby looked out the window. He said, I guess they didn't want to leave each other.

Guthrie glanced at him. Maybe so, he said. Maybe that's what happened, son.

At the highway Guthrie and the two boys turned north and it was quieter in the pickup now because they were on the blacktop, pointed toward town. Guthrie turned the radio on to receive the evening news.

Victoria Roubideaux.

When she said her name the middle-aged woman sitting on the other side of the window looked at her and said, Yes, Mrs. Jones called, and then she made a check mark on the chart in front of her and handed the girl three sheets of paper on a clipboard to fill out. She took them back across the waiting room to her seat and held the papers on her knees, leaning over them with her hair fallen about her face like a thick dark curtain, until she lifted it deftly in a motion familiar and automatic and settled it behind her shoulders. There were questions she had no answer to. They wanted to know was there cancer in the family, heart disease among her father's people, syphilis in her mother's relations. Altogether more than a hundred questions. She answered the ones she could, the ones she had some certain knowledge of, believing it would not be right to guess on the others as it might be if this were some test she was taking at school. When she was finished she took the clipboard and sheets of paper to the woman and handed them through the window.

I didn't know all of these, she said.

Did you answer what you did know?

Yes.

Then take a seat. We'll call you.

She sat down again. The waiting room was a long narrow room with potted plants tied upright to sticks and set in front of the four windows. There were three other people in the room waiting too. A woman with a little boy whose face looked as yellow as tablet paper and whose eyes looked too big for his head. The boy leaned listlessly against his mother while she caressed the back of his head, and after a time he put his face down in her lap and shut his eyes and she smoothed her hand over his yellow sick-looking cheek while she herself stared blankly toward the windows. The other person in the room was an old man with a new pearl-gray felt hat that rode squarely on his head like a statement. He sat against the opposite wall and he was holding the thumb of his right hand forward on his knee. The thumb of that hand was wrapped thickly in white bandages and it stuck up like some kind of hastily wrapped exhibit in a freak show. He regarded the girl with merry eyes as if he were going to say something, explain to her all that had happened, but he didn't. He looked at her, and no one said anything. Presently a nurse called the woman with the sick boy, and then she came back and beckoned the old man with the bad thumb, and after a while they called her.

She rose and followed the woman in the white smock and slacks down the narrow corridor past a number of closed doors. They stopped at a scale and she was weighed and her height was taken, then they went into a little room where there was an examination table and a sink counter and two chairs. The woman took her pulse and checked her blood pressure and temperature, all without talking, and wrote the results of her findings in the file.

Then she said, Now get undressed please. And put this on. He'll see you in a minute. She went out and shut the door.

The girl felt discommoded but she did what she was told to do. She put on the paper jacket that was open in the front, then she sat on the examination table with a paper sheet over her legs, both the sheet and jacket starkly white and scratchily uncomfortable to her, and waited and looked toward the wall in front of her at the picture of autumn trees growing up in some place that was altogether foreign to Holt, Colorado, since the trees were tall and dense and were of a species of hardwood and were colored so spectacularly that they seemed in the girl's experience altogether unlikely if not impossible. Then he came in, the old man, the old doctor, stately and formal and elegant and kindly in a dark blue suit and wearing an absolutely white shirt with a maroon bow tie knotted expertly at his starched collar, and after he closed the door he shook her hand cordially and introduced himself.

You saw me once before, she said.

Did I? I don't recall.

Six or seven years ago.

He looked at her closely and smiled. The eyes behind the rimless spectacles were lighter than his suit. His face was gray but his eyes were very lively. There were age spots at his temples.

That's a long time, he said. Probably you've changed somewhat since then, since the last time I saw you. He smiled again. Now then, Miss Roubideaux, I need to examine you. And after I'm finished with that we'll have a little talk about what I find out. Have you ever had a pelvic exam before?

No.

I see. Well, it's not very comfortable. I'm afraid you'll just have to endure through it, and I'll try to be careful and not hurt you, and be as quick but as thorough as I need to be. He picked up a silver instrument from the tray on the counter. I'll be using this speculum. Have you seen one of these before? It opens like this inside you—he showed her, as illustration, by sliding it into the circle made by his finger and thumb, and then opening it—and you may hear me screwing this little nut so that it stays open. Try not to tighten the muscle at the bottom—he indicated the muscle web between his finger and thumb—because that makes it more difficult for me and more uncomfortable for you. This is the light which shines inside you so I can see the cervix, and I'll also be taking a smear with this swab. Do you have any questions?

The girl looked at him and looked away. She shook her head.

The old man removed his blue suitcoat and folded it over the back of the chair and rolled up his white starched cuffs and went to the sink and scrubbed his hands. Then he came over to her at the examination table.

Now I'll ask you to lie back, he said, and put your feet up here, please.

She did as he instructed. Her feet were in the stirrups and he draped the paper sheet over her knees and thighs and he put on rubber gloves and took up the speculum and squeezed a little lubricant onto it from a tube. Then he sat down on a stool between her knees and patted down the drape so he could see her face.

This is the uncomfortable part, he said. He adjusted the sheet. Slide all the way forward, please. Thank you. That's right. This may feel cold. He warmed the instrument for a moment in his hands.

She felt it then and flinched.

Did I hurt you? I'm sorry.

She stared straight up. He was seated low, eye-level between her open legs.

That's right, he said. Try to relax. Now I'm just going to take a look.

She stared up at the ceiling and felt what he was doing and waited and endured it and listened to his calm voice telling her all the time what examinations he was making and why and what was next, and that everything was fine and he was almost finished. She didn't say anything. He continued his examinations. Then in a little while he was finished and he removed the discomfort of the metal instrument and said, Yes. That's fine. Now I just need to do this, and felt the ovaries and the size of the uterus, one hand outside and one inside, again telling her what he was doing, and afterward he took the rubber gloves off and examined her breasts while she was still lying down and told her that she needed to do the same for herself regularly and how she should do it. After that he stood back and moved to the sink and washed his hands again and turned down the cuffs of his stiff white shirt and put his suitcoat on. You may get dressed now, he said. Then I'll come back and we'll talk.

The girl sat up and removed the paper jacket and put on her own clothes once more. When he returned she was seated on the table waiting for him.

So, he said. Miss Roubideaux, as I expect you already know, you are pregnant. Something over three months, I'd say. Closer to four. When was your last period?

She told him.

Yes. Well, you can expect to have a baby in the spring. The middle of April, I calculate, give or take two weeks on either side. But I'm wondering, I don't know whether this is good news to you or not.

I already knew, if that's what you mean, the girl said. I felt sure of it.

Yes. I thought you must have, he said. But that doesn't answer my question.

He put her chart out of the way on the counter. He drew a chair up and sat near her in his blue suit and white shirt, looking at her where she sat slightly above him on the examining table, her hands in her lap, waiting, her face flushed and guarded.

I want to be straightforward with you, he said. This doesn't have to go anywhere but right here. Do you understand? You and I talking. Having a brief conversation in the privacy of this room.

What do you mean? the girl said.

Miss Roubideaux, he said. Do you want this baby?

Quickly she raised her eyes to him. She was frightened now, her eyes dark and intent, waiting.

Yes, she said. I want it.

You feel certain of that, do you? Absolutely certain.

She looked at his face. Do you mean if I want to put it up for adoption?

That too, perhaps, he said. But more, I meant are you going to keep this baby? Carry it full-term and give birth to it?

I plan to.

And you do want it, don't you.

Yes.

And now that you've told me that, you're not going to do anything foolish such as trying to stop it by yourself by some means.

No.

No, he said. That's fine then. I believe you. That's what I need to know. You will have various kinds of trouble, I expect. That's what happens. Many teenage mothers do. You're not supposed to be having babies yet. Your body's not ready. You're too young. On the other hand, you do seem strong. You don't appear to be the hysterical kind. Are you the hysterical kind, Miss Roubideaux?

I don't think so.

Then you should be all right. Do you smoke?

No.

Don't start. Do you drink alcohol?

No.

Don't start that either, not now. Do you take any drugs of any kind?

No.

You're telling me the truth? He looked at her and waited. That's important. Because everything you take in goes to the baby. You know that, don't you.

Yes. I know.

You need to eat right. That's important too. Mrs. Jones can help you with that. I expect she's a good cook. You need to gain some weight but not too much. Yes, well. All right then. I'll see you again in a month, and once each month until the eighth month, then I'll see you every week. Do you have any questions?

For the first time the girl released the hold on herself a little. Her eyes welled up. It was as if what she wanted to ask him was more important and more frightening than anything either one of them had said or done so far. She said, Is the baby all right? Would you tell me that?

Oh, he said. Why yes. So far as I can tell, everything is fine. Didn't I make that clear? There is no reason why that should change, so long as you take care of yourself. I didn't mean to frighten you.

She let herself cry silently just a little, while her shoulders slumped forward and her hair fell about her face. The old doctor reached up and took her hand and held it warmly between both of his hands for a moment and was quiet with her, simply looking into her face, serenely, grandfatherly, but not talking, treating her out of respect and kindness, out of his own long experience of patients in examination rooms.

Afterward, when she was calm again, after the doctor had left, she went into the air outside the Holt County Clinic next to the hospital, and the light in the street seemed sharp to her and hard-edged, definite, as if it were no longer merely a late fall afternoon in the hour before dusk, but instead as if it were the first moment of noon in the exact meridian of summer and she was standing precisely under the full illumination of the sun.

Guthrie.

In the last period of the day he sat at his desk at the front of the room, listening to their speeches and glancing out the window toward the place where the sun shone aslant on the few bare trees risen up along the street. It looked cold and bleak outside.

The tall girl talking at the head of the class was just finishing. Something to do with Hamilton. She had spent half of her speech on the duel with Burr. What she was saying was scarcely coherent. She finished and glanced at Guthrie and approached his desk and handed over her notes. Thank you, he said. She turned and sat down at her desk near the west windows, and he made a note about what to say to her in conference and again consulted the list before him and looked out at their faces. They looked as if they were waiting for some inevitable doom and disaster. Unless they had already given their speeches. Then they were bored and indifferent. Glenda, he said.

A girl in the middle row said, Mr. Guthrie?

Yes.

I'm not ready today.

Do you have your notes?

Yes. But I'm not ready.

Come ahead. You'll have to do what you can.

But I don't know about this, she said.

Come ahead.

She got up and walked to the front and began to read rapidly from her papers without ever once looking up, a stream of uninflected talk that would have bored even her, even as she uttered it, if she weren't so terrified. About Cornwallis, evidently. The Battle of Yorktown. She didn't get as far as the surrender. Suddenly she was finished. She turned her paper over and there was nothing on the other side. She looked at Guthrie. I told you I wasn't ready, she said.

She stood facing him, then she advanced and handed him her papers and went back in a rush to her seat in the middle of the room, her face hotly red, and sat down and peered into the palms of her hands as though she might discover some explanation or at least some form of consolation and succor there, and then she looked at the girl next to her, a large brown-haired girl who gave her a little nod, but it didn't seem to be enough because lastly she hid her hands under her skirt and sat on them.

At the front of the room at his desk Guthrie made a note and consulted the list of names before him. He called the next one. A big boy in black cowboy boots rose up and stomped forward from the back of the room. Once he got started he talked haltingly for something less than a minute.

That's it? Guthrie said. You think that just about covers it?

Yeah.

That was pretty short.

I couldn't find anything, the boy said.

You couldn't find anything about Thomas Jefferson?

No.

The Declaration of Independence.

No.

The presidency. His life at Monticello.

No.

Where did you look?

Everywhere I could think of.

You must not have thought very long, Guthrie said. Let me see your notes.

I just got this page.

Let me see that much.

The big boy handed over the single sheet of tablet paper and stomped back and sat down. Guthrie watched him. The boy had sulled up now. He was staring straight ahead. The room was quiet, the students all waiting and watching him. He looked away and stared out the window. The trees along the curb in front of the school still showed sunlight at the tops; in the slanting afternoon sun the trees cast the thinnest of shadows as though they had been sprayed onto the street and the brown grass. For weeks it had been very dry and in the nights there were hard freezes. He turned back and called Victoria Roubideaux to make her speech.

When she came forward she was in a black skirt and a soft yellow sweater and her coal black hair fell down her back, and he noticed that her hair was cut off squarely and neatly at the bottom in a straight thick line. She looked better now, better kept. She stopped in front of the class and turned slowly and began at once to speak very softly. He could barely hear her.

Could you talk a little louder, please? Guthrie said.

From the beginning? she said.

No. From where you are.

She began to read from the notes again in a voice that had scarcely more volume. He watched her in profile. The girl was staying in Maggie Jones's house now. Maggie had told him about it. That was better. She already looked better. Probably Maggie had been the one to trim her hair that way.

Then there was a commotion in the room. Abruptly she stopped reading because somebody had said something from the back of the room and now all of the girls were turned in their seats looking at Russell Beckman. He sat at the very back corner, his red curly hair combed down over his forehead, a big boy wearing a tee-shirt under his red and white Holt County Union High School jacket.

She wouldn't start reading again. She was still staring out at their faces, holding her papers before her. She looked as though she were in a kind of panic.

What's wrong? Guthrie said.

She turned her head and looked at him, her eyes guarded and dark.

What's wrong here?

She would not speak nor make any complaint, but turned back toward the class, the rows of suddenly blank faces staring back at her, and looked over their heads toward the Beckman boy who sat at the back row cramped in his desk and who gazed forward blankly, his hands folded on his desk as though he were no more responsible for any disturbance than he was for the setting of the sun. At the front of the classroom the girl watched him. Then without saying any word at all she started walking across the front of the room. By the time she reached the door she was running. Behind her the door crashed against the wall and rebounded and they could hear her rapid steps diminishing in the tiled hallway.

The students sat looking at the door, which was still shuddering. Guthrie rose from his desk. Alberta, he said. Go catch up with her and see what you can do.

A small blond girl in front stood up. But what if I can't find her?

Go look for her. She can't be far.

But I don't know where she went.

Just go look for her. Go on now.

She hurried out of the room into the hall.

Guthrie walked back in the aisle between the desks toward Russell Beckman who still sat with his hands folded. The other students turned to watch as Guthrie passed. He stopped and stood over the boy. What did you say to her?

I didn't say nothing to her. He made a gesture with his hand. He was brushing something away.

Yes you did. What was it?

I wasn't even talking to her. I was talking to him. He ducked his head sideways toward the boy next to him. Ask him.

Guthrie looked at the boy in the black cowboy boots in the next desk. The boy stared straight ahead with a sullen look on his face. What'd he say?

I never heard it, the boy said.

You never heard it.

No.

How come everybody else did?

I don't have any idea. Ask them.

Guthrie looked at him. He turned back to Russell Beckman. I'll see you out in the hallway.

I never did nothing.

Let's go.

Russell Beckman glanced at the boy in the next desk. There was a faint expression on the other boy's face now. Beckman gave a little snort and the expression on the other boy's face got slightly bigger, and now something was showing in his eyes too. Russell Beckman sighed loudly, as if he were greatly oppressed, and stood up and walked very slowly down the aisle between the other students and out into the empty hall. Guthrie followed him and shut the door. They faced each other.

You said something to Victoria that hurt her. I want to know what's going on here.

I didn't do nothing to her, the boy said. I wasn't even talking to her. I already told you that.

And I'm going to tell you something, Guthrie said. You're already in serious trouble in this class. You haven't done anything for weeks. I'm not going to pass you until you do.

You think I care about that?

You will.

No I won't. You don't know a goddamn thing about me.

I know more about you than I want to know.

You can go to hell.

Guthrie grabbed the boy's arm. They struggled and the boy fell back against the metal lockers. He jerked his arm away. His jacket was halfway off his shoulder and he pulled it straight.

The fuck you think you're doing? he said. You can't touch me. Keep your fucking hands off me. He stood up straight. His face was dark red now.

You shut your filthy mouth, Guthrie said. And you keep it shut. Whatever you said to her, don't you ever say something like that again.

Fuck you.

Guthrie grabbed him once more but he jerked away and then the boy swung and hit Guthrie at the side of the face, and then he whirled and ran away down the hallway and on outside, headed toward the parking lot. Guthrie watched him through the hallway windows. The boy got into his car, a dark blue Ford, and drove off, screeching across the parking lot and out of sight. Guthrie stood in the hallway and made himself breathe until he was calm again. The side of his face felt numb. He supposed he would feel it more later on. He took out a handkerchief and wiped it across his mouth and felt something on his tongue and spat it into the handkerchief and looked at it. A bloody piece of a tooth. He put it in his shirt pocket and wiped his mouth again and put the handkerchief away. Then he opened the door to the classroom and entered in on an immediate unnatural quiet. The students were all watching him.

Take out your books, he told them. Read until the bell. I don't want to hear anything more from any one of you today. You can finish your speeches tomorrow.

The students began to open their books. Just before the bell rang, the door opened and Alberta came back into the room. She came in and stood beside his desk. She wouldn't look at him.

Did you find her?

She must of went home, Mr. Guthrie.

You looked in the rest rooms?

Yes.

And outside? Out front?

I didn't want to go out of the building. You're not suppose to leave the building without a pass.

You could have this time.

But you're not suppose to.

All right. Take your seat.

The girl sat down in her desk. He looked out at the students and none of them was reading. They were all watching him and just waiting. Then the bell rang and they began to rise and Guthrie looked outside across the street again where the sunlight was red now against the trees.

Ike and Bobby.

Just once they took another boy with them to the vacant house and the room where it had happened. They wanted to see it again themselves, to walk in it and feel what that would feel like and what it might be to show it to somebody else, and afterward they were sorry they had ever wanted to know or do any of that at all. He was from Ike's class in the school, a tall skinny boy with thick hair. Donny Lee Burris.

It was after school was released for the day. They had come through the town park and crossed the railroad tracks already. Then they were out in the road in front of their house, a little past it, out on Railroad Street, and Ike stopped and squatted in the fine dirt. It was a bright cool windless day in November, far enough along in the afternoon that their shadows reached out behind them like dark rags stretched in the dirt road. The road was as dry as powder. Here. This might be his car tracks, he said. Leave them alone.

Bobby and the other boy, Donny Lee, squatted down beside him and studied the double tracks of the high school boy's car in the dust. They looked up the road toward the place where the tracks must have originated, where the car had been stopped that night in front of the old vacant house at the end of

Railroad Street a hundred yards away, and beyond, where the trafficless road ended in sagebrush and soapweed. The other boy stood up. How come they are? he said. They're probably somebody else's.

They're his, Ike said.

The boy looked up the road; he turned and looked back the other way. Then he scraped the toe of his shoe across the tire track, obliterating a piece of it.

What are you doing? Ike said. Quit that.

I thought we was going to look at that old house, the boy said.

All right, Ike said.

They started west toward the vacant building. Alongside the road the old man's house in the lot adjacent to their own house was quiet and pale as usual, behind the overgrown bushes and the tall ragweed, and there was no sign anywhere of the old man himself.

When they were in front of the empty house at the end of the road they stopped to study it and everything around it. The broken-down neglected locust trees, shaggy barked, the overgrown yard, the dead sunflowers grown up everywhere with their heads loaded and drooping, everything dry and brown now in the late fall, dust-coated, and the sunken house itself diminished and weathered, with the front door swung open carelessly and the windows broken out over the years, and the sole square intact window in the attic bearing a fly screen that was turned down loose from one corner in a way that looked peculiar, like it was sleepy-eyed.

What you waiting on now? the boy said.

Nothing. We're just looking at it.

I'm going in.

There were tracks still showing at the road edge, where the car had been parked, and shoe prints in the dirt where the two high school boys and the girl with them had climbed in and out of the car. Ike and Bobby were bent over inspecting the tracks.

I'm going, the boy said.

You wait, Ike said. You have to follow me. They stepped around the footprints and entered the lot through the weeds on the path and climbed onto the porch, the old boards dry as kindling and absolutely paintless, and passed through the open door. A broken chair stood in the middle of the room like something crippled that the last tenants had left behind because it couldn't keep up, and high up on the north wall the plaster was stained by long runs of rainwater. The chimney showed a soot-blackened hole where a stovepipe had vented into it, and on the floor were yellowed newspapers. Also old cigarette butts and sharp pieces of green-looking glass. A rusted can.

They done it in here? the other boy said.

Ike and Bobby looked around the room.

She was in the bedroom, Ike said.

Let's see that, the boy said.

They moved into the next room. The mattress lay on the bare floor with the candle stubs fitted into the beer bottles on either side. The jar lid still had her cigarette butts, the ends of them stained red from her lipstick. The army blanket was spread out on the mattress. Ike and Bobby moved across the room toward the window through which they'd seen the girl and the two high school boys taking use of her in the night, and leaned out and noted the trampled grass where they themselves had stood in the night, watching.

The other boy knelt next to the mattress. I guess she bout screamed her head off, he said.

Ike looked at him. Why?

Cause that's how they always do. Holler their heads off when they take it in the pussy. On account of how big it is and how much they like it.

The two brothers studied him with suspicion. Where'd you ever hear something like that? Ike said.

That's the way they do.

That's a lie. I don't believe that.

It don't matter what you believe.

Well, she didn't do any of that, Ike said.

She was just on her back, Bobby said. She was just laying on her back looking up and waiting for him to quit bothering her.

Sure, the other boy said. All right. He bent over the rough army blanket and put his face to it and sniffed and raised his eyes dramatically.

What's that? What are you doing now? Ike said.

Smelling if she's still here, the boy said.

They watched what he was doing, his antics. He was holding parts of the blanket up to his face and shifting it about, sampling it. They didn't want him to be acting in such a way in this room. They didn't approve of it.

You better stop that, Bobby said.

I'm not hurting nothing.

You better leave that alone, Bobby said.

You better stand up from there, Ike said. You quit that.

The boy made a face as if the blanket were too dirty to touch, and he dropped it. He reached and pulled out one of the candle stubs from the throat of a beer bottle. Then I'll just take me one of these, he said.

You leave them alone too, Ike said.

You don't own this place. It's just junk. Old-time shit. What's wrong with taking something?

They were going to tell him what was wrong with taking something but suddenly there was someone outside on the front porch. They could hear him distinctly. The hard soles of the shoes on the floorboards and then the footsteps coming into the house.

Who's in here?

It was the old man's voice, high and whining, crazy. They didn't answer. They glanced wildly at the window.

Here now, he called. You hear me? Who's in this goddamn house?

They could hear him coming across the front room and

then he stood in the doorway looking at them, the old man from next door in his dirty overalls and high-topped black shoes and his worn-out blue work shirt, his eyes red and maddened, watery-looking, and his cheeks covered with a two-days' growth of whiskers. In his hands he was waving a rusty shotgun.

You little sonsabitches, he said. What you think you're doing in here?

We were looking, Ike said. We're leaving now.

You got no business coming in here. You goddamn kids coming in here breaking things.

We're not doing nothing, the other boy said. It's not your place either, is it? This don't belong to you, mister.

Why, you little smart sonofabitch. I'll blow your head off. He raised the gun up and leveled it at the boy. I'll blast you to hell.

No, wait now, Ike said. It's all right. We're going. You don't have to worry. Come on, he said.

He pushed Bobby out ahead of him and pulled the other boy by the arm. When they passed the old man he smelled of kerosene and sweat and of something sour like silage. He turned as they passed, following them with the shotgun raised up in his shaking hands.

Don't you little shitasses ever come back in here, he said. I'll come in a-shootin next time. I won't ask no questions first.

We weren't doing a thing in there, the other boy said.

What's that? the old man said. By Jesus, I got a mind to blow your shittin little head off right now. He raised the gun again, dangerously, waving it.

No. Now look out, Ike said. We're leaving. Wait a minute.

The boys went out of the house back through the weeds onto Railroad Street. The old man came out onto the porch and watched them. They turned and looked at him one time and he was still there on the porch standing in the lowering sun in his dirty overalls and blue shirt, still holding the gun up. When he saw them stop in front of the house he pointed the gun at them again, like he was taking aim. They went on.

When they had walked far enough down the road so that the old man couldn't see them clearly, the other boy said, I got this much anyhow. He stopped and withdrew a candle stub from his back pocket.

You took that? Bobby said. You shouldn't even of touched that.

What's wrong with you? It's a candle.

That doesn't matter, Ike said. It wasn't yours. You didn't see her.

I never had to see her. I don't care a turd about her.

You didn't see the way she was that night.

Oh, I seen lots of them without their clothes on. I seen their pink titties, lots of times.

You never saw her, Ike said.

What of it.

She was different. She was pretty, wasn't she, Bobby?

I thought she was pretty, Bobby said.

I don't give a rat's ass. I'm keeping this candle.

They started back along the dirt road toward the house. At the gravel drive the other boy went on by himself toward town, but the two brothers turned and went back past their empty house toward the lot where the two horses were standing dozing by the barn. They went out to the corral to be in the place where there were horses.

Victoria Roubideaux.

One night when she had finished washing dishes at the Holt Café and afterward had eaten her own supper sitting at the café counter, she didn't go back to Maggie Jones's house immediately. Instead she walked about town by herself with her coat buttoned up to her chin and her hands pulled up into the sleeves.

She made the call from a pay phone on the highway out at the town limits of Holt where there was a short turnout for cars and where a summer picnic table was set out under four scrubby and leafless Chinese elm trees. Cattle buyers used the phone during the day, leaning over the hoods of their dusty pickups while they talked, carrying the phone out on its cable as far it would allow them and writing their figures on pads of paper. Now it was dark. The sun had gone under two hours ago and a sharp cold winter wind was blowing dirt across the highway in brown skeins, pushing it into ridges along the gutters at the curbing. The new yellowish streetlamps were burning all along the empty blacktop, showing the entrance into town. She called for information in Norka, where he came from, the next town going west from Holt. The operator gave the number that was listed for his mother.

When she dialed the number, the woman on the other end answered at once, and the woman sounded angry from the outset.

May I speak to Dwayne? the girl said.

Who is this?

This is a friend of his.

Dwayne isn't here. He doesn't live here.

Is he in Denver?

Who is it wants to know?

Victoria Roubideaux.

Who?

The girl said it again.

I never heard him mention that name before, the woman said.

I'm a friend of his, the girl said. We met last summer.

That's what you say. How do I know that? the woman said. I wouldn't know you from Nancy Reagan.

The girl looked out across the highway. There was a scrap of paper blowing along the gutter, tumbling with the dirt. Can't you just give me his phone number? she said. Please, I need to talk to him. There's something I want to tell him.

Now you listen to me, the woman said. I told you, he isn't here. And he isn't here. I'm not giving out his number to everybody that wants it. He's got his privacy to think of. He's working a job and that's what he needs to be doing. Whoever you are, you leave him alone. You hear me? She hung up.

The girl put the phone back. She felt very alone now, cut off and frightened for the first time. She was not sick in the morning very often anymore, but she still wanted to cry too much of the time, and lately her jeans and skirts were so tight at the waist that she'd begun wearing them unbuttoned with a little piece of elastic strap pinned inside, holding them together, a solution that Maggie Jones had given her. The girl looked up and down the highway. It was empty save for a big tanker truck that was rattling in from the west. She could hear the whistle of its brakes as it slowed, passing under the first streetlights. When it rattled by, the driver sitting up high in the tractor cab looked her over thoroughly, his head turned sideways like he had a broken neck.

Across the highway and up a block toward town was Shattuck's, and she decided to go there. She didn't want to go back to Maggie's yet. She would still be out of the house at a teachers' meeting, and the old man was there alone. The girl started walking back toward Shattuck's. She felt emotional and softhearted toward it, as though she were being pulled there by the past. It was where he had bought hamburgers and Cokes for the two of them in the summer, and afterward they had taken the sack of food in the car and driven out into the flat open country north of town on the unnamed gravel roads, driving out alone at that hour when the sky was only beginning to deepen and color up and the first stars were just coming clear, when all the scattered birds of the fields were flying homeward.

Shattuck's had a narrow room at the side with three café tables positioned along the wall where you could sit and eat your food if you weren't ordering from a car. When she entered this room there was a young woman with two little girls eating at one of the tables. The woman had stiff red hair that looked dyed. She was eating chili from a Styrofoam bowl and the little girls were each having a hot dog and sipping chocolate milk from straws.

At the order window the girl asked for a Coke and old Mrs. Shattuck brought the glass to the counter and she carried it to the table in the corner where a window looked out on the highway. She sat down and put her red purse on the table. She unbuttoned her coat. She took a drink and looked out toward the street. A car went by loaded with high school kids, the windows rolled down and the music blaring. After a while two cattle trucks rattled past, one immediately behind the other, making the café windows vibrate. She could see the brown hides of the cattle through the ventilation holes in the aluminum sides, and all along the panels the manure had run down in ragged stains.

Inside Shattuck's, country music was playing from the ceiling speakers. The young red-haired mother at the other table had finished with the chili and was smoking a cigarette. She was jiggling her foot to the music, her loose shoe half off. From the speakers overhead a girl's voice was singing, You really had me going, baby, but now I'm gone. The woman's foot moved with the music. Then suddenly she jumped up from the table and cried, Oh, Jesus Christ. Oh, my God. What is wrong with you? She jerked the smaller of the two girls by the arm, lifting the little girl out of her chair, and stood her violently on her feet. Couldn't you see that was going to happen? There was a pool of chocolate milk spreading across the table from an upended glass, the dark milk spilling off the edge like a little dirty waterfall. The small girl stood away from the table watching it, her face was as white as paper and she began to whimper. Don't you dare, the woman said. Don't you even start that. She grabbed napkins from the dispenser and swiped at the table, spreading the mess around, then she dabbed at her hands. Shit, she said. Look at this. Finally she snatched up her purse and rushed out of the room. Behind her the two little girls clattered in their hard shoes across the tiled floor, calling for her to wait.

The girl watched them through the café window. The woman had already cranked the car and was beginning to roll it backward on the gravel lot, and then the older of the girls managed to open the passenger door and they hopped alongside trying to get in. Suddenly they leaped in one after the other but the door had swung out too wide and they couldn't close it. The car jerked to a stop. The woman came rushing out and around to the other side and slammed the door shut and got back in and raced the car backward onto the highway where she put it forward and they roared away.

On the floor under the table the chocolate milk had made a

thin muddy pool. Mrs. Shattuck appeared from the kitchen dragging a mop and began to soak up the chocolate milk by swiping the mop back and forth. She stopped and looked at the girl. Did you ever see such a mess? she said.

She didn't mean to, the girl said.

I'm not referring to that, Mrs. Shattuck said. Is that what you thought?

It was after ten when the girl returned to the house. But it was still too early. Maggie Jones had not come home yet. The girl stepped quietly down the hall to the old man's room and opened the door slightly and peered in. He was asleep in the bed in this back room where he could control the level of heat and it was turned up to a degree that seemed suffocating to the girl, but even so he was asleep in all his clothes with a blanket pulled up to his chin. His shoes formed a sharp bump under the blanket. A book was folded over his chest. She closed the door and went back to the sewing room she used as a bedroom and got undressed and put on her nightgown.

Afterward she was in the bathroom, scrubbing her face, when the door suddenly opened. She turned from the mirror. He stood in the doorway, his white hair standing up on his head like wisps of dried corn silk. His eyes appeared bloodshot and glazed, staring at her.

What are you doing in this house? he said.

She watched him carefully. I live here, she said.

Who are you? Who said you could just come in here?

Mr. Jackson—

Get out. Before I call the authorities.

Mr. Jackson, I live here. You remember me.

I never saw you before in my life.

But Mrs. Jones invited me, the girl said.

Mrs. Jones is dead.

No. Your daughter. That Mrs. Jones.

Then where is she? he said.

I don't know. At a meeting, I think. She said she'd be here by now.

That's a filthy lie.

He stepped into the room and began to move toward her. The girl stepped back. Suddenly he brought his arm up and slapped her face with his open hand and slapped her again. Her nose began to bleed.

Mr. Jackson, she cried. Don't. She was backed up against the shower door, turned a little to the side, with one hand over her stomach to protect herself in case he should try to hit her somewhere other than the face. Don't. Please. You don't want to do this.

I'll do it again. You better get out of here.

I will. If you just step out for a minute, I'll leave.

He stood still, waiting. His eyes were wild. It's at the bank, he said. You'll never touch it in your life.

What? No. If you'll just step back.

I have it. Not you. You don't have the key.

Yes, I know. But just wait outside. Just for a minute. Will you do that?

Why should I?

I want to dry my face.

He looked at her. I can't take much more of this, he said. He surveyed the bathroom, his eyes still wild and red. At last he shuffled his feet, backing out.

Immediately she locked the door and he stayed outside, muttering. She could hear him guarding the door, waiting for her. For an hour she stayed in the bathroom. She put the lid down and sat down on the toilet and held toilet paper to her nose and all the time she could hear him talking and arguing in the hallway. It sounded as though he had seated himself against the wall.

. . .

He was still there when Maggie Jones came home after eleven. She came into the hall and found him sitting on the floor. Oh, Dad, she said. What have you done?

She's in there, he said. I got her trapped. But she won't come out.

Mrs. Jones? the girl called. Is that you?

That's her, he said. That's her yapping in there.

Dad, Maggie Jones said, she lives here. That's Victoria. Don't you remember? She turned toward the door. Honey, are you okay?

I don't know what I did, the girl said through the door. I don't know what upset him.

I know. It's all right. I know you didn't do anything, honey.

She wants my key. That's what she wants.

No, now Dad. That's not so. You know it isn't. Come on. Let's get you to bed.

That's what they all want.

She raised her old father by the arm and led him back to his room. He came along docilely now. She helped him out of his clothes and removed his shoes and set them on the floor beside the bed and he stood naked in the hot room, his arms at his sides, his skin sagging at the elbows and knees, his thighs as skinny as sticks. His old gray buttocks had fallen forlornly. He stood like a child waiting for what she would do next. She helped him step into his pajamas and buttoned his top, then he lay down in the bed. She covered him with the blankets.

Dad, she said. She brushed his wispy hair flat on his head. You can't do that again. Please. You can't. Listen to me now.

Do what? he said.

Please, she said. Just don't do that. That girl has enough trouble.

She can't get to it anyway.

No. Hush now. We'll talk in the morning. Try to sleep. She bent and kissed him and held her face against his cheek for a long while. He began to relax. She smoothed her hand over his eyes and he closed them. She continued to caress his face. At last he was asleep. Then she went back into the hall. She found the girl in the makeshift bedroom at the back of the house, standing at the dresser. The girl looked large-eyed and very tired and pale in the long white nightgown. Just a young high school girl with dark hair, with something swollen beginning to show at her stomach.

Did he hurt you? Maggie Jones said.

Not really, the girl said.

You're sure you're all right?

I'm okay. But Mrs. Jones. I think I have to go someplace else. He doesn't like me.

Honey, he doesn't even know you.

He scares me. I don't know what to do.

Can you stay with a friend?

I don't know who, the girl said. I don't like to ask.

Go to bed then, honey, Maggie Jones said. I'm here now.

Ike and Bobby.

In the afternoon they sat on their bikes at the curb on Chicago Street directly across the way, looking at it. A little pale stucco house no bigger than a cottage, standing back behind three low elms that grew in the front yard, one of the trees with a long weep of sap from upwards in its trunk where a limb had been taken off. A sidewalk led to the front door. It was a little rental house, one story and no basement, in this country where most houses had basements or root cellars, and it was faded to a dim green with a gray shingled roof and even though they knew she was inside it looked empty and unlived in. Beyond the windows there was no movement. They watched for a long while.

Then they crossed the street walking their bikes and stopped and looked at it again, put down their kickstands and parked the bikes on the sidewalk and walked up to the front door. Go on, Bobby said.

Ike tapped on the unvarnished wood door.

She won't even hear that, Bobby said.

Then you do it.

Bobby looked away.

All right then.

Ike tapped again, only slightly louder, and they waited, staring at the door. Behind them the street was quiet and without traffic. When they no longer expected anything from inside, the door swung inward slowly and there was their mother. She stood in the doorway looking at them with dull lusterless eyes. She looked bad now. She appeared to be completely worn out. They could see that. She had been a pretty woman with soft brown hair and slim arms and a thin waist. But now she looked sick. Her eyes were sunken behind dark circles and her face was pasty-looking, thin and drawn, as if for days she'd fogotten to eat or as if nothing she brought to her mouth tasted good enough anymore, even to take in and chew and swallow. She was still wearing a bathrobe in the middle of the afternoon and her hair was flattened against one side of her head.

Yes, she said. Her voice was dry and flat, without inflection.

Hello, Mother.

Is something wrong? She cupped one hand over her eyes against the bright afternoon sun.

We just wanted to see you. They felt embarrassed and they turned away, looking back across the empty street toward the spot at the curb from which they had watched the house.

Did you want to come in? she said.

If you don't care.

They followed her into the little front room where at any time, day or night, her clothes had been discarded and dropped over the anonymous furniture and where dishes from the kitchen, coffee cups and saucers and bowls of shrinking drying food, had been put down at random on the bare rug.

I wasn't expecting anyone, she said.

She sat down on the couch and drew her feet up under her. The boys were still standing.

Can't you find a place to sit?

They seated themselves on the two wood chairs opposite the couch and looked in her direction and after the first time they didn't look at her eyes again. She was playing with the belt of her bathrobe, wrapping it around one finger and then unwrapping it. Her pale legs, the pale shins and her yellowish sallow feet, were visible beneath the hem of her robe.

Did your father send you here? she said.

No, Ike said. He didn't send us.

He doesn't even know we came, Bobby said.

Does he ask about me?

We talk about you, Ike said.

What do you say?

We say we miss you. We wonder how you are.

We wonder how you're doing all alone in this new house, Bobby said.

I appreciate that, she said. Knowing that much makes me feel better. She looked across the room. How is he?

Dad?

Yes.

He's okay.

I understand he stays out all the time now.

He goes out at night sometimes after we're in bed, Ike said.

Where does he go?

We don't know.

Doesn't he tell you?

No.

I don't like that, she said. She examined her hands, the ends of her long slender shapely fingers. He must think I'm crazy now. That I've gone over the other side. He must think that about me. She looked up. Did you know he doesn't want me to come back anymore. Even if I wanted to. He told me as much.

We want you to come back, Mother.

I'm not crazy yet, she said. I don't think I am. Do you think I'm crazy?

No.

No. I haven't gotten there yet. I don't think I'm going to now. She stared off fixedly across the room. I thought I would but I don't think so now. It's just that I don't know what to do about what I'm thinking. I think all the time and I can't seem to stop, but I don't know what to do about that yet either. She was looking at them again. Isn't that a nice fix to find yourself in?

Maybe you should go outside more, Ike said.

Do you think that would help me?

It might.

But when do you think you will be coming home again? Bobby said.

I can't say about that. You mustn't rush me. I need time. Don't ask me that now, all right?

All right.

She smiled at him sadly. Thank you, she said.

Mother, do you want us to pick up for you? Ike said.

Why? What do you mean?

The things here. In this house. He looked around the room and waved his hand.

Oh. No. That's nice of you. But I'm feeling kind of tired. She pulled the neck of her robe together. I think I'll lie down. I feel kind of sick.

You should see the doctor.

I know. Would you mind if I lie down now?

You look tired, Mother.

We'll come back later, Bobby said.

Can we bring you anything? Ike said.

She looked into their faces. Well. I don't know. I am out of coffee, she said. Could you get me some coffee?

Yes.

You could charge it at Johnson's in my name.

She stood up and went back slowly to the bedroom, and they went outside and talked about it between themselves on the street curb and then rode downtown to Johnson's grocery store on Main Street and went back along the wood floor to the ranked shelves of coffee that were arranged by brand and price and chose a green can that looked familiar to them and charged it to their mother at the register. Afterward they went over to Duckwall's, still on Main Street in the middle of the same block, and stood in front of the perfume counter, debating for fifteen minutes, while the clerk behind the glass case showed them little bottles.

How much is that one? Ike said.

This one here?

Yes.

This one is five dollars.

Finally they chose the one they could afford out of their paper-route money and from what was left of the dollars Raymond McPheron had given them for helping work cattle—a little blue bottle that said Evening in Paris on the label and had a very sweet scent and a silver stopper that closed it, and they still had enough money left over to buy a small box with a clear lid that contained a dozen round soft vari-colored balls of bubble bath. They had the clerk, the middle-aged woman, wrap the two boxes in paper with a bow.

Then they rode back to her house on Chicago Street. By now it was late afternoon and getting cold outside. The long shadows were reaching across the street. They waited a long time before she answered their knock, and when she came to the door she looked as though she had risen from a deep sleep.

They offered the can of coffee to her and she took it fumbling and then they held out the two boxes from Duckwall's.

Did you buy these too?

Yes.

What are they?

Open them why don't you, Mother?

But what are they?

They're for you.

She slowly untied the bows and unwrapped the bright paper and saw what was in the boxes. She began to cry then. The tears ran unregarded down her face. Oh, dear God, she said. She was crying. She hugged the two boys with the boxes still clutched in her hands. Oh God, what am I going to do about any of this?

McPherons.

Maggie Jones drove out to the McPherons' on a cold Saturday afternoon. Seventeen miles southeast of Holt. Beside the black-top there were patches of snow in the fallow fields, drifts and scallops wind-hardened in the ditches. Black baldy cattle were spread out in the corn stubble, all pointed out of the wind with their heads down, eating steadily. When she turned off onto the gravel road small birds flew up from the roadside in gusts and blew away in the wind. Along the fenceline the snow was brilliant under the sun.

She drove up the track to the old house set back off the road a quarter mile. Beside the house a few low elm trees stood leafless inside the yard that was closed in by wire hogfencing. When she got out of the car a mottled old farm dog scuttled up to her and sniffed her leather boots and she patted his head and went through the wire gate up to the house and knocked on the screen door. Above the steps was a little screened porch, the mesh mended in places with white cotton string where it had been torn or poked through with something sharp. Beyond was the kitchen. She went up the steps onto the porch and knocked again. She looked in, the kitchen was more or less orderly. The table was cleared of dishes and the dishes laid in the sink, but there were stacks of *Farm Journals* and newspapers loaded up against the far walls, and greasy pieces of machinery—cogwheels, old bearings, shank bolts—were set out on mechanics' rags on each of the chairs except the two that were placed opposite each other at the pine table. She opened the door and hollered in. Hello? Her voice echoed, it died out in the far room.

She came back off the porch and out to the car. Now there was the far-off sound of a tractor muttering and popping, coming up from the pasture to the south. She walked down to it and stood around the corner of the horse barn out of the wind. She could see them now. Both brothers were on the tractor, Raymond standing up behind Harold, who sat behind the wheel driving an ancient red sun-faded Farmall with the canvas wings of the heat houser bolted over the block onto the fenders for protection from the wind, pulling an empty flatbed hay wagon. They'd been feeding cattle out in the winter pasture, hay bales and pellets of cottonseed cake, scattering the cake in the feedbunks. They jolted through the gate and stopped and Raymond got off and swung the gate closed and climbed back on, and they came banging and clattering past the corrals and past the loading chute up to the barn. The lid on the tractor's exhaust stack flapped with bursts of black smoke, then they shut the engine off and the lid dropped shut and suddenly Maggie Jones could hear the wind again.

She stepped away from the barn and stood waiting for them. They got down and approached her slowly, calmly, as deliberately as church deacons, as if they were not at all surprised to see her. They moved heavily in their winter coveralls and they had on thick caps pulled low and cumbersome winter gloves.

You're going to freeze yourself standing there, Harold said. You better get out of this wind. Are you lost?

Probably, Maggie Jones said. She laughed. But I wanted to talk to you.

Oh oh. I don't like the sound of that.

Don't tell me I scared you already, she said.

Why hell, Harold said. You probably want something.

I do, she said.

You better come up to the house, Raymond said.

Thank you, she said. At least one of you is a gentleman.

They went back to the old house across the frozen lot in the wind. The dog came out to meet them and sniffed at her again and retreated once more into the open garage. They mounted the steps to the house. On the little porch the brothers bent over and unbuckled their manure-caked overshoes. Go on in, Raymond said. Don't wait on us. She opened the door and entered the kitchen. The house was not warm but it felt better out of the wind. They came in after her, closed the door and took their gloves off and set them out on the counter where they looked as stiff as firewood curled open in the permanent shapes of their hands. They unzipped the tops of their coveralls. Underneath they wore black button-up sweaters, flannel shirts and long underwear.

You want any coffee? Raymond said.

Oh, that's too much trouble, Maggie said.

It's only what's left over from noon dinner.

He set a pan on the stove and poured the coffee from the pot into it. Then he removed his cap and the hair stood up in short gray stiff shocks on his round head. She thought his head looked beautiful, had a clean perfect shape. They both looked that way. Harold had removed the greasy pieces of machinery from one of the extra chairs and had dragged it up to the table. He sat down solidly. When they were inside the house the McPheron brothers' faces turned shiny and red as beets and the tops of their heads steamed in the cool room. They looked like something out of an old painting, of peasants, laborers resting after work.

Maggie Jones unbuttoned her coat and sat down. I came out here to ask you a favor, she said to them.

That so? Harold said. Well, you can always ask anyhow.

What is it? Raymond said.

There is a girl I know who needs some help, Maggie said. She's a good girl but she's gotten into trouble. I think you might be able to help her. I would like you to consider it and let me know.

What's wrong with her? Harold said. She need a donation of money?

No. She needs a lot more than that.

What sort of trouble is she in? Raymond said.

She's seventeen, Maggie Jones said. She's four months pregnant and she doesn't have a husband.

Well yeah, Harold said. I reckon that could amount to trouble.

I've had her staying with me in my house for a while, but my father won't accept her being there anymore. His mind's gone. He's all mixed up and sometimes he gets violent. He's made her afraid to be in the house with him.

What about her kinfolk? Harold said. Don't she have any family?

Her father left her years ago. I don't know how many years exactly. Now, lately, her mother won't have her in the house.

On account of her carrying the baby?

Yes, Maggie said. Her mother has problems of her own. You probably know who I'm talking about.

Who?

Betty Roubideaux.

Oh, Harold said. Leonard's wife.

Did you know him?

Enough to drink with.

What ever became of him, I wonder.

Nothing good. You can bet on that.

Well, he might of went to Denver, Raymond said. Then he might of went back to the Rosebud in South Dakota. I doubt anybody knows. He's been gone a long time.

But the girl's still here, Maggie said. That's my point. His daughter's still here. She's a good person too. Her name is Victoria.

What about the sire? Harold said.

Who? she said. Oh. You mean the baby's father.

Where does he come into this?

He doesn't. She won't even tell me who he is except to say he doesn't live here. He lives somewhere else. He doesn't want her anymore, she says. Or the baby either, apparently. Well, I don't know if he even knows about the baby. Whether she told him.

On the stove the coffee had begun to boil. Raymond stood up and set three cups out and poured out the coffee, the pan hissing wildly as he tipped it up. The coffee was black and thick as steaming tar. You take something in it? he said.

Maggie looked in her cup. Maybe some milk?

He brought a jar of milk from the refrigerator and set it on the table and sat down again. She took the lid off and poured a little into her cup.

All right then, Harold said. You got our attention. You say you don't want money. What do you want?

She sipped from her coffee and tasted it and looked in the cup again and set it back on the table. She looked at the two old brothers. They were waiting, sitting forward at the table across from her. I want something improbable, she said. That's what I want. I want you to think about taking this girl in. Of letting her live with you.

They stared at her.

You're fooling, Harold said.

No, Maggie said. I am not fooling.

They were dumbfounded. They looked at her, regarding her as if she might be dangerous. Then they peered into the palms of their thick callused hands spread out before them on the kitchen table and lastly they looked out the window toward the leafless and stunted elm trees.

Oh, I know it sounds crazy, she said. I suppose it is crazy. I don't know. I don't even care. But that girl needs somebody and I'm ready to take desperate measures. She needs a home for these months. And you—she smiled at them—you old solitary bastards need somebody too. Somebody or something besides an old red cow to care about and worry over. It's too lonesome out here. Well, look at you. You're going to die some day without ever having had enough trouble in your life. Not of the right kind anyway. This is your chance.

The McPheron brothers shifted in their chairs. They watched her suspiciously.

Well? she said. What do you think?

They didn't say anything.

She laughed. I believe I have robbed you of speech. Will you at least think about it?

Hell, Maggie, Harold said at last. Let's go back to the money part. Money'd be a lot easier.

Yes, she said. It would. But not nearly as much fun.

Fun, he said. That's a nice word for what you're talking about. More like pandemonium and disruption, you mean. Jesus God.

All right, she said. I tried. I had to do that much. She stood up and buttoned her coat. You can let me know if you change your minds.

She went outside to the car. They followed her and went down the little walk and stood at the wire gate in the freezing wind, waiting for her to back up and come forward in the rutted driveway and drive back out past the house toward the county road. As she passed she waved at them. They lifted their hands and gestured back to her.

When she had gone they didn't talk to each other but returned to the kitchen and drank down the coffee in their cups and put on their winter caps and gloves and pulled on their overshoes and buckled them, and then went back down the porch steps into the yard to return to work as mutely and numbly as if they had been stunned into a sudden and permanent silence by such a proposal.

But later, when the sun had gone down in the late afternoon, after the sky had turned faint and wispy and the thin blue shadows had reached across the snow, the brothers did talk. They were out in the horse lot, working at the stock tank.

The tank had frozen over with ice. The shaggy saddle horses, already winter-coated, stood with their backs to the wind, watching the two men in the corral, the horses' tails blowing out, their breath snorted out in white plumes and carried away in tatters by the wind.

Harold chopped at the ice on the stock tank with a wood axe. He flailed at it and finally broke through into the water below, the head of the axe sunken helve-deep out of sight and suddenly heavy, and he pulled it out and chopped again. Then Raymond scooped out the ice chunks with his cob fork and flung the ice away from the tank onto the hard ground behind him where it landed among other frozen blocks and pieces. When the tank was clear they lifted the lid from the galvanized watertight box that floated in the water. Inside the box was the tank heater. When they looked inside they could see that the pilot light had blown out. Harold took off his gloves and withdrew a long firebox match from his inside pocket, popped it on his thumbnail and cupped the little flame and held it down into the box. When the pilot light took he adjusted the flame and drew his arm out, and Raymond wired the lid tight again. Then they checked the propane bottle that was standing out of the way. It looked all right.

So for a while they stood below the windmill in the failing light. The thirsty horses approached and peered at them and sniffed at the water and began to drink, sucking up long draughts of it. Afterward they stood back watching the two brothers, their eyes as large and luminous as perfect round knobs of mahogany glass.

It was almost dark now. Only a thin violet band of light showed in the west on the low horizon.

All right, Harold said. I know what I think. What do you think we do with her?

We take her in, Raymond said. He spoke without hesitation, as though he'd only been waiting for his brother to start so they could have this out and settle it. Maybe she wouldn't be as much trouble, he said.

I'm not talking about that yet, Harold said. He looked out into the gathering darkness. I'm talking about—why hell, look at us. Old men alone. Decrepit old bachelors out here in the country seventeen miles from the closest town which don't amount to much of a good goddamn even when you get there. Think of us. Crotchety and ignorant. Lonesome. Independent. Set in all our ways. How you going to change now at this age of life?

I can't say, Raymond said. But I'm going to. That's what I know.

And what do you mean? How come she wouldn't be no trouble?

I never said she wouldn't be no trouble. I said maybe she wouldn't be as much trouble.

Why wouldn't she be as much trouble? As much trouble as what? You ever had a girl living with you before?

You know I ain't, Raymond said.

Well, I ain't either. But let me tell you. A girl is different. They want things. They need things on a regular schedule. Why, a girl's got purposes you and me can't even imagine. They got ideas in their heads you and me can't even suppose. And goddamn it, there's the baby too. What do you know about babies?

Nothing. I don't even know the first thing about em, Raymond said.

Well then?

But I don't have to know about any babies yet. Maybe I'll have time to learn. Now, are you going to go in on this thing with me or not? Cause I'm going to do it anyhow, whatever.

Harold turned toward him. The light was gone in the sky and he couldn't make out the features of his brother's face. There was only this dark familiar figure against the failed horizon.

All right, he said. I will. I'll agree. I shouldn't, but I will. I'll make up my mind to it. But I'm going to tell you one thing first.

What is it?

You're getting goddamn stubborn and hard to live with. That's all I'll say. Raymond, you're my brother. But you're getting flat unruly and difficult to abide. And I'll say one thing more.

What?

This ain't going to be no goddamn Sunday school picnic.

No, it ain't, Raymond said. But I don't recall you ever attending Sunday school either.

Ella.

When he drove to Chicago Street to her little house after she had called him at school it was late in the afternoon. He parked and walked up the sidewalk past the three elm trees, the one with the sap still showing the dark stain but no longer so raw nor fresh this late in the year, and then when he stepped onto the porch he discovered that she was already waiting for him at the door. She opened it even before he could knock. She let him in and he entered the little front room of the place and saw at once that she had been packing. Her two suitcases were set out on the floor and the room itself was clean and spruce and neat again, as it had been when she'd moved in. Dustfree and anonymous again, it was returned once more to its former state: a little rental house on Chicago Street on the east side of Holt.

When he had a good look at Ella he could see that she too was better now. Not as good as she had looked once, but her hair was pretty again, just washed and brushed back from her face, and she was dressed in wool slacks and a good white blouse. She had lost weight since he'd last seen her, but it didn't appear that she would lose any more.

He gestured toward the suitcases. Are you going somewhere?

I'm going to tell you about it, she said. That's why I called you.

So tell me, he said.

She looked at him. Her eyes still bore a kind of wounded fierceness, as though the sadness and the anger were both just below the surface. I hoped you weren't going to be that way today, she said.

What way?

I didn't want it to be like this, not this time.

Why don't you go ahead and tell me what you have in mind, he said. You called school and I came.

Can we at least sit down? she said. Will you do that?

Yes.

She seated herself on the couch and he sat opposite her on one of the wooden chairs. On the couch she looked small, almost frail. He picked out a cigarette from his shirt pocket. Are you going to object if I smoke?

I'd prefer that you didn't.

He looked at her. He held the cigarette but didn't light it. Go ahead and talk, he said. I'm listening.

Well, she said, I wanted you to know that I've decided to go to Denver to my sister's. To stay with her for a while. I called her and it's all set. She has an extra bedroom and I can have the use of that. I won't be in the way and it'll give me time to think. We both think it'll be for the best.

For how long?

I don't know. I can't tell that yet. For as long as it takes.

When?

You mean when am I going?

Yes, when do you plan to leave?

Tomorrow. In the morning. I'll be taking the car.

You'll be taking the car. That's news.

You don't need it. You have the pickup.

He looked around, out into the little dining room and

through the arched doorway into the kitchen. He turned back. And you think this'll be the answer? Taking off like this?

She regarded him steadily. You know, you make me really tired sometimes.

I guess that goes both ways, he said.

They looked at each other, and it seemed obvious to Guthrie that she was thinking hard, trying to get back to how she wanted this to be. But it wasn't going to happen. Too much had gone on.

She spoke again. I'm sorry about that for both of us, she said. I'm sorry about a lot of things. And I've decided I'm finally tired of being sorry.

He started to speak, but she cut him off.

Let me finish, please.

I was only going to say—

I know. Let me finish. I don't want to forget this. I want something more than this. I understand that now. I've been submerged and abstracted. I wanted something more from you all these years. I wanted someone who wanted me for what I am. Not his own version of me. It sounds too simple to say it that way, but that's what it is. Someone who wanted me, for myself. You don't.

I used to, he said. I did once.

What happened to it?

Lots of things. It wore out. He shrugged. I didn't get back what I gave you, what I wanted in return.

What you wanted? She flared up now, speaking heatedly. What about me? What about what I want?

What do you want? he said. He was angry now too. I don't think you know. I wish you did but I don't think you do. This is just another example of it.

You can't say that, she said. That's not for you to say. I'll take care of that.

They sat facing each other across the room, and Guthrie thought, So they had reached this point again. It hadn't taken them long. They'd arrived at this place one more time despite whatever good intentions they'd started with. It didn't matter, this is where they would end up. It had been this way for the past three or four years. He looked at her. They were waiting, both trying privately to regain some calm in themselves. At the back of the little house the heater clicked on and the fan blew warm air into the room.

What about the boys? he said.

I've been thinking about that. You'll just have to keep them.

You mean as opposed to what I've already been doing.

I know you've been taking care of them by yourself, she said. I can't do anything else right now. But I want them to come stay with me here tonight. Then I'll leave in the morning. I'll bring them back to the house before I leave.

They still have their papers in the morning.

They'll be home in time.

What about money? he said.

I'm going to take half of our savings.

The hell.

It's half mine, she said. It's only fair.

He took out matches and lit the cigarette he'd been holding. He blew smoke toward the ceiling light and looked across at her. All right, he said. Take the money.

I already have, she said. And you'll be good to the boys, won't you. And you'll pay attention to them. And I want them to call me and for you to let me talk to them. I want you to promise you won't make that a problem.

You can call any time, he said. They can call you any time.

And I want them to come and see me too. After a while. After I've gotten settled.

I think they should, he said. They'll want to. They already miss you now. It'll be worse after you leave.

He smoked and looked around for an ashtray but there wasn't any and she didn't get up to find him one. He tapped ashes into his cupped palm.

So that's it?

Yes, I think so.

All right. I think I'll go.

He rose without saying anything more and he walked out onto the front porch and she followed him and shut the door. Outside, he brushed the ashes off his hand and that evening he drove the two boys back to their mother's house, driving across town in the old pickup with a grocery bag containing their clean pajamas on the seat between them, with the blue streetlights turned on at all the street corners and the town itself looking quiet and serene. He pulled up and stopped in front of the house. The lights were on inside.

Mom'll bring you home in the morning, he said. And you've got your pajamas.

They nodded.

You're all set then.

Can we call you if we need anything? Bobby said.

Of course. But you'll be all right. I know you will. You're going to have a good time here.

Guthrie and the two boys sat in the heated cab, looking at the little stucco house with the lights showing in the windows. Once they saw her pass before the window carrying something. Patches of snow under the bare trees in the yard were shining in the house light.

All right? Guthrie said. That'll be good. You'll have a fine time. Who knows, maybe you won't even want to come home again. He patted them on the legs. A joke.

But they didn't smile. They didn't say anything.

Well. You better go. Your mom's waiting. I'll see you in the morning.

Good night, Dad.

Good night, he said.

They climbed out of the pickup and walked one after the other up the sidewalk and knocked on the door and stood waiting without turning to look back at him, and then she opened the front door. She had changed clothes since the afternoon and now was wearing a handsome blue dress. He thought she looked slim and pretty framed in the doorway. She let them in and closed the door, and afterward he drove up Chicago past the little houses set back from the street in their narrow lots, the lawns in front of them all brown with winter and the evening lights turned on inside the houses and people sitting down to dinner in the kitchens or watching the news on television in the front rooms, while in some of the houses some of the people too, he knew well, were already starting to argue in the back bedrooms.

When they entered the house Ike and Bobby found that she had already set the table in the little dining room. It was pleasant, with lighted candles and the flames reflecting in the glasses and silverware, and out in the kitchen she had hamburger chili ready to dish up and a round chocolate cake, which she had made specially for them. She wanted it to be festive.

Well come in, come in, she said. Don't be strangers. Take off your coats. I have everything ready.

We ate at home, Bobby said, looking at the table. We didn't know you'd have supper.

Oh. Didn't you? She looked at him. She had both hands on the back of a chair. She looked at his brother. I thought you would eat here. I thought that was understood.

We can eat some more, Ike said.

Don't be foolish. You don't have to make yourselves sick.

No. We're still hungry, Mother.

Are you?

Yes, we are.

I am, Bobby said.

They sat down and ate the supper she had prepared. They were able to eat quite a lot while she told them about her decision to go to Denver. They listened to her without saying anything since Guthrie had already told them about it. She said she wanted them to come visit her soon and that her leaving was going to be better for everyone, including the two of them, even if they couldn't see it yet, because soon she'd be able to act like their mother again, and then when she was feeling completely better they would all decide what to do next, didn't they think that would be all right? They didn't know, they said. Maybe, they said. She said she guessed that would have to do, that it was about as much as she could hope for right then.

After supper they played a game of blackjack which she had taught them a year ago. She went to the closet and opened her purse and took out some coins and they used these to bet with, determining for the sake of the game that the coins were all the same worth, even the quarters and pennies. During the card game she sat across from them on the carpet with her stockinged legs folded back to the side and her dress covering her knees. She acted as though she were happy, as though they were having a real party, and made little jokes to tease them, and once she stood up and brought each of them more cake from the kitchen and they ate it sitting on the floor together. They watched her with their heads down and smiled when she said things.

Later they put on their pajamas in the bathroom and then went into her bedroom and got into the bed that she used.

She undressed in the bathroom too. She brushed her hair and washed her face and put on a long nightgown, then came into the bedroom. She said she'd made up the bed in the other room for them. But they asked to sleep in this room with her. Couldn't they, this once? They were already in the bed. She stood beside the bed looking at them. They wanted to sleep one on each side of her but she said that would be too hot. She got in on the outside and Bobby lay in the middle with Ike next to him. The ceiling light down the hallway shone in through the half-open door. They settled down and lay quietly. Occasionally a car went by outside on Chicago Street. They talked a little in the dim light.

Mother, are you going to be all right in Denver? Ike said.

I hope so, she said. I want to be. I'll call you when I get there. Will you call me back sometimes?

Yes, he said. We'll call you every week.

Does Dad have your number? Bobby said.

Yes, he does. And you know how much I love you, don't you. Both of you. I want you always to remember that. I'm going to miss you so much. But I know you're going to be all right.

I wish you didn't have to go, Ike said.

I don't understand why you are, Bobby said.

It's hard to explain, she said. I just know I have to. Can you try to accept that, even if you don't understand it?

They didn't say anything.

I hope you can.

After a while she said, Do you have any more questions?

They shook their heads.

Do you think you can go to sleep?

In the night after they were asleep she got up and looked out the window at the front yard and the empty street, at the stark trees that stood in the lawn like arrested stickfigures. She went out to the kitchen. She made coffee and took it to the front room and lay down on the sofa and after an hour or more she went to sleep. But she woke early, in time to wake them and set out cereal, and then she drove them in the car back to the house in the early cold winter morning. She leaned across in the front seat of the car and kissed them both, and Guthrie came out on the porch to meet them, and then she turned the car around and went out the drive onto Railroad Street and drove through Holt, which didn't take long, and then she was in the country on US 34 driving west to start her next life in Denver.

Victoria Roubideaux.

The second time she drove out there she had the girl with her, beside her in the front seat of the car. The girl looked frightened and preoccupied, as if she were going to confession or jail or some other place that was so unpleasant that she was willing to go only under force of circumstance and nothing else. It was Sunday. A cold and bright day and the snow still as brilliant as glass under the sun, with the wind blowing as usual in sudden but regular gusts so that outside when they got beyond the town limits it was the same as before except that the wind had turned west in the night. The cattle, the same shaggy black baldy cattle spread out in the corn stubble as the day before, were still there. It was only as if the cattle had made a collective rightface in the night when the wind had changed and had then gone on slicking up the spilled corn, wrapping their tongues around the dry corn husks, raising their heads and staring off into the distance, all the time chewing steadily.

Maggie Jones had driven more than halfway to the McPherons before the girl said any word at all. Then she said:

Mrs. Jones. Would you stop the car?

What is it?

Please, would you pull over?

Maggie slowed and steered the car off onto the rutted shoulder. A bank of snow alongside was packed into the barrow ditch and from behind the car the white smokelike exhaust tore away in the gusting wind.

What is it? Are you sick?

No.

What then?

Mrs. Jones, I don't know if I can do this.

Oh. Well honey, yes you can.

I don't know, the girl said.

Maggie turned to face her. The girl was looking straight ahead with one hand on the door handle, sitting up rigid and tense in the seat as though she were waiting for the right moment to jump out and run.

All right, I'll tell you again, Maggie said. I can't guarantee anything about this. Don't ask that. But you need to regard this as an opportunity. They called last night and said they would take you, that they'd try it. That's a great deal for them to say. I think it will be all right. You don't have to be at all afraid of them. They're about as good as men can be. They may be gruff and unpolished but they don't mean anything by that, it's only they've been alone so much. Think of living your life alone for half a century and more, like they have. It would do something to you. So you can't let their gruffness bother you or deter you. Yes, they are rough around the edges, of course they are. They haven't been rounded off. But you'll be safe out here. You can still come in to school, ride the bus back and forth and complete your course work as usual. But you have to try to remember what it's been like for them. Both their folks died in a highway truck wreck when these old men were younger than you are now. Afterward they just quit attending school, if they'd ever gone very much anyway, which I don't think they did, and they stayed at home and went to work ranching and farming, and that's about all they've known in the world or had to know. Up to now that's been enough.

She stopped. She studied the girl's face to see what effect her talking had had.

The girl was looking out over the nose of the car toward the straight two-lane highway. After a while she said, But Mrs. Jones. Do you think they'll like me?

Yes, I do. If you give them a chance they will.

But it seems crazy to be going out here to live with two old men.

That's right, Maggie said. But these are crazy times. I sometimes believe these must be the craziest times ever.

The girl turned her head to look out the side window at the native pasture beyond the ditch and fenceline. The flower spikes of the soapweed stuck up like splintered sticks, the seed pods dry and dark-looking against the winter grass. Do they have a dog? she said.

There's an old farm dog.

Do they have any cats?

I didn't see any. But I would guess they do. I've never heard of a farm yet without at least one or two stray cats around to keep down the mice and rats.

I'd have to quit my job at the Holt Café. I'd have to tell Janine.

Yes. But you wouldn't be the first one to quit washing dishes for Janine. She expects that.

Does she?

Yes.

The girl continued to look out the window. Maggie Jones waited. Whenever there was a gust of wind the car was rocked on its wheels. After a while the girl turned back and faced forward again. You can go on if you want to, she said. I'm okay now.

Good, Maggie said. I thought you would be. She steered the car back onto the blacktop and they drove down the narrow highway. After a time they turned east onto the gravel county road and then onto the track which led back to the old house with the rusted hogwire strung around it and the stunted elm trees standing up leafless inside the rusted wire. Maggie stopped the car in front of the gate. She and the girl got out.

The McPheron brothers had been watching for them. They came out of the house at once onto the little screened porch and stood waiting for the women to come up to the house. But they neither spoke nor made any gesture. They looked as stiff and motionless as if they'd been shaped out of plaster and then stood up on the porch like two lifelike statues of minor saints.

When she got out of the car the wind had wrapped the girl's hair across her face so that her first view of the McPherons was obscured by her own thick dark hair. But the old men had dressed for the occasion. They wore new shirts with pearl snaps and had on clean Sunday trousers. Their red faces were clean-shaven and their iron-gray hair was combed down flat on their heads with a considerable excess of hair oil, leaving it so heavy and stiffened that even the gusting wind couldn't move it. The girl followed Maggie Jones up onto the porch.

Maggie made the introductions. Harold and Raymond McPheron, she said, this is Victoria Roubideaux. Victoria, this is Harold. This is Raymond.

The two brothers stepped forward one after the other in a kind of vaudeville drill, without yet looking directly into the girl's face, and both shook her hand, each in his own turn, giving her one quick brisk hard-clenched squeeze and release, feeling her hand so small and soft and pliable in their own big hard cal-lused hands, and then stepped back. Then they did look at her. She stood silently beside Maggie Jones in her winter coat and blue jeans, a young girl with long black hair and black eyes, carrying a red purse over the shoulder of her dark coat. But they couldn't tell whether she was pregnant or not, she seemed so young and slight.

Well, Harold said. I guess you better come on in the house. It's a booger out here.

They let the girl enter the kitchen ahead of them. Then

Maggie followed and they followed her. Inside, it was apparent at once that the McPheron brothers had made an effort. The sink was empty of dishes, the table was scrubbed clean, the kitchen chairs were free of the mechanics' rags and the pieces of machinery they had held the day before, and the floor looked as hard-swept as if an immigrant woman had used her broom on it.

This here is the kitchen, Harold said, what you're looking at. Over here's the sink. Next to it there is the gas range. He stopped. He looked about him. I reckon all that'd be more or less obvious to anybody. It don't require me to tell you. In here's the dining room and parlor.

They moved farther into the house, into two larger rooms which were intersected by shafts of daylight since the cracked brown shades bracketed above the windows had been rolled up at some point years ago, leaving both rooms filled with unshaded light as in a country schoolhouse or a rural train depot. In the first, the dining room, positioned under a hanging light fixture was an old square walnut table supported by a heavy pedestal, with four wood chairs gathered about it. The table had been cleared only very recently and the sunbleached outlines of books and magazines were still visible on its surface. Beyond, in the next room, were two worn-out plaid recliner chairs placed like housebroken outsized animals in front of a television set, with a floor lamp located at exact equidistance between the chairs and piles of newspapers and *Farm Journals* spread on the linoleum at the chairs' feet. The girl turned and looked, taking it all in.

I expect you'd like to have a idea where your bedroom's at, Harold said. He motioned toward the small room off the dining room. They entered it. It was almost completely filled by an old soft double bed covered by an ancient quilt, and standing against the inside wall was a heavy mahogany chest of drawers. The girl walked around the foot of the bed and opened the closet door. Inside were dusty cardboard boxes and the dark clothes of a man and woman hanging from a silver rod, the clothes so old that they were no longer black but almost purple.

All this here was theirs, Harold said. They used to sleep in here in this room.

Your mother and father? Maggie said.

After they was gone, he said, I expect we got use to thinking of it as storage space. He glanced at the girl. Course, you move things around however you want.

Thank you, the girl said.

Because we don't come in here, Raymond said. This'll be just yours alone. Our bedrooms is upstairs.

Oh, she said.

Yes, he said.

Well, Harold said. And out here's where you step out.

The girl turned toward him, questioning.

Right next door to you. Convenient.

The girl looked puzzled yet. She turned to Maggie Jones.

Don't look at me, Maggie said. I don't know what he's talking about.

What? Harold said. Why hell. You know. The commode. The indoor outhouse. Well, what do you call it?

That'll do fine, Maggie said.

Our mother always called it where you step out.

Did she?

That's what she always called it, he said. He scratched his head. Well, damn it, Maggie, I'm just trying to be proper. I'm just trying to get us started off on the right chalk. I don't want to scare her off already.

Maggie patted his smooth-shaven cheek. You're doing just fine, she said. Keep going.

They went out of the bedroom. And while the others waited in the dining room the girl stepped into the bathroom. Another small room, it had a sink and toilet and a freestanding enameled tub with a red hose and showerhead coiled under the faucet at one end. On the shelves above the sink were various half-used jars of liniment and salve and Cornhuskers handbalm, and tubes of back-rub and sore-muscle ointment, and there was also tooth powder and denture adhesive and shaving equipment, and hanging over one of the drying rods next to the bathtub, together with two old towels, was a single fresh new pink towel that still had the store tag stapled to it. The girl came back out of the room. Should I get my suitcase now? she said.

I think that would be a good idea, Maggie Jones said.

You need any assistance? said Raymond.

No thank you. I think I can do it, the girl said, then went out through the kitchen to the car.

When she had gone Harold said, She ain't very big, is she. Why, she's just a little thing. She don't even show the baby any that I can see.

Not much yet, Maggie said. Some of her clothes are beginning to get tight. You'll notice it more when she takes her coat off.

Is she scared of us? Raymond said. She don't say much.

What do you think? Maggie Jones said.

Raymond looked out the window toward the car where the girl stood at the trunk gathering her belongings. She don't have to be, he said. We wouldn't hurt her. We wouldn't do her a harm for anything in this world.

I know that, Maggie said. But she doesn't know it yet. You'll have to give her time.

The girl returned to the house carrying a single cardboard suitcase and dragging a plastic trash bag. These she took into the bedroom. They could hear her in the room, moving about on the wood floor, temporarily arranging things, then she came back out.

I'm afraid this is a hard trial for you, Raymond said to the girl. He was not looking at her, but peering past her into some distance of his own. But we want to hope . . . What I want to say is, Harold and me, we want to think that you might come to feel a little at home out here. In time, I mean. Not right away, I don't guess.

She looked at him, then at his brother. Thank you, she said. Thank you for letting me stay here with you.

Well, you're welcome, Raymond said. You sure are.

They stood awkwardly inspecting the floor.

Very well then, Maggie said. I believe I've done my part. So I think I'll just go home and let you three souls get acquainted.

The girl looked startled. On the McPheron brothers' faces there was the look of panic. Do you have to leave already? the girl said.

I think so, Maggie said. I think I better. It's time.

We thought you might stay to supper, Harold said. Wouldn't you care to do that?

Another time, she said. I'll be back.

She went outside and the McPheron brothers and the girl followed her out and stood on the little screened porch in the wind, watching until she had driven away in the car. Then they turned and came back inside and stood looking at one another from across the bare wooden table in the kitchen.

Well, Harold said. I reckon—

The house was quiet. From outside came the faint sound of birdsong, coming up from the red cedar trees next to the garage, and there was the rising and falling noise of the wind.

—I reckon Raymond and me better go out and feed before it gets full dark, he said. Then we'll come back in. We'll have to see about getting some supper.

The girl looked at him.

It won't take us long, he said.

What is it you're feeding?

Cattle.

Oh.

Mother cows and heifers, Raymond said.

Oh.

The McPheron brothers and the girl stood looking at one another.

I guess I can get unpacked, the girl said.

McPherons.

When supper was finished they sat on in the dining room in the quiet. The table had been cleared already and the dishes washed and rinsed and left to dry. Raymond sat at one end of the table bent over the *Holt Mercury* newspaper spread out before him, reading, licking his finger when he turned the pages, his wire glasses low down on his nose. While he read he rolled a flat toothpick back and forth in his mouth without once touching it. Harold sat at the other end of the table. He was turned out from it, his knees spread open, and he was rubbing Black Bear Mountain mink oil into the thick leather of a work boot. Beside his chair the other boot was flopped over empty on the patterned and cracked linoleum.

Outside the house the wind had risen higher than it had been in the afternoon. They could hear it crying around the house corners, heaving and whining in the bare trees. The dry snow was lifted by the wind and blown past the windows and it carried in sudden gusts across the frozen yard under the farm-light that hung from a telephone pole out back. The snow swirled and sped in the bluish light. In the house it was quiet.

Across the room the door was closed. She had gone into her bedroom after supper and they had not heard anything from her since. They didn't know what to think of this. They wondered privately if all seventeen-year-old girls disappeared after eating supper.

When he had both boots oiled to his requirements Harold stood up and set them out in the kitchen where they gleamed mutely against the wall. Then he came back and crossed to her door and stood listening with his head canted and his eyes staring. He knocked on the door.

Victoria? he said.

Yes.

Everything all right in there?

You can come in, she said.

So he entered her room. It was hers already. She had made it so. It was female now, cleaner and tidier, with little things set out in place. For the first time in half a century someone had taken an interest in the room. The old cardboard boxes were pushed under the bed and the clothes in the closet had been shoved back farther into the dark. Against the wall the old mahogany chest of drawers, its oval mirror darkened and finely cracked at the edges, had been dusted and polished, and her belongings were now arranged on it, hair ribbons and comb and brush, lipstick and liner, hair clasps, a little cedar box of jewelry whose lid was closed by a tiny brass lock.

She herself was sitting up in the bed in a square-necked winter nightgown with a sweater pulled over her shoulders, a schoolbook and a blue notepad propped up in her lap, while the lamp beside the bed cast yellow light onto her clear face and her shining dark hair.

I just was wondering, he said. If you was warm enough in here.

Yes, she said. It's fine.

They're saying how it's suppose to get kind of cold tonight. Is it?

And this old house ain't very warm.

I'm fine, she said again. She watched him. He was standing

just inside the door, his hands poked into his pockets, his weather-blasted red face shining in the lamplight.

Anyhow, he said. He peered around. You think of something, you can let us know. We don't know much about this sort of thing.

Thank you, she said.

He looked at her once more, quickly, as some shy country animal might, and closed the door.

In the dining room Raymond sat at the table waiting, curious, the newspaper held up captured in his hands. She all right? he said.

I guess so.

She need more blankets?

She never said she wanted any.

Maybe we ought to get her some anyhow. In case.

I don't know. You about done with that paper?

It's going to be a goddamn cold night tonight.

I told her that. She knows. Why don't you let me have the front page. You're done with that much.

Raymond handed him the newspaper, and he took it and shook it out and began to read. After a while Raymond said, What was she doing in there? When you was inside her room.

Nothing. Reading. Working over her schoolbooks.

Was she in bed?

Harold looked up at him. I don't know where else was she going to be.

Raymond stared back at his brother. Then Harold began to read again. The wind blew and whistled outside. After a time Raymond spoke again. She didn't eat very much supper, he said. I don't think she did.

Harold didn't look up.

I reckon maybe she just don't like steak.

Oh, she ate enough. She's just a small eater.

I don't know if she did. She didn't hardly touch none of what I give her. I had to scrape most of it to the dog.

Did he eat it?

Who?

Did the dog eat it?

What in hell do you think? Course he did.

Well, Harold said. He looked up again now, peering at his brother from above the top of the newspaper. Not everybody likes their beefsteak covered in black pepper.

Who doesn't?

Victoria, maybe.

He bent back to the paper and Raymond sat at the table watching him. His face took on a disturbed and arrested look, as though he'd been caught in some sudden and disquieting act. You think she didn't like my cooking? he said.

I wouldn't know, Harold said.

The wind howled and cried. The house creaked.

An hour later Raymond stood up from the table. I never considered that, he said.

Considered what?

About peppering her steak.

He started upstairs. Harold followed him with his eyes.

Where you going?

Up.

To bed already?

No.

He went on. Harold could hear him walking on the pine floorboards overhead. Then he came back down carrying two thick wool blankets that smelled of dust and disuse, and he carried them to the front door and stood in the open doorway in the howling gusts of snow and wind and shook them out. Afterward he crossed to the door and tapped lightly, not wanting to wake her if she were asleep. There was no sound from inside. He stepped in and found that the girl was lying deep under the covers and that the light from the high purple farmlight outside was shining palely onto the bed. He stood for a quiet moment looking at her, at the room and all its new disturbances and the things in it, and then he spread the two blankets over her in the bed. When he turned to come back out, Harold was standing in the doorway watching. They came out together and left the door slightly ajar.

I didn't want her to take a chill, Raymond said. Not on her first night.

Much later in the night she woke up sweating and shoved the blankets aside.

Guthrie.

All parties seem to be present, Lloyd Crowder said, so we can get started.

The five of them were convened in a small room next to the school library, seated at a square table in the middle of the room and Lloyd Crowder, the principal, was presiding. Russell Beckman sat opposite him with his parents on either side. His mother was a short heavy woman who wore a pink sweater that was too tight on her arms and chest, and his father was a big dark-haired man in a shiny white-satin athletic jacket that had HOLT HAWKS lettered across the back. Off to the side of the Beckmans sat Tom Guthrie. He had looked at the Beckmans once when they came in and had then sat waiting silently for the meeting to begin. On the table in front of him were the duplicates of the forms he'd signed, and more forms and more papers were spread out in front of the principal. It was late in the afternoon, two hours after school had been let out for the day.

I believe you already know one another, Lloyd Crowder said. So I'm going to begin without introductions. And we'll have this over with. He put his big meaty hands out on the table on top of the papers and leaned forward. What we're doing here today, as you have been duly informed of, is because a discipline referral has been filed in regard to your son—he looked across the table at the Beckmans—and once that happens, when a referral has been filled out, I'm required by statute to do something about it and I'm going to do that. He surveyed the four faces watching him. I'll just put it simple. Russell here, the other day in school during the hours that school was in session, acted wrongful and inappropriate, and so we're here to discuss what all he's done and to decide what the consequences should be.

You can stop right there, Mrs. Beckman said, interrupting him. What you just said, that's a bunch of crap. Her cheeks had turned pink and her sweater was starting to inch upward. Because that's like you already convicted him without a trial. What's he done? He never did nothing. What do you say he did?

I'm going to get to that, Lloyd Crowder said. In due time. If you will let me proceed. He spoke evenly to her, looking directly at her. He held up a small pamphlet and went on: But first, I'm going to read to you from the Student Handbook. On page nine. Where it reads, Following are the behaviors that may result in suspension or other disciplinary action. Then I skip down to Level Three Violation. Where it says, Repeat of any Level Two Violation. Use of or possession of tobacco or drugs on school grounds. Fireworks in school. Harassment. Insubordination. Fighting. Physical and or verbal assault on a staff member. Intimidation or confrontation of a student. Theft. Damage or destruction of school property. Possession or use of weapons. And so on. He looked up. That's the pertinent regulation. The one Russell here violated.

How come it is? Mrs. Beckman said. Russell never had his weapons at school. What damage did he ever do to school property?

Wait, the principal said. You haven't let me finish. I'm not done yet. Now then, you will want to look at this. He handed her a copy of the discipline referral. She looked at it suspiciously and spread it before her on the table. Her husband and son leaned forward with her to look at it.

Look it over with me, Lloyd Crowder said. That's his name at the top and the date of the occurrence. Under that it reads in detail what he did and said. Under that you can read what the recommended punishment is and the consequences for what he did. Which in a case like this one here is a period of suspension up to five days. What it says in so many words, it states that Russell has said something injurious and profane to one of his classmates which caused her public harm and humiliation, and after that, when he was called out into the hallway to discuss it, he cursed and acted in a violent manner against his teacher. Which refers us back to the paragraph in the Student Handbook I just read you. Intimidation and confrontation of a student. Physical and or verbal assault on a staff member.

Who wrote this? Mrs. Beckman said.

The secretary made it out, based on the information provided by Mr. Guthrie. She applied the necessary language.

Then I can tell you what this is, Mrs. Beckman said. This is a pile of shit.

Guthrie looked across the corner of the table at her. Do you think so? he said.

Yes, I think so, she said, glaring at him. It is to me. He told us about you. You just don't appreciate him. That's what this is about. You got your favorites and he's not one of them. You haven't never been fair to Russell since the first day of school. This paper here with these fancy words on it is a pack of lies, and if you want to know what I think, I think you are too.

Here, the principal said. We're not going to have this.

But this is just his side of it, Mrs. Beckman cried. She swung back to face the principal. She picked up the paper and shook it disgustedly in the direction of Tom Guthrie. It's only what he says. Why don't you ask Russell what he has to say? Or don't you care about telling the truth either?

Careful now, the principal said. You don't want to say something you're going to regret tomorrow. I intend to let the boy say his piece. How about it, Russell?

The big high school boy sat stonelike between his parents. He neither moved nor spoke. He eyed the principal.

Go ahead, his mother said. What are you waiting on? Tell him what you told us.

He looked at his mother, then he stared ahead. I never said nothing to her. I don't care what he says. I was talking to somebody else. He don't have no proof. He don't even know if I said anything or not.

He said something, Guthrie said. Everybody heard it. And after he said it the girl stopped reading and looked at him. Then she ran out of the room.

What was it? Ask him that. He don't know.

Do you, Tom?

No. I didn't hear it clearly, Guthrie said. But I can about guess what it was. I asked the other students, but none of them would repeat it. Whatever it was, it caused her to flee the room.

How does he know that? Mrs. Beckman said. That's just his assumption.

No, Guthrie said. It was more than an assumption. Everybody in the room knew it. Why else would she run out?

Well my God, Mrs. Beckman said. There's lots of reasons. She's pregnant, isn't she? The little bitch got herself knocked up. Maybe she had to run out and piss in the toilet.

Lady, Tom Guthrie said, looking at her, you've got a filthy mouth. You're about as ignorant as they come.

And you're a dirty liar, she cried.

Here, the principal said. I already warned you. We're going to keep this civil and orderly.

Tell him, then.

I'm telling both of you. I'll stop it right now.

Mrs. Beckman glared at the principal, then she peered at her husband and lastly at her son. She pulled the sweater down tightly over her chest and stomach. All right, she said. What about out in the school hallway? What about that? Tell him your side of what happened there. See how he weasels out of that.

The high school boy sat as before, sullen and rigid, staring silently across the table.

Go on, his mother said. Tell him.

What for? It won't make no difference. He already made up his mind.

Tell him anyhow. Tell him like you told us. Go on now.

He sat looking ahead, looking at nothing, then he began to talk in a flat monotone, as though what he was saying was some indifferent and irksome rehearsal. He called me out of the room out in the hall, he said. I went out there with him. We were talking. Then all of a sudden he grabs me by the arm and twists it up behind my back and shoves me against the lockers. I told him to stop it. Told him he couldn't touch me. Then I got loose and went outside and went home.

The principal waited. And that's all? That's it. That's all that happened?

Yeah.

You didn't hit him?

No.

You didn't say anything else?

Like what?

You tell me.

No. I never said nothing else.

That's not what it says here, the principal said.

So. The boy stared sullenly forward. That's just his bullshit anyway.

The principal looked at the boy for a long moment. Studying him, thinking. Then he appeared to have made a decision. He began to put the papers and pamphlets before him into order and to slide them into a manila folder. The others at the table watched him silently. When he finished collecting his papers, he looked up. I think that'll about do it for today, he said. I think I've heard enough. I've made up my mind. Son, I'm going to suspend you for five days starting tomorrow like the rules call for. You'll get zeros in all your classes for that period of time, and you'll be required to stay completely away from school; I don't want to see you anywhere near this building for the next five school days. Understand? You might just manage to learn something yet even if it doesn't come out of a book.

As soon as he finished, Mrs. Beckman jumped up violently from her seat, knocking her chair over backward. It clattered on the floor. Her entire face had turned red and her sweater had risen again, showing a little of her soft stomach. She whirled on her husband. Well, my God, she cried. I never thought I'd see this. Aren't you going to say something? You heard him. You heard what he said. You're his father. Are you just going to sit there like nothing happened?

Her tall thin husband, sitting next to her in his satin athletic jacket, was not even looking at her. He was looking at the principal across the table. When you think you can shut your goddamn mouth, he said quietly, and can keep it shut, I'll say something. His wife glared at him. She started to say something more but thought better of it and pinched her lips shut. He continued to look across the table at Lloyd Crowder. After a moment he spoke again. I don't know nothing about this referral and suspension happy-horse-shit, he said. I don't care about it. It don't concern me. But this better not mean my boy can't play basketball this weekend.

That's exactly what it does mean, the principal said. He can't practice. He can't dress out. He can't play in any basketball game of any kind for the next five school days.

You know there's two games this weekend, Beckman said. You know that. It's a tournament.

I ought to know it. I've been on the phone all day about it.

And now you're telling me you won't let him play.

Not till five school days have passed.

On account of what Guthrie here claims my boy said to some little knocked-up half-breed schoolgirl.

That. And what happened out in the hallway.

And that's your final word. You made up your mind.

Yes.

Your final decision.

That's right.

All right then, you fat son of a bitch, Beckman said. There's other ways to deal with this.

The principal leaned heavily forward across the table toward Beckman. You want to hold up right there, he said. Are you threatening me? I want to know.

Take it how you want. You heard what I said.

No, by God. I don't have to take this. I've been here a long time. I'm going to be here till I'm ready to quit. And you nor nobody else in this room had better think otherwise. Now this meeting is over.

Beckman stared at him. Then he rose up from the table and made a violent backward motion at his wife and son. They started out of the room and he followed, but at the door he turned back. Just remember, he said, you fat tub of guts, there's always ways. I'm not forgetting this. I'm going to remember. I won't forget none of this. Then he turned and shoved his wife and boy out of the room and the three of them went down the hallway.

When they were gone the principal sat for a moment musing, gazing distractedly at the open doorway. After a while he shook himself and turned toward Tom Guthrie. Well, he said. You see what you got us into. This here has got me upset and I wasn't going to let it. I told myself I wouldn't. I didn't plan on it. It's not how I like to conduct my business. But I'll tell you something. You better be careful now.

You mean with them? Guthrie said.

That's right.

What about you?

Oh, he's not going to do anything to me. That's only show. He had to do that. But you better just take it easy. You don't want to mess with these folks. And that boy when he comes back, ease up on him for God's sake. I told you before, we want him graduated and out of here.

He better do the work then.

Even if he doesn't, the principal said.

I'm not changing my mind, Guthrie said.

You better listen to me, the principal said. You better hear what I'm telling you.

Ike and Bobby.

They went up the wood stairs and back along the narrow dim-lit corridor after school in the afternoon, but not to collect. When she opened the door Iva Stearns said, It's not Saturday. What is it? Are you collecting early?

No, Ike told her.

What then? What'd you come for?

They turned their heads and peered into the corridor behind them, too humble and embarrassed to say what it was they wanted even if they could have said exactly what that was.

Mrs. Stearns watched them. I see, she said. You better come in here in that case.

They passed into the room wordlessly. Her apartment was just as it always was: crowded rooms that were too hot, the stores of papers and old bills on the floor and the grocery sacks of her saved remnants loaded onto the ironing board and the portable tv on top of the big hardwood console, and over it all the inevitable smell of her cigarette smoke and the accumulation of Holt County dust. She shut the door and stood looking at them, thinking, considering, a humpbacked woman in a thin blue housedress and apron, wearing a pair of men's wool socks inside her worn slippers, leaning on her twin silver canes.

I tell you what we better do, she said. I've been thinking of making cookies. But I don't have all of the ingredients and I've been too lame and too lazy to go get them. You might go purchase them for me, would you?

What do you need? they said.

I'll make a list. Do you boys eat oatmeal cookies?

Yes. We like them.

Very well. That's what we'll make.

She lowered herself into the stuffed chair against the wall. It took a considerable period of time. When she was seated she caught her breath and stood the two canes beside the chair. She settled the skirts of her dress and apron over her thin knees, then she said, Bring me my purse from the table in there. You know where it is.

Bobby stepped into the next room, where it was just as crowded and just as hot, and found her purse and brought it back and set it in her lap. They stood in front of the chair, watching. Her head was bent forward and they could see that the fine thin yellow-white hair scarcely covered her skull and that her ears looked raw where the bows of her glasses fit over them. The cord of her old-fashioned hearing aid curled down into the neck of her housedress where it disappeared.

She opened the leather purse and took out a wallet, then extracted ten dollars. She gave the money to Ike. That should be more than enough, she said. Bring back the change.

Yes, ma'am.

Now what do we need? She peered at them as if they might know. They stared back at her patiently, simply waiting, standing in front of her. We need most of it, she said.

She took out an ink pen and scratched about in the purse but could not find what else she wanted.

Here, she said. Give me something to write on. That paper will do. Hand me that newspaper. It was the morning's *Denver News*, still rolled in the rubber band the boys had put on it early that morning at the depot. She unrolled it and from the front page tore off a ragged piece and began to write along the white margin, listing the ingredients—oatmeal, eggs, brown sugar—writing in the old school-taught Palmer script in the fluid style, but shaky now as though she were shivering from cold or fever. There, she said. I gave you the money. She looked at Ike. I'm giving you the shopping list, she said to Bobby. She handed him the scrap of newspaper. Go ahead now. Go on. I'll be waiting.

But where should we get these, Mrs. Stearns? Ike said.

At Johnson's. You know the grocery store.

Yes. We know it.

That's where.

They turned and started out.

Wait, she said. How are you going to get back in here? I don't want to have to get up and answer the door again. She took a key from the purse and handed it to them.

They left her apartment and went down the stairs to the sidewalk and into the sharp winter air on Main Street and on to Johnson's at the corner of Second. When they were inside the store it was a good deal more complicated than they had thought it would be. On the ranks of shelves were two brands of brown sugar. Also, there were quick oats and regular oats and two measures of the cardboard barrels they came in. And with eggs, three sizes and two colors. They debated the matter between themselves, standing in the aisles of the store while around them the other shoppers, middle-aged women and young mothers, looked at them curiously and went on pushing their full carts.

We settled on the cheap brown sugar, Ike said.

Yes, Bobby said.

And the big one of regular oats.

Yes.

So now with eggs we take the medium ones.

Why?

Because they're in the middle.

So?

It makes a difference, Ike said. The one between the other two ones. It makes it even.

Bobby looked at him, considering. All right, he said. Which color?

Which color?

Brown or white.

They turned toward the refrigerated case once more and regarded the tiers of cardboard egg cartons. Mother bought white ones, Ike said.

She's not our mother, Bobby said. Maybe she wants brown ones.

Why would she want brown ones?

She had us get brown sugar.

So?

Because it comes in white too, Bobby said. Only she said brown.

All right, Ike said. Brown eggs.

All right, Bobby said.

Medium sized.

All right then.

They carried the eggs and oats and sugar up to the front of the store to the cash register and paid the checkout woman. She smiled at them. You boys making something good? she said. They didn't answer but took the change from her hand and went back outside and up the stairs to the old woman's dark and overheated rooms above the alley. They used the key and went in without knocking and discovered her asleep in the chair they'd left her in. She was breathing faintly, a quiet sigh and recover, her head lapsed forward onto the yoke of her blue housedress. They approached and stood before her, hesitant, and seeing how faint the movement was in her chest, watching the meager rise and collapse of the housedress, they felt a little frightened. Ike leaned forward and said, Mrs. Stearns. We're back. They stood before her, waiting. They watched her. Mrs. Stearns, he said. He leaned forward again. We're here. He touched her arm.

Abruptly she stopped breathing. She choked a little. Her eyes fluttered open behind the glasses and she raised her head to look about. Well. Are you back?

We just came in, Ike said. Just now.

What trouble did you have at the grocery store?

None. We got everything.

Good, she said.

They handed her the leftover money and the grocery receipt and she held her open palm in front of her face, counting the money with her finger, and put the bills and coins away in her purse. They handed her the front-door key but she said, I'm going to trust you with that. You can come in if you need to. And I won't have to get up to let you in. Maybe you'll want to sometime. She looked at them. All right? They nodded. Very well, she said. Let me see if I can stand up. Slowly she began to rise from the chair, pushing back with her fisted hands against the armrests. They wanted to help her but didn't know where she might be touched. At last she stood erect. It's ridiculous to get so old, she said. It's stupid and ridiculous. She took up her canes. Stand back so I don't trip on you.

They followed her scraping into the kitchen, where they hadn't been before: a little room with a small window overlooking the tarred roof of the next building, and a plain wood table with a toaster on it, a half-refrigerator, a trash can and an old hard enameled sink containing a single dirty coffee cup and the toast crumbs of her breakfast.

Wash your hands, she said. That's first. Here.

They stood next to one another before the sink. Afterward she handed them a towel. Then she told them to take down the additional ingredients from the cupboard and set them out on the table, following the order of the old recipe she'd cut from the top of an oatmeal barrel, the recipe gray and worn now, grease-smeared but still legible.

What's next? she said. Read it.

Vanilla.

Up there. On the middle shelf. Then what?

Baking soda.

There. She pointed. Anything else?

No. That's all.

All right, she said. You understand? If you can read you can cook. You can always feed yourselves. You remember that. I'm not just talking about here. When you go home too. Do you understand what I'm saying?

They looked at her gravely. Bobby read the scrap of recipe print again. What does cream mean? he said.

Where?

It says cream the butter and sugars.

That means mix them together until they're soft, she said. Like heavy cream.

Oh.

You use a fork for that.

They began to put it all in and they stirred it together in the bowl while she stood beside them overseeing, instructing, then they spooned dollops of batter onto the greased sheet and set the raw cookies in the oven.

I've been thinking, she said. I'm going to show you something. While we wait.

She shuffled into the next room and came back carrying a flat and ragged cardboard box and set it on the table and removed the lid, then she showed them photographs that had been much-handled in the long afternoons and evenings of her solitary life, photographs that had been lifted out and examined and returned to the black picture book album, the album itself of an old shape and style. They were all of her son, Albert. That's him, she told them. Her tobacco-stained finger pointed at one of the photographs. That's my son. He died in the war. In the Pacific.

The boys bent forward to see him.

That's my Albert in his Navy uniform. That's my favorite picture of him as a grown man. Do you see that look on his face? Oh, he was a handsome boy.

He was a tall thin boy in a dark Navy uniform, wearing his dress blues, and his white dixie cup pushed back on his head, his shoes gleaming. In the picture he was squinting into the sun. Behind him there was a tree in leaf and a pool of dark shade. He was grinning terrifically.

I miss him every day, she said. I still do.

She turned the page and there was a photograph of the same boy standing with his arm draped around the shoulders of a slender woman with dark wavy hair in a white gabardine dress.

Who's that? they said. That lady with him.

Who do you think? she said.

They shrugged. They didn't know.

That's me. Couldn't you guess?

They turned to look at her, examining her face.

That's how I used to look, she said. I was young once too, don't you know.

Her face was close to theirs, old and bespectacled, age-spotted; she had soft loose cheeks, her thin hair was pulled back. She smelled of cigarette smoke. They looked again at the picture of her when she was a young woman wearing a handsome white dress in the company of her son.

That was when Albert was home for the last time, she said.

Where was his father? Ike said. Was he home too?

No, he was not. Her voice changed. She sounded bitter and tired now. He was gone by then. His father was nowhere. That's where he was.

Bobby said, Our mother's in Denver now.

Oh, she said. She looked at him. Their faces were close. Yes, I think I heard something about that.

Because she was just renting that house, Ike said. She's in Denver staying with her sister.

I see.

We'll be going to visit her pretty soon. At Christmastime.

That'll be good, won't it. She must miss you terribly. I would. Like breath itself. I know she does too.

She calls on the phone sometimes, Ike said.

The timer dinged on the stove. They took the first oatmeal cookies out of the oven and now there was the smell of cinnamon and fresh baking in the dark little room. The boys sat at the table and ate the cookies together with the milk Mrs. Stearns had poured out into blue glasses. She stood at the counter watching them and sipped at a cup of hot tea and ate a small piece of a cookie, but she wasn't hungry. After a while she smoked a cigarette and tapped the ashes in the sink.

You boys don't say very much, she said. I wonder what you're thinking all the time.

About what?

About anything. About the cookies you made.

They're good, Ike said.

You can take them home with you, she said.

Don't you want them?

I'll keep a few. You take the rest home when you go.

Guthrie.

Maggie Jones said, You're not leaving so soon?

Guthrie stood in the front hall with his winter coat in his hand, while behind Maggie other teachers stood about in groups holding little paper plates of food, drinking and talking, and still others sat in chairs and on the davenport. In the corner of the living room one of them was listening to Maggie Jones's father. The old man had on a corduroy shirt and a green tie and he was gesturing with both hands, telling the woman something, some story out of his own old time when he was young.

Why so soon? Maggie said. It's still early.

I'm not much for these things, Guthrie said. I think I'll go on.

Where are you going?

Over to have a drink at the Chute. Why don't you come with me.

I can't leave these people here. You know that.

Guthrie pulled his coat on and zipped it.

Wait for me, she said. I'll come join you when I can.

All right. But I don't know how long I'll be there.

He opened the door and went outside. He felt the cold air

at once on his face and ears and inside his nose. There were cars parked all along the street in front of her house and around the corner. He walked up half a block and climbed into his pickup. It turned over grudgingly, then it caught and he shoved his hands in his pockets while it warmed up a minute, then he pulled out into the street. Three blocks south on the almost empty highway he stopped at the Gas and Go, leaving the pickup engine idling, and bought a pack of cigarettes and came back out and drove over a couple of blocks east to the Chute Bar and Grill. It was smoky inside and somebody had fed the jukebox. The usual crowd was there, for a Saturday night.

He sat down at the bar and Monroe came over, drying his hands on a white bar towel. Tom, what's it going to be? Guthrie ordered a beer and Monroe drew it and set it down in front of him. He wiped at a spot on the polished wood but it was something in the grain of the wood itself. You want to start a tab?

I don't guess so. Guthrie handed him a bill and Monroe turned and made change at the cash register in front of the big mirror and brought it back and set the bills and coins alongside the glass.

Anything happening?

It's still early, Monroe said.

He went down the bar and Guthrie looked around. There were three or four men on his left and people at the booths behind them and others in the far room at the tables and booths and at the shuffleboard table against the wall. Judy, the high school secretary, was sitting with another woman at one of the tables. She saw him looking at her and raised her glass and waggled two fingers like a young girl would. He nodded to her and turned and looked the other direction back toward the entrance. A couple more men, and slumped on the end stool was a woman in an army jacket. The man next to him turned. It was Buster Wheelright.

That you, Tom?

How's it going? Guthrie said.

It isn't any use to complain, is it?

Not that I know of.

Not around here, Buster said.

Guthrie drank from his glass and looked at him. What'd you do, lose some weight? I didn't recognize you.

Hell yeah. How's it look on me?

It looks good.

I just got out of detox. I lost some weight in there.

How was that?

Detox?

Yeah.

It was all right. Except once I got sobered up I was depressed as hell. Crying all the time. Doctor give me some antidepression pills. Then I was okay. Except I couldn't shit.

Guthrie grinned and shook his head. Hell of a deal.

It's a hell of a deal, Tom. You can't live if you can't shit. Can you?

I don't believe so.

No. So then he give me some laxatives. Cleaned me out thorough. That'll make you lose some weight, let me tell you. Only I couldn't keep up with it. All the time I was in there I eat like a horse but I kept shittin like a full growed elephant. Buster laughed. He was missing teeth on the upper left side of his mouth.

Sounds like a radical cure to me, Guthrie said.

Oh, you don't want to do it every day, Buster said.

They both drank. Guthrie looked back into the other room. Judy was laughing about something with the people at the table. A big curly-haired man was there now too.

Where's your partner? Guthrie said. I don't see him anywhere.

Who?

Terrel.

Oh, hell. Didn't you hear about that?

No.

Well hell. Terrel he was coming into town yesterday morning driving in his truck on the north side of town there and that little spotted bitch dog of Smythe's run out in the street in front of him. Terrel feared he run over it. So he slowed down and opened the door and leant out to look behind him and be goddamned if he didn't fall out of the truck right out in the street. The truck went on without him and runt into Helen Shattuck's backyard privacy fence. They took him to the hospital, thinking he'd had a cardiac arrest. When he come to he had to tell what it was. Fell out of the truck, all it was. On account of he's overweight and got to leaning out too far. Overbalanced hisself, I guess. Dumped out on his head right there on Hoag Street.

Guthrie shook his head, grinning. How bad was he hurt?

Oh, he's all right. Give him a good headache is all.

Did he hit the dog?

Nah. Hell. The dog wasn't even involved. The dog skedaddled. You reckon there's a lesson there?

I wouldn't be surprised, Guthrie said.

My mama use to say it's a lesson in everything you do if you just have eyes to see it, Buster said.

I believe that, Guthrie said. Your mama was a smart woman.

Yes sir, she was, Buster said. She's been dead now twenty-seven years.

Guthrie lit a cigarette and offered the pack to Buster. Buster took one and inspected it and put the filter end in his mouth. They smoked and drank for a while. Monroe brought Guthrie another beer and brought a beer and a shot for Buster. Take it out of that, Guthrie said. Buster nodded thanks to him and picked up the little glass and threw the shot back and immediately afterward bent over and had a long drink of beer.

As he was finishing it Judy came up from the back room.

She stopped behind Guthrie and tapped him on the shoulder.
When he turned around she said, I thought you'd be at the
party at Maggie Jones's house.

I was. I didn't see you there.

I get enough of school at school, she said. It's just the teachers. The same old talk.

Well, Guthrie said, you're looking good.

Why, thank you. She turned completely around in front
of him, making a little dance. She had on a low-cut white top
and tight blue jeans and boots fashioned from soft red leather.
The tightness of the top she was wearing made smooth pretty
mounds of her breasts.

Can I buy you a drink?

I came over to buy you one, she said.

You can buy the next one, Guthrie said.

All right. I won't forget.

Monroe brought her a rum and Coke and handed it to her
and she tasted it and stirred it with the straw and tasted it again.

You want to sit down? Guthrie said.

Where?

You can have my seat. I'll stand up awhile.

Shoot. I'm younger than you are.

Are you?

I'm younger than anybody here. I'm the youngest girl out
on a Saturday night. She raised her fist and waved it.

The man on the barstool to Guthrie's left was listening and
he turned around and looked at her. He was wearing a big black
hat with a bright feather in the band. I'll tell you what, he said.
You can have my seat if you give me a good-night kiss first. I was
just about to leave anyhow.

Do I know you? she said.

No. But I'm not hard to get to know. I don't have nothing, if
that's what you mean.

All right, she said. Lean forward, you're too tall. He leaned
forward from the waist and she took his face in both of her

hands, ducked under the brim of his hat and kissed him hard on the mouth.

How's that? she said.

Jesus Christ, he said. He licked his lips. Maybe I better just stay here.

No you don't, she said. She pulled him by the arm.

He stood up and patted her on the shouder and went outside. She sat at the bar with Guthrie and turned in his direction. Who was that? she said.

He lives out south, Guthrie said. He comes in here once in a while. I don't know his name.

I've never seen him before.

He comes in about every other week.

Guthrie and Judy sat and talked about various things, about school, about Lloyd Crowder, some of the students, but not for long. Instead she told Guthrie about her daughter, who was a freshman at Fort Collins, and how it was to have the house just to herself now, how it was so quiet too much of the time. And Guthrie said a few things about his boys, told her what they were doing. Then she told him the story about the blonde on the charter plane to Hawaii, and in turn he asked if she knew what the worst thing was for someone to say to you when you were standing at the urinal. They had another drink, which she insisted on buying.

After it came she said, You mind if I ask you something?

What.

Is your wife still in Denver?

Guthrie looked at her. Yes, she's still there.

Is she?

Yes.

What's going to happen, do you think?

I can't say. She might stay there. She's staying with her sister.

Aren't you two going to get back together?

I doubt it.

Don't you want to?

He looked at her. You think we could talk about something else?

Sorry, she said.

He lit a cigarette. She watched him smoke. Then she took the cigarette out of his hand and drew on it, blew two jets of smoke from her nostrils and drew on it again and gave it back.

Keep it.

No, I just wanted that much. I quit.

You can have this one.

No, that's all right. But listen. Why don't you come over sometime and let me cook you a steak or something. You seem so lonely. And it's too quiet over there in my house all the time when it's just me.

I might do that.

Why don't you. You ought to.

I might.

A few minutes later the other woman came in from the other room and dragged Judy back to their table. My God, the woman said, don't leave me with him.

See you later, Judy said, and Guthrie watched them go back into the other room. The two women pulled the curly-haired man to his feet and walked him over to the shuffleboard table and Guthrie watched them play for a while. When he turned back to the bar he found that Buster Wheelright had disappeared. He'd left some change on the bar and then he'd gone off. Guthrie looked around. The woman in the army jacket was still asleep down the bar. He finished his beer and went out into the cold air again and drove up Main Street toward home.

Victoria Roubideaux.

In December the girl appeared in the doorway of Maggie
Jones's classroom during the teacher's planning hour. Maggie was
sitting at her desk, marking student papers with a red ink pen.

Mrs. Jones? the girl said.

The teacher looked up. Victoria. Come in.

The girl entered the room and stopped beside the desk.
Nobody else was in the room. The girl was heavier now, beginning to show, and her face looked wider, fuller. Her blouse had
drawn more tightly over her stomach, making the material
appear polished and shiny. Maggie set the papers aside. Come
around here, she said. Let me look at you. Well, my yes. You're
getting there, aren't you. Turn around, let me see you from the
side.

The girl did so.

Are you feeling all right?

It's been moving lately. I've been feeling it.

Have you? She smiled at the girl. You seem to be eating
enough. Is there something you wanted? You don't have a class
now?

I told Mr. Guthrie I had to be excused to the rest room.

Is something wrong?

The girl glanced around the room and looked back. She stood beside the desk and picked up a paperweight, then put it back. Mrs. Jones, she said, they don't talk.

Who doesn't?

They don't say more than two words at a time. It's not just to me. I don't think they even talk to each other.

Oh, Maggie said. The McPheron brothers, you mean them.

It's so quiet out there, the girl said. I don't know what I'm supposed to do. We eat supper. They read the paper. I go into my room and study. And that's about it. Every day it's like that.

Is everything else all right?

Oh, they're kind to me. If that's what you mean. They're nice enough.

But they don't talk, Maggie said.

I don't know if they even want me out there, the girl said. I can't tell what they're thinking.

Have you tried talking to them? You know you could start a conversation yourself.

The girl looked at the older woman with exasperation. Mrs. Jones, she said, I don't know anything about cows.

Maggie laughed. She laid the red pen down on the stack of student papers and leaned back in her chair, stretching her shoulders. Do you want me to talk to them for you?

I know they mean well, the girl said. I don't think they mean any harm.

Two days later that week, in the afternoon, after school was let out for the day, Maggie Jones discovered Harold McPheron standing in front of the refrigerated meat case at the rear of the Highway 34 Grocery Store on the east side of Holt. He was clenching a package of pork roast to his nose. She walked up beside him.

This look recent to you? he said. He held the meat out toward her.

It looks bloody, she said.

I can't tell if it smells good. They got it wrapped up in all this goddamn plastic. You couldn't tell the working end of a skunk with this stuff on it.

I didn't know you ate skunks.

That's what I'm talking about. I can't tell what I'm eating with this goddamn plastic wrapped around it. It ain't like our own beef from the meat locker—when we get it I know what I'm getting. He shoved the pork roast back into the meat case and picked up another package. He held it close to his face, sniffing at it, grimacing, his eyes squinted. He turned it over and peered suspiciously at the underside.

Maggie watched him, amused. I was hoping I'd run into you, she said. But I guess it'll have to wait. I wouldn't want to interrupt your shopping.

Harold looked at her. What for? What'd I do now?

Not enough, she said. Neither one of you has.

He lowered the meat package and turned to face her. He was dressed in his work clothes, worn jeans and his canvas chore jacket, and on his head, canted toward one ear, was an old dirty white hat.

What are you talking about? he said.

You and your brother want to keep that girl out there with you, don't you?

Why yeah, he said. What's the trouble? He looked surprised.

Because you think it's kind of nice having a girl in the house, don't you? You've gotten kind of used to having her out there with you?

Where'd we go wrong? he said.

You're not talking to her, Maggie Jones said. You and Raymond don't talk like you should to that girl. Women want to hear some conversation in the evening. We don't think that's too much to ask. We're willing to put up with a lot from you men, but in the evening we want to hear some talking. We want to have a little conversation in the house.

What kind? Harold said.

Any kind. Just so you mean it.

Well damn it, Maggie, Harold said. You know I don't know how to talk to women. You knew that before you ever brought her out there. And Raymond, he don't know a thing about it either. Neither one of us does. In particular a young girl like her.

That's why I'm telling you, Maggie said. Because you better learn.

But damn it, what would we talk to her about?

I expect you'll think of something.

She said no more. Instead she walked away into one of the aisles of the grocery store, pushing her shopping cart ahead of her, her long dark skirt swirling briskly about her legs. Gazing after her, Harold followed her progress with considerable interest, watching from under the dirty brim of his hat. In his eyes there was the look of mystification and alarm.

When he returned to the house it was just before dark. Raymond was still outside. He located him out back of the horse barn and pulled him inside into one of the plank-sided stalls as if there were a need for privacy. With some excitement in his voice he reported to Raymond what Maggie Jones had said to him in the Highway 34 Grocery Store while he stood before the meat case considering pork roast for their supper.

Raymond received the news in silence. Afterward he looked up and studied his brother's face for a moment. That's what she said?

Yes. That's what she said.

That's all of it? The sum and total?

All I can remember.

Then we got to do something.

That's what I think too, Harold said.

I'm talking about we got to do something today, Raymond said. Not next week.

That's what I'm telling you, Harold said. I'm trying to agree with you.

The McPheron brothers made their attempt that same evening. They had decided it was safe to wait until after supper, but believed they could wait no longer. After supper they sallied forth together.

They and the girl had just finished eating a meal of fried meat and red onions, boiled potatoes, coffee, green beans, sliced bread and equally divided portions of canned peaches, bright yellow in their own syrup. It had been the customary nearly silent evening meal, eaten almost formally out in the dining room, and afterward the girl had cleared the square walnut table of their dishes and had taken the dishes to the kitchen and washed them and put them away, and then she was started back to her bedroom when Harold said:

Victoria. He had to clear his throat. He started again. Victoria. Raymond and me was wanting to ask you a question, if you don't mind. If we could. Before you started back to your studies there.

Yes? she said. What did you want to ask?

We just was wondering . . . what you thought of the market?

The girl looked at him. What? she said.

On the radio, he said. The man said today how soybeans was down a point. But that live cattle was holding steady.

And we wondered, Raymond said, what you thought of it. Buy or sell, would you say.

Oh, the girl said. She looked at their faces. The brothers were watching her closely, a little desperately, sitting at the table, their faces sober and weathered but still kindly, still well meaning, with their smooth white foreheads shining like polished marble under the dining room light. I wouldn't know, she said. I couldn't say about that. I don't know anything about it. Maybe you could explain it to me.

Well sure, Harold said. I reckon we could try. Because the market . . . But maybe you'd like to sit down again first. At the table here.

Raymond rose at once and pulled out her chair. She seated herself slowly and he pushed the chair in for her and she thanked him and he went back to the other side of the table and took his place. For a moment the girl sat rubbing her stomach where it felt tight, then she noticed they were watching her with close interest, and she put her hands forth on the table. She looked across at them. I'm listening, she said. Do you want to go ahead?

Why sure, of course, Harold said. As I was saying. He began in a loud voice. Now the market is what soybeans and corn and live cattle and June wheat and feeder pigs and bean meal is all bringing in today for a price. He reads it out every day at noon, the man on the radio. Six-dollar soybeans. Corn two-forty. Fifty-eight-cent hogs. Cash value, sold today.

The girl sat watching him talk, following his lecture.

People listen to it, he said, and know what the prices are. They manage to keep current that a-way. Know what's going on.

Not to mention pork bellies, Raymond said.

Harold opened his mouth to say something more, but now he stopped. He and the girl turned to look at Raymond.

How's that? Harold said. Say again.

Pork bellies, Raymond said. That's another one of em. You never mentioned it. You never told her about them.

Well yeah, of course, Harold said. Them too. I was just getting started.

You can buy them too, Raymond said to the girl. If you had

a mind to. He was looking at her solemnly from across the table.
Or sell em too, if you had some.

What are they? the girl said.

Well that's your bacon, Raymond said.

Oh, she said.

Your fat meat under the ribs there, he said.

That's right, Harold said. They're touted on the market too.
So anyway, he said, looking at the girl. Now do you see?

She looked from one old man to the other. They were waiting, watching for some reaction, as if they'd been laying out the
intricacies of some last will and testament or perhaps the necessary precautions to take against the onset of fatal disease and
the contagion of plague. I don't think so, she said. I don't understand how he knows what the prices are.

The man on the radio? Harold said.

Yes.

They call them up out of the big salebarns. He gets the market reports from Chicago or Kansas City. Or Denver maybe.

Then how do you sell something? she said.

All right, Raymond said, taking his turn. He leaned forward
toward her to explain these matters. Take for instance you want
to sell you some wheat, he said. Take, you already got it there in
the elevator in Holt next to the railroad tracks where you carried it back in July at harvest time. Now you want to sell some
of it off. So you call up the elevator and tell him to sell off five
thousand bushel, say. So he sells it at today's prices and then the
big grain trucks, those tractors and trailers you see out on the
highway, they haul it away.

Who does he sell it to? the girl said.

Any number of places. Most likely to the milling company.
Mostly it goes for your baking flour.

Then when do you get your money?

He writes you out a check today.

Who does that?

The elevator manager.

Except if there's a storage charge, Harold said, taking his turn again. He takes that out. Plus your drying charge, if there is one. Only, since it's wheat we're talking about, there's never much drying charge with wheat. Mostly that's with your corn.

They stopped again and studied the girl once more. They had begun to feel better, a little satisfied with themselves. They knew they were not out of the woods yet, but they had begun to allow themselves to believe that what they saw ahead was at least a faint track leading to a kind of promising clearing. They watched the girl and waited.

She shook her head and smiled. They noticed again how beautiful her teeth were and how smooth her face. She said, I still don't think I understand it. You said something about cattle. What about them?

Oh, well, Harold said. Okay. Now with cattle.

And so the two McPheron brothers went on to discuss slaughter cattle and choice steers, heifers and feeder calves, explaining these too, and between the three of them they discussed these matters thoroughly, late into the evening. Talking. Conversing. Venturing out into various other matters a little too. The two old men and the seventeen-year-old girl sitting at the dining room table out in the country after supper was over and after the table was cleared, while outside, beyond the house walls and the curtainless windows, a cold blue norther began to blow up one more high plains midwinter storm.

Ike and Bobby.

As per agreement they spent Christmas week in Denver with their mother. Guthrie drove them to the city in the pickup and went up with them to the seventh floor of the apartment building on Logan Street where their mother's sister lived. They took the elevator and followed a runner of carpet in the long bright corridor. Guthrie saw them into the front room and talked briefly to their mother without heat or argument, but he wouldn't sit down and he left very soon.

Their mother seemed quieter now. Perhaps she was more at peace. Her face looked less pinched and pale, less drawn. She was glad to see them. She hugged them for a long time and her eyes were wet with tears while she smiled, and they sat together on the couch and she held their hands warmly in her lap. It was clear she had missed them. But in some way their mother had been taken over by her sister who was three years older. She was a small woman, precise and particular, with sharp opinions, pretty instead of beautiful, with gray eyes and a small hard chin. She and their mother would contend now and then over little things—the table setting, the degree of heat in the apartment—but in the matters of consequence their mother's sister had her way. Then their mother seemed remote and passive as though she could not be roused to defend herself. But the two boys didn't think in such terms. They thought their aunt was bossy. They wanted their mother to do something about the way their aunt was.

The apartment had two bedrooms and the boys stayed with their mother in her room, chatting and telling little jokes and playing cards, and at night they slept on the floor on pallets, with warm blankets folded over them at the foot of her bed. It was like camping. But much of the time they couldn't be in the bedroom since their mother was having her silent spells again, when she wanted to be alone in a darkened room. The spells started the fourth day they were in Denver, after Christmas. Christmas had been disappointing. The red sweater they'd bought their mother was too big for her, though she said she liked it anyway. They hadn't thought to buy their aunt anything. Their mother had bought them each a bright shirt, and later, one day when she was feeling better, she took them shopping downtown and bought them new shoes and new pants and several pairs of socks and underwear. When they stopped at the register to pay Ike said, It's too much, Mother. We don't need all this.

Your father sent me some money, she said. Should we go back now?

It was very quiet in their aunt's apartment. Their aunt was a supervisory clerk in the municipal court system with an office in the civic center downtown, and she had been there for twenty-three years and as a result she had developed a stark view of humanity and its vagaries and the multitude of ways it found to commit crimes. She had been married once, for three months, and since that time had never considered marrying anyone again. She was left with two passions: a fat yellow neutered cat named Theodore and the television soap opera that came on at one o'clock every weekday while she was at work, a program she taped religiously and watched without fail every night when she was home again.

The boys were bored right away. Their mother had seemed better, but after the silent spells began she appeared defeated again and went back to bed, and their aunt told them they must be quiet and let her rest. This was after she'd gone into their mother's room one evening and they'd talked for an hour behind the closed door, and then she had come back out and said, You will have to be quiet and let her rest.

We have been quiet.

Are you arguing with me.

What's wrong with Mother?

Your mother is not strong.

So their aunt went to work and their mother went back to bed lying with her arm folded over her eyes in a darkened room, and they were left alone in the seventh-floor apartment in Denver and were told strictly not to go outside. They spent their time reading a little and they watched tv until they were blind, while still being careful at the critical hour not to interfere with the taping of their aunt's soap opera. Their only recourse was the balcony at the front of the apartment, which they entered by sliding back a glass door. It overlooked Logan Street and the sidewalk and there were cars parked all along the curbing and they could see into the tops of the leafless winter trees. They began to go out on the balcony to watch the cars go by in the street and to see people walking their dogs. They put their coats on and stayed for longer and longer periods of time. After a while they took to dropping things off the balcony. They started by leaning over the rail to watch what the wind did with their spittle, then they made up a game to see who could sail scraps of paper the farthest, floating the paper like feathers, and they invented a system of points for distance and placement. But that was too unpredictable. Wind had too much to do with it. They found that dropping things that had weight was better. And eggs were best.

After this had gone on for a couple of days someone in the building told their aunt about it. When she came into the apartment that evening she removed her coat and hung it up, and then she took them both by the wrist and led them into their mother's room. Do you know what these two have been doing?

Their mother leaned up in bed. No, she said. She looked pale and drawn again. But it couldn't be very bad, she said.

They've been smashing eggs on the sidewalk.

How?

Dropping them off the balcony. Oh, it's very intelligent.

Have you? she said, looking in their faces.

They stood looking at her impassively. Their aunt was still holding their wrists.

Yes, they have.

Well, I'm sure they won't do it anymore. There's too little for them to do up here.

They can't do that anymore. I won't have it.

So that was the end of that. They were forbidden to go out onto the balcony.

At the end of the week they woke one night in the dark and discovered that their mother wasn't in the room. They opened the door and went out into the living room. No lights were on, but the curtain was drawn back from the glass balcony door and the lights of the city came in through the glass. Their mother was sitting on the davenport with a blanket wrapped around her. Though she was awake, so far as they could see, she wasn't doing anything.

Mother?

What is it? she said. What woke you?

We wondered where you were.

I'm just out here, she said. It's all right. Go back to bed.

Can't we sit here with you?

If you want. It's cool out here though.

I'll get a blanket, Ike said.

But you won't like it, their mother said. I'm not very good company.

Mother, can't you come home again? Bobby said. What good is it here?

No. Not yet, she said.

When?

I don't know, she said. I'm not sure. Here. Slide closer. You're getting cold. I should make you go back to bed. They sat for a long time watching out the window.

The boys were glad the next day when their father returned to pick them up. They wanted to go home again, but they felt confused and uneasy about leaving their mother in Denver in the apartment with her sister. Guthrie tried to make them talk on the way back. They wouldn't say very much of anything, though. They didn't want to be disloyal to their mother. The trip seemed to take a long time. Once they were in the house upstairs in their own bedroom it was better. They could look out and see the corral and windmill and horse barn.

McPherons.

There was no school between Christmas and New Year's. Victoria Roubideaux stayed out in the country in the old house back off the county road with the McPheron brothers, and the days seemed slow. The ground was covered in thin dirty patches of ice and the weather stayed cold, the temperature never rising above freezing, and in the night it was bitterly cold. She stayed inside the house and read popular magazines and baked in the kitchen, while the brothers came and went from the house, haying cattle and chopping ice in the stock tanks, paying close attention all the time to the steady advance of pregnancy in the two-year-old heifers, since they would be the most trouble during calving, and returned to the kitchen from the farm lots and pastures, ice-bound and half frozen, with their blue eyes watery and their cheeks as red as if they had been burnt. In the house Christmas had been quiet and there were no particular plans for New Year's.

By the middle of the week the girl had begun to spend long hours in her room, sleeping late in the morning and staying up at night listening to the radio and fixing her hair, reading about babies, thinking, fiddling in a notebook.

The McPheron brothers didn't know what to make of this

behavior. They had grown accustomed to her school-week routine, when she had gotten up and eaten breakfast with them every morning and then gone to school on the bus and afterward had come home from her classes and was often out in the parlor reading another magazine or watching television when they came in for the evening. They had begun to talk more easily with her and to rehearse together the happenings of the passing days, finding the threads of things that interested them all. So it bothered them now that she'd begun to spend so many hours by herself. They didn't know what she was doing in her room, but they didn't want to ask her either. They didn't think it was their right to ask or query her. So instead they began to worry.

Late in the week, driving back to the house in the pickup in the evening, Harold said, Don't Victoria seem kind of sorry and miserable to you lately?

Yes. I've noted it.

Because she stays in bed too late. That's one thing.

Maybe they do, Raymond said. Young girls might all do like that, by their natures.

Till nine-thirty in the morning? I went back into the house for something the other day and she was just getting up.

I don't know, Raymond said. He looked out over the rattling hood of the pickup. I reckon she's just getting bored and lonesome.

Maybe, Harold said. But if she is, I don't know if that's good for the baby.

What isn't good for the baby?

Feeling lonesome and sorry like that. That can't be good for him. On top of staying up all manner of hours and sleeping all morning.

Well, Raymond said. She needs her sleep.

She needs her regular sleep. That's what she needs. She needs regular hours.

How do you know that?

I don't know that, Harold said, not for a certified fact. But you take a two-year-old heifer that's carrying a calf. She's not up all night long, restless, moving around, is she.

What are you talking about? Raymond said. How in hell does that apply to anything?

I started thinking about it the other day. The similarities amongst em. Both of them is young. Both of them's out in the country with only us here to watch out for em. Both is carrying a baby for the first time. Just think about it.

Raymond looked at his brother in amazement. They had arrived at the house and stopped on the frozen rutted drive in front of the wire gate. Goddamn it, he said, that's a cow. You're talking about cows.

I'm just saying, is all, Harold said. Give it some thought.

You're saying she's a cow is what you're saying.

I'm not either saying that.

She's a girl, for christsakes. She's not a cow. You can't rate girls and cows together.

I was only just saying, Harold said. What are you getting so riled up about it for?

I don't appreciate you saying she's a heifer.

I never said she was one. I wouldn't say that for money.

It sounded like it to me. Like you was.

I just thought of it, is all, Harold said. Don't you ever think of something?

Yeah. I think of something sometimes.

Well then.

But I don't have to say it. Just because I think of it.

All right. I talked out before I thought. You want to shoot me now or wait till full dark?

I'll have to let you know, Raymond said. He looked out the side window toward the house where the lights had been switched on in the darkening evening. I just reckon she's getting bored. There's nothing to do out here. No school nor nothing else now.

She don't appear to have many friends to speak of, Harold said. That's one thing for sure.

No. And she don't call nobody and nobody calls her, Raymond said.

Maybe we ought to take her in to town to a picture show sometime. Do something like that.

Raymond stared at his brother. Why, you just flat amaze me. What's wrong now?

Well, do you want to attend a movie show? Can you see us doing that? Sit there while some Hollywood movie actor pokes his business into some naked girl on the screen while we're sitting there eating salted popcorn watching him do it—with her sitting there next to us.

Well.

Well.

Okay, Harold said. All right then.

No sir, Raymond said. I didn't think you'd want to do that.

But by God, we got to do something, Harold said.

I ain't arguing that.

Well, we do, goddamn it.

I said I know, Raymond said. He rubbed his hands together between his knees, warming them; his hands were chafed and red, cracked. It does appear to me like we just did this, he said. Or something next to it. That night when we was talking to her about the market. I tell you, it seems like you get one thing fixed and something else pops up. Like with a young girl like her, you can't fix nothing permanent.

I hear what you're saying, Harold said.

The two brothers looked toward the house, thinking. The house was old and weathered, nearly paintless, the upstairs windows looked down blankly. Next to the house the bare elm trees blew and tossed in the wind.

I'm going to tell you what though, Harold said. I'm beginning to have a little more appreciation for these people with kids nowadays. It only appears to be easier from the outside. He looked at his brother. I think that's the truth, he said. Raymond was still looking toward the house, not saying anything. Are you listening to me? I just said something.

I heard what you said, Raymond said.

Well? You never said nothing.

I'm thinking.

Well, can't you think and talk to me at the same time?

No, I can't, Raymond said. Not with something like this. It takes all my concentration.

All right then, Harold said. Keep thinking. I'll shut my mouth if that's what it takes. But one of us had better come up with something pretty damn quick. Her staying in that bedroom all the time can't be any good for her. Nor for that baby either she's carrying inside her.

That night Harold McPheron put in a call to Maggie Jones. Harold and Raymond had decided that he should do that. It was after the girl had gone back to her bedroom for the night and had shut the door.

When Maggie picked up the phone Harold said to her, If you was to buy a crib, where would you think to get it?

Maggie paused. Then she said, This must be one of the McPheron brothers.

That's right. The good-looking smart one.

Well, Raymond, she said. It's nice of you to call.

That's not as comical as you think, Harold said.

Isn't it?

No, it ain't. Anyhow, what's your answer? Where would you buy a crib if you was to need one?

I'm to understand that you don't mean a corn crib. You wouldn't have to ask me about that.

That's right.

I believe I'd drive over to Phillips. To the department store. They'd have a baby section.

Whereabouts is it?

On the square across from the courthouse.

On the north side?

Yes.

Okay, Harold said. How you doing, Maggie? You doing all right?

She laughed. I'm doing fine.

Thanks for the information, he said. Happy New Year's to you, and hung up.

The next morning the McPheron brothers came up to the house from work about nine o'clock, covered up against the cold, stomping their boots on the little porch, taking their thick caps off. They had purposely timed their return to the house so as to find the girl still seated in the dining room at the walnut table, eating her solitary breakfast. She looked up at them where they stood hesitating in the doorway, then they came in and sat down across from her. She was still in her flannel nightgown and heavy sweater and stockings and her hair was shining in the winter-slanted sun coming in through the uncurtained south windows.

Harold cleared his throat. We've been thinking, he said.

Oh? the girl said.

Yes ma'am, we have. Victoria, we want to take you over to Phillips to do some shopping in the stores. If that's all right with you. If you don't have something else planned for the day.

This announcement surprised her. What for? she said.

For fun, Raymond said. For some diversion. Don't you want to? We thought you might appreciate getting out of the house.

No. I mean, what are we shopping for?

For the baby. Don't you think this little baby you're carrying is going to want some place to put his head down some day?

Yes. I think so.

Then we better get him something to do it in.

She looked at him and smiled. What if it's a girl though?

Then I guess we'll just have to keep her anyway and make

the best of our bad luck, Raymond said. He made an exaggerat-edly grave face. But a little girl's going to want a bed too, isn't she? Don't little baby girls get tired too?

They left the house about eleven that morning after the McPheron brothers had finished the morning feeding. They had come back in and washed up and changed into clean pants and clean shirts, and by the time they had put on the good hand-shaped silver-belly Bailey hats that they wore only to town the girl was already waiting for them, sitting at the kitchen table in her winter coat with the red purse looped over her shoulder.

They set out in the bright cold day, riding in the pickup, the girl seated in the middle between them with a blanket over her lap, with the old papers and sales receipts and fencing pliers and the hot wire testers and the dirty coffee mugs all sliding back and forth across the dashboard whenever they made any sharp turn, driving north toward Holt, passing through town and beneath the new water tower and carrying on north, the country flat and whitepatched with snow and the wheat stubble and the cornstalks sticking up blackly out of the frozen ground and the winter wheat showing in the fall-planted fields as green as jewelry. Once they saw a lone coyote in the open, running, a steady distance-covering lope, its long tail floating out behind like a trail of smoke. Then it spotted the pickup, stopped, started to move again, running hard now, and crossed the highway and hit a section of woven fence and was instantly thrown back but at once sprang up again and hit the fence again and at last in a panic scrambled up over the wire fence like a human man would, and ran on, loping again in the open, tra-versing the wide country on the other side of the road without once pausing or even slowing down to look back.

Is he all right? the girl said.

Appears like it, Raymond said.

Until somebody gets after him, Harold said, chasing after him in a pickup with coyote dogs. And shoots him.

Do they do that?

They do.

They drove on. There were farm houses scattered and isolated in the flat sandy country, with barns and outbuildings down below them, and dark windbreaks of trees in the far distances, showing where a farmstead was now or once had been. They drove past one farm beside the highway where there were quarter horses and a red barn and where the man had poked worn-out cowboy boots upside down over the tops of the fence posts along the road for an eighth of a mile, for decoration. At Red Willow they turned west and drove on, past the country schoolhouse at Lone Star and across the high open wheatland, and after a while they topped a rise and could see down into the South Platte River valley, wide and tree-lined, the cliffs far away on the other side, with the town laid out below. They fishtailed down, crossed the interstate highway and entered the outreaches of Phillips.

By now it was about one-thirty. They parked at the curb across from the courthouse and went into a little local café for lunch and sat down at a table with a green tablecloth quartered over it. The noon-hour rush was finished and they were the only customers. In a moment a woman got up from the counter where she'd been smoking and resting and brought them water glasses and menus. The girl ordered a grilled cheese sandwich and tomato soup. Raymond said to her, You better get you more than that. Don't you think, Victoria? It's a long time till supper.

The girl asked for a glass of milk.

Bring her a tall glass, would you, ma'am? Raymond said.

What about you two gentlemen? the woman said.

Both of the McPheron brothers ordered chicken fried steaks which came with mashed potatoes and green beans and canned corn and a carrot Jell-O salad.

Them are good to eat, the woman said.

That so? Harold said.

I like em myself, she said.

That sounds encouraging, if the help eats the food, he said. What kind of gravy comes with it?

Yellow.

Put some of that on the steaks too, would you?

I can tell him. I don't do it myself.

If you would, he said. And some black coffee too, when you get a decent chance. Thank you kindly.

The woman put in their order and brought their coffee and milk, and in a short while she brought out their platters of food. They sat at the table in the little café and ate quietly, deliberately. When the brothers were finished they ordered themselves and the girl Dutch apple pie with a scoop of ice cream on top, but she could only eat half of hers. They paid the bill and walked up the block to the department store.

The shop windows out front had sets of bedroom furniture and living room sofas and lamps on display. They went inside the store and were met at once by a brisk short middle-aged woman in a brown dress. May I help you? she said.

We're looking for the crib section, Harold said.

Baby cribs?

Yes, ma'am. We're in the market for one. He winked at the girl. We want to consider your selection.

If you will follow me, the woman said.

They followed her back through the store aisles to a far corner. Here you see what we offer, she said. There were a dozen new baby cribs assembled and set up, fitted with mattresses and baby blankets, displayed among matching chests of drawers and changing tables. The brothers surveyed them and were astonished. They glanced at the girl. She stood aside, not saying anything at all.

Maybe you better just tell us about em, Harold said.

I'd be happy to, the woman said. The features you look for

in a baby crib include this nontoxic easy-care finish. This plastic teething rail. This one side which raises and lowers for easy access. These hooded casters. This one-piece mattress support here. The brackets like these on this model so the mattress can be adjusted to various levels. This one offers a rail which lowers by knee pressure while the rail on this one lowers when you release these two catches. This model here permits you to convert it to a toddler's daybed by removing the rail altogether.

She stopped and waited, her hands behind her back. Did you have any questions?

Why ever would you want hooded casters? Harold said.

For decoration.

Ma'am?

It looks better.

I expect that's important, how the wheels look.

It's an added attraction, she said. Some people prefer it.

I see, he said.

The McPheron brothers approached the baby cribs and began to inspect them closely. They manipulated the moveable sides, raising them and lowering them, and walked around each of the cribs and adjusted the height of the supports and peered underneath, and they pushed them and rolled them forward and backward. Raymond leaned over and punched down on one of the crib mattresses, causing it to bounce.

What do you think, Victoria? he said. How about this one?

It's too expensive, she said. Every one of them is.

You let us worry about that. Which one of these do you like best?

I don't know, she said. She looked around. This one, maybe. She indicated the least costly one.

That's a nice one, Raymond said. I kind of like this one here, myself. They went on looking.

Finally the McPheron brothers chose the crib which converted to a daybed, the most expensive of the lot. It had carpenter-turned spindles and actual wood headboards. It seemed substantial to them and the side that was adjustable moved easily on its slides. They believed the girl would have no difficulty with it.

You have this in stock, I guess, Harold said.

Surely, the woman said.

Why don't you bring one of em out.

But you understand it doesn't include the mattress.

Doesn't?

No. Mattresses are not included. Not at this price.

Well, ma'am, Harold said. We need a crib. And we'd rather to have a mattress to go with it. This girl's going to have a baby and it can't sleep on a board. Even if the board can be adjusted to three different levels.

Which one would you care to have? the woman said. They come in these possibilities.

She began to show them the mattresses. They chose a solid one which felt sufficiently firm when they squeezed it and turned it over, and afterward they selected several crib sheets and warm blankets.

The girl watched it all from a kind of abject distance. She had grown increasingly quiet. At last she said, Can't you wait? It's too much. You shouldn't be doing all of this.

What's the matter? Harold said. We're having us some fun here. We thought you was too.

But it's too expensive. Why are you doing this?

It's all right, he said. He started to put his arm around her, but stopped himself. He looked down into her face. It's all right, he said again. It is. You'll just have to believe that.

The girl's eyes filled with tears, though she made no sound. Harold took out a handkerchief from the rear pocket of his pants and gave it to her. She wiped at her eyes and blew her nose and handed it back to him. You want to keep it? Harold said. She shook her head.

The woman said, You do still want these?

Harold put the handkerchief away and turned to face her.

That's right, ma'am. We haven't changed our minds. We still want em.

Very well. I just wanted to be positive.

We're positive.

She called a stock boy and sent him back to the storeroom and he came out wheeling two large flat cardboard boxes on a dolly. He drew up at the counter.

The woman rang up their purchases. She said, Will this be cash or charge?

I'll sign you a bank check, Raymond said. He bent over the counter, leaning on his elbow, and wrote stiffly into his checkbook. When he had finished he inspected what he had written, then he folded it once and tore it off and blew back and forth over it and handed the check to the woman. She looked at it.

May I see some identification, please?

He took out his old wallet from the inner pocket of his coat and picked out his driver's license. She read it, then she looked up at him.

I didn't know they would allow you to have your picture taken with your hat on, she said.

They do in Holt, he said. What's the trouble? Don't it favor me?

Oh, there's a clear resemblance, she said.

She handed the license back to him and he put it away. Then she finished ringing up their purchases and gave them the receipt. And we thank you very much, she said.

The stock boy started toward the front of the store, dollying the new mattress and the new crib in the flat cardboard boxes printed with the bright factory lettering, moving out into the main aisle in a flourish. He advanced only a short way.

Son, Harold said. You can hold up there. That won't be necessary.

I was going to take them out for you.

That's all right.

The McPheron brothers hefted the two boxes and together

carried them ladder-fashion under their arms, one old man in his good hat following directly behind the other, out onto the sidewalk and up the block toward the pickup. The girl came after, with the store bag of sheets and blankets. Together they made a kind of parade. People on the square, shoppers, women and teenage girls and old retired men, watched them pass, turning to stare as the two old men and the pregnant girl went by. Out in the winter air it was colder now and the sun was already starting to lean toward the west, while across the street the granite-block courthouse loomed up gray and solid under its green tiled roof. At the curb they set the boxes in the bed of the pickup and lashed them down with yellow binder twine from the toolbox. Then they backed out into the street and drove slowly out of town, riding up out of the South Platte River valley onto the cold winter flatlands of the high plains.

It was evening when they got home. The early dark of late December. That low sky closing down. As they drove up over the last little rise before the turnoff to the house they saw that there were cattle out on the gravel road. Their eyes glinted red as rubies in the headlights—one of the old mother cows and three of the heavy-bodied two-year-old heifers. Wait up, Raymond said.

I see em, Harold said.

The cow stood broadside in the middle of the road, her head lifted in the lights, staring as the pickup came closer, then she wheeled and dropped down into the ditch and the heifers dropped down with her.

You make it four?

Harold nodded.

They drove past them slowly, watching them, and took the girl back to the house and went inside with her and put on their work boots and coats and warm caps, and then they went back into the cold and located the cows and headed them trotting in the ditch alongside the road until they passed the gate. Raymond got out and swung the gate open and Harold gunned the pickup ahead and turned the cattle back. They whirled back along the fence in the bright headlights of the truck, moving in the ditch weeds, their bellies swinging, their flanks swaying, their feet thrown out sidways in that awkward bovine manner and kicking up clots of snow. Raymond stood out in the road waiting. When the cattle got up to the gate he hollered and flapped his arms and without any trouble they trotted in. He climbed into the cab and they pushed the cattle farther into the pasture away from the fence. They watched for a while to see which way they'd go. By now it was completely dark and hard-cold. They drove out of the pasture and when they got up to the house the yardlight had come on, shining purplish-blue from the lightpole next to the garage.

They mounted the porch steps and scraped their feet. But as soon as they entered the kitchen they stopped. They discovered that the girl had the room warm and brightly lighted, and on the stove she had supper already heated up and ready to be served and the square wooden kitchen table was set for the three of them with the old plates and the old silverware already ranged in order about the table.

Well, by God, Harold said. I want you to look at here.

Well, yes, Raymond said. It makes me think of the way Mother used to do.

If you want to sit down, the girl said. She stood next to the stove with one of the white dish towels tied about her thickening waist. Her face looked flushed from the cooking, but her black eyes shone. It's all ready, she said. Maybe we could eat out here tonight. If that's all right. It seems homier.

Well, surely, Harold said. I don't see why not.

The brothers washed up and the three of them ate together in the kitchen and talked a little about the trip to Phillips, about the woman in the store with the brown dress and the boy with the dolly, the look on his face, and after supper the girl read the page of directions while the two McPherons assembled the crib. When it was finished they stood it up against a warm interior wall in the girl's bedroom with one of the new sheets stretched tight on the mattress and the warm blanket folded down neatly. Afterward the brothers went out back to the parlor and watched the ten o'clock news while the girl washed the supper dishes and cleaned up in the kitchen.

Later, when the girl was lying in the old soft double bed that had once been the elder McPherons' marriage bed, she lay awake for a while and looked with pleasure and satisfaction at the crib. It gleamed against the faded pink-flowered wallpaper. The varnish shone. She imagined looking at a little face lying there, what that would feel like. At ten-thirty she heard the brothers mounting the stairs to their bedrooms and heard them overhead on the pinewood floorboards.

The next morning she stayed asleep in her room until mid-morning, as she had the previous six days of vacation, but it was different now. It was all right now. The McPheron brothers had decided that seventeen-year-old girls did that. It didn't matter. They couldn't say what they would do about it even if they still wanted to do something, and now they didn't care to.

Two days later it was New Year's, and school started again the day afterward.

Guthrie.

It appeared to him there were ruffles everywhere. Ranged around both bedroom windows, sewn on the bedcover, tacked on the pillows. Still more surrounding the mirror over the chest of drawers. Judy must get something out of it, he thought. She was in the bathroom doing something to herself, inserting something. He smoked a cigarette and looked at the ceiling. A pool of light was showing directly above the bedside lamp on the pink plaster.

Then she came out of the bathroom wearing a little night-gown and nothing under it and he could see the dark medallions of her nipples and the outlines of her small breasts and the dark vee of her hair below.

You didn't need to do that, he said. I've been cut.

How do you know what I've been doing?

I assumed.

Don't assume too much, she said. Then she smiled. Her teeth shone in the light.

She got into bed with him. It had been a long time. Ella and he hadn't slept together for almost a year now. Judy felt warm beside him in the bed.

Where'd you get this scar? she said.

Where?

This one on your shoulder here.

I don't know. Fence wire, I guess. Don't you have any scars?

Inside.

Do you?

Of course.

You don't act like it.

I don't intend to. It doesn't do much good, does it?

Not in my experience, he said.

She was lying on her side looking at him. What made you come over here tonight?

I don't know. I was lonely, I guess. Like you said at the Chute the other night.

Aren't we all, she said.

She raised up higher and leaned forward and kissed him and he brushed her hair away from her face, and then without saying anything more she moved over on top of him and he could feel her warm against himself and he felt up under the back of her nightgown with both hands, feeling her small waist and her smooth hips.

What ever became of Roger? Guthrie said.

What? She laughed. You're asking about him at this time?

I got to wondering about him while you were in the bathroom.

He left. It was better for everybody.

So what was his story?

How do you mean? she said.

Well, how did you meet? Guthrie said.

She pushed herself up and looked at him. You want to talk about that right now?

I was just wondering.

Well. I was at this bar in Brush. It was a long time ago. A Saturday night. I was younger then.

You're still young. You said that the other night too.

I know. But I was even younger then. I was at this bar and I met this guy who turned out to be my husband. He was a sweet talker. Old Roger sweet-talked me into seeing things his way.

Did he?

Then after a while it wasn't sweet anymore.

She looked sad suddenly and he was sorry he'd said anything. He brushed her hair away again. She shook her head and smiled, bent to kiss him. He held her for a while and she felt very warm and smooth. In the bathroom she had put on cologne in addition to the nightgown. She kissed him again.

What if I was to ask you something else? Guthrie said.

What is it?

How about taking your nightgown off?

That's different. I don't mind that.

She raised up again and pulled the nightgown over her head. She looked very good in the lamplight.

That better?

Yes, Guthrie said. I believe it is.

Two hours earlier that evening he had driven past Maggie Jones's house and all the lights had been turned off. So he'd driven around Holt awhile and had stopped and bought cigarettes and a six-pack of beer and afterward he'd driven out of town a ways, and about five miles south of town on the narrow highway he had made up his mind and turned around and driven back and stopped at her house, at Judy's, the secretary from school. When she opened the door and let him in she smiled and said, Well, hello. Do you want to come in?

Now, afterward, as he was leaving, she said, You going to come back?

Maybe.

You know you don't have to. But I'd like it if you did.

Thank you, Guthrie said.

For the rest of that night and the following day he believed it was just between the two of them. But other people in Holt knew too. He didn't know how Maggie Jones knew, but she did. At school on Monday she came into his room in the afternoon after the last class.

Is this the way it's going to be now? she said.

Is what the way it's going to be, Guthrie said, looking at her face.

Don't do this, damn you. You're too old to play dumb.

He looked at her. He took his glasses off and wiped them and put them back on. His black hair looked thin under the light. He said, How did you know?

How big of a town do you think this is? Do you think there is somebody in Holt who doesn't know your pickup?

Guthrie turned in the chair and looked out the window. The same winter trees. The street. The curbing across the way. He looked back at her. She was standing just inside the door watching him. No, he said, it's not going to be like this.

So what was that, last night?

That, he said, was somebody that was turned out free for a night and didn't know what to do with it.

You could have come over to see me. I would've been glad to see you.

I drove by. The lights were all off.

So you decided to go over to her house, is that it?

Something like that.

She stared at him for a long time. So is this something that's going to be permanent? she said finally.

I don't think so. No, he said. It isn't. She wouldn't want it to be either.

All right, Maggie said. But I will not compete for you. I

won't get into some kind of contest for you. I will not do that. Oh, goddamn you anyway, you son of a bitch.

She walked out of the room and down the hallway, and for the remainder of that day and on into the night Guthrie felt mixed up and wooden in all his movements and thoughts.

Victoria Roubideaux.

She was in the hallway at the high school in the afternoon when Alberta, the small blond girl from history, came up to her bearing something in her hand and said, He's outside. He said to give you this. Here.

Who said?

I don't know his name. He just stopped me and said give this to you when I saw you. Here, take it.

She opened the note. It was a folded scrap of cheap yellow tablet paper, with pencil writing scrawled on it: *Vicky. Come out to the parking lot. Dwayne.* She turned it over, there was nothing on the other side. Though she had never seen any of his handwriting before she believed this was what it would look like, this pencil-scrawl slanted backward. She didn't think it was a joke. It was from him, no one else. She didn't even feel much surprised. So he'd come back now. What did that mean? For most of the fall she had wanted that. Now late in the winter it had happened when she no longer believed in it or expected it. She looked at Alberta. Alberta's eyes were wide and excited as if she were engaged in some daytime soap opera and some new shocking pronouncement was about to be made and she was only waiting for the cue to react to it.

She reached past Alberta matter-of-factly and opened the metal door of the student locker and took out her winter coat. She put it on and drew out her red shiny purse.

Vicky, what are you going to do? Alberta said. You better be careful. That's him, isn't it.

Yes, she said. That's him.

She left Alberta and walked down the hall and out of the school building into the cold afternoon air, walking without rush, without hurry, in a kind of numbed trance, moving toward the icy parking lot behind the school. When she passed the last corner of the building she saw his black Plymouth waiting at the edge of the paved lot. He had the motor running and there was the familiar low muttering of the muffler, a sound that took her back to the summer. He was sitting slumped down in the front seat, smoking a cigarette. She could see the smoke drifting thinly out of the half-opened window. She walked up to him. He was watching her as she approached, then he sat up.

You don't look too pregnant, he said. I figured you'd be bigger.

She said nothing to him yet.

Your face got rounder, he said. He studied her, looking at her steadily, a little critically as he always did, as he regarded everything. That calmness, a kind of distance he had, that you couldn't touch. She remembered that now. It looks okay on you, he said. Turn sideways.

No.

Turn sideways. Let me see if it shows that way.

No, she said again. What do you want? What are you doing here?

I haven't made up my mind yet, he said. I come back to see how you're doing. I heard you were pregnant and living out in the country with two old men.

Who told you that? Haven't you been in Denver all this time?

Sure. But I still know people here, he said. He sounded surprised.

Well, what of it? she said.

You're mad now. I can see that much, he said.

Maybe I have a reason to be.

Maybe you do, he said. He seemed to be considering something. He reached forward and stubbed out his cigarette in the ashtray. His motions seemed unhurried and calm. He looked at her again. Don't be like this, he said. I come back to see you, is what I'm saying. To see if you'd want to go to Denver.

With you?

Why not?

What would I do in Denver?

What does anybody do in Denver? he said. Live in my apartment with me. We could take up our lives together. We could take up where we left off. You're carrying my baby, aren't you?

Yes. I have a baby in me.

And I'm the father, aren't I?

Nobody else could be.

That's why, he said. That's what I'm talking about.

She looked at him in the front seat of the car. The motor was still running. She felt cold standing out in the open air in the parking lot. Six months had passed since he'd left and things had happened to her, but what had changed for him? He looked no different. He was thin and dark and his hair was curly and she still thought he was very good looking. But she didn't want to feel anything at all for him anymore. She had thought she was over those feelings. She believed she was. He had left without telling her he was leaving and she was already pregnant then, and afterward her mother wouldn't let her in the house and then she couldn't stay any longer with Mrs. Jones because of her old father, so she had gone out into the country with the two McPheron brothers and as unlikely as that had seemed that was turning out all right, and lately it was better than all right. Now, unexpectedly, here he was again. She didn't know what to feel.

Why don't you get in? he said. At least you could do that. You're going to freeze like a hunk of ice standing out there. I didn't come back to make you get cold, Vicky.

She looked away from him. The sun was bright. But it didn't feel warm. It was a bright cold winter day and nothing was moving, no one else was even outside, the other high school kids were in their afternoon classes. She looked at their cars in the parking lot. Some had frost forming inside the windows. The cars had been there since eight in the morning. They looked cold and desolate.

Aren't you even going to talk to me? he said.

She looked at him. I shouldn't even be here, she said.

Yes you should. I come back for you. I should of called during these months, I know. I'll apologize for that. I'll say I was wrong. Come on, though. You're getting cold.

She continued to look at him. She couldn't think. He was waiting. From across the pavement came a gust of wind; she felt it on her face. She looked out toward the patches of snow on the football field and toward the empty stands rising up on either side. She looked back at him once more. He was still watching her. Then, without knowing she was going to, she walked around the rear of the car and got in on the other side and closed the door. It was warm inside. They sat facing each other. He didn't try to touch her yet. He knew that much. But after a while he turned forward and put the car in gear.

I missed you, he said. He was speaking straight ahead, talking over the steering wheel of the black Plymouth.

I don't believe you, she said. Why don't you tell me the truth.

That is the truth, he said.

They left Holt driving west on 34, driving out into the winter landscape. When they got out past Norka after half an hour they began to see the mountains, a faint jagged blue line low on the horizon a hundred miles farther away. They didn't talk very much. He was smoking and the radio was playing from Denver and she was looking out the side window at the brown pastures and the dark corn stubble, the shaggy cattle and the regular intervals of telephone poles, like crosses strung beside the railroad tracks, standing up above the dry ditch weeds. Then they arrived in Brush and turned up onto the interstate and went on west, going faster now on the good road, and passed Fort Morgan where in the freezing air the fog from the sewage plant drifted across the highway, and about then she decided to say what she had been thinking for the last five minutes. I wish you wouldn't smoke in the car.

He turned toward her. You never cared before, he said.

I wasn't pregnant before.

That's a fact.

He rolled the window down and flicked the burning cigarette outside into the rushing air and turned the window up again.

How will that be? he said.

Better.

How come you have to sit so far away? he said. I never bit you before, did I?

Maybe you've changed.

Why don't you come a little closer and find out. He showed his teeth and grinned.

She slid across the seat toward him and he put his arm over her shoulders and kissed her cheek and she set her open hand on his thigh, and they rode as they had ridden in the summer when they had driven out in the country north of Holt before stopping at the old homestead house under the green trees in the evening, and they were still riding that way when they drove into Denver at dusk in the midst of city traffic.

After that she didn't know what to do with herself. She had made a sudden turn. She was seventeen and carrying a baby and she was alone most of every day in an apartment in Denver while Dwayne, this boy she had met last summer and wasn't sure she knew at all, went to work at the Gates plant. His apartment was two rooms and a bathroom, and she had it completely cleaned and swept in the first morning. And his cupboards rearranged on the second morning, and the laundry done, the single set of sheets he owned and his dirty jeans and work shirts, all done in the first three mornings, and the only person she had met so far was a woman in the laundry room in the basement who stared at her the whole time, smoking and not speaking to her even once so that she thought the woman must be mute or maybe angry at her for some reason. In the first few days in Denver she did what she could, washed the clothes and cleaned the apartment and had something cooked for supper in the evening, and on the first Saturday afternoon when he got off work she went out with him to a shopping mall and he bought her a few things, a couple of shirts and a pair of pants, to make up for what she had left in Holt. But there wasn't enough for her to do, and she was more alone than she had ever been.

That first night when they had arrived at the apartment they had gotten out of the car in the parking lot with its rows of dark cars and he had led her up the stairs and down a tiled hallway to the door and unlocked it. You're home, he said. This is it. It was two rooms. She looked around. And in a little while he took her into the bedroom and they had never been in bed together before, not an actual bed, and he undressed her and looked at her stomach, the round smooth full rise of it, and he noted the blue veins showing on her breasts, and her breasts swollen and harder now, and her nipples larger and darker too. He shaped his hand over the hard ball of her stomach. Is it moving yet? he said.

It's been moving for two months.

He held his hand there, waiting, as if he expected it to move now, for him, then he bent and kissed her navel. He rose and took his clothes off and got back in bed where she was and kissed her and stetched out beside her, looking at her.

You still love me?

I might, she said.

You might. What does that mean?

It means it's been a long time. You left me.

But I missed you. I told you that already. He began to kiss her face and to caress her.

I don't know if you should do this, she said.

Why not?

Because. The baby.

Well, people still do this after she has a baby in her, he said.

But you have to be careful.

I'm always careful.

No, you're not. Not always.

When wasn't I?

I'm pregnant, aren't I?

He looked in her face. That was a accident. I didn't mean to do that.

It still happened.

You could of done something yourself too, you know, he said. It wasn't just up to me.

I know. I've thought about that a lot.

He looked into her face, her dark eyes. You seem different some way now. You've changed.

I'm pregnant, she said. I am different.

It's more than that, he said. But you're not sorry, are you?

About the baby?

Yeah.

No, she said. I'm not sorry about the baby.

You going to let me kiss you, then?

She didn't say anything, she didn't refuse. And so he began to kiss her and caress her once more and after a while he lay on top of her, holding himself up, and after a while longer he came inside and began to move slowly, and in truth it seemed to be all right. But still she was worried.

Later, they lay in bed quietly. The room was not a very big one. He had nailed a couple of posters on the walls for decoration. There was one window which had a shade pulled down over it and outside the window was the noise of nighttime Denver traffic.

Still later they got up from bed and he called on the phone for pizza and the delivery boy brought it and he paid the boy and made a little joke which made the boy laugh, and after he was gone they ate the pizza together in the front room and watched what there was on television until midnight. The next morning he got up early and went to work. And then she was lonely as soon as he left the apartment and she didn't know what to do with herself.

McPherons.

Three hours after dark they stopped the pickup at the curb in front of Maggie Jones's house and got out in the cold and went up onto the porch. When she came to the door she was still in her school clothes, a long skirt and sweater, but she had taken her shoes off and was in her stocking feet. What is it? she said. Will you come in?

They got as far as the front hall. Then they began to speak, almost at the same time.

She never come home today, Harold said. We been driving all over these streets looking for her.

We don't even know where to start looking, Raymond said.

We been driving the streets more than three hours, looking everywhere we could think of.

You're talking about Victoria, of course, Maggie said.

There don't seem to be any friend we could talk to, Raymond said. Least we don't know of one.

She didn't come home on the bus after school this evening? No.

Has she not come home like this before?

No. This is the first.

Something must of happened to her, Harold said. She must of got taken off or something.

Watch what you say, Raymond said. We don't know that. I'm not going to think that yet.

Yes, Maggie said, that's right. Let me make some calls first. You want to come in and sit down?

They entered her living room as they would some courtroom or church sanctuary and looked around cautiously and finally chose to sit on the davenport. Maggie went back to the kitchen to the phone. They could hear her talking. They sat holding their hats between their knees, just waiting until she came back into the room.

I called two or three girls in her class, she said, and finally called Alberta Willis. She said she'd given Victoria a note from a boy waiting in a car out in the parking lot. I asked her if she knew what was in the note. She said it was private, it wasn't to her. But did you read it? I asked her.

Yes. But just once, she said.

Tell me please. What did it say?

Mrs. Jones, it didn't say anything. Only come see me in the parking lot, and then his name. Dwayne.

Do you know him? I said.

No. But he's from Norka. Only he doesn't live there no more. Nobody knows where he lives.

And did Victoria go out to him in the parking lot, like the note said?

Yes, she went out to him. I tried to tell her not to. I warned her.

And did you not see her after that?

No. I didn't see her again after that at all.

So, Maggie said to the McPherons. I think she must have gone with him. With this boy.

The old brothers looked at her for a considerable time without speaking, watching her, their faces sad and tired.

You know him yourself at all? Harold said finally.

No, she said. I don't believe I've ever seen the boy. The kids know him somewhat. He was at some of the dances last year, this past summer particularly. That's when Victoria met him. She told me a little about that. But she wouldn't ever tell me his name. This is the first I've heard any part of his name.

Did that girl on the phone know the rest of it?

No.

They stared at her again for a time, waiting for anything more.

So she isn't hurt, Harold said. Or lost.

No, I don't think so.

She isn't lost, Raymond said. That's all we know. We don't know about hurt.

Oh, I want to believe she is all right, Maggie said. Let us think that.

What brought her to leave though? Raymond said. Can you tell me that. You think we did something to her?

Of course not, Maggie Jones said.

Don't you?

No, she said. Not for a minute.

Harold looked slowly around the room. I don't think we did anything to her, he said. I can't think of anything we might of did. He looked at Maggie. I been trying to think, he said.

Of course not, she said. I know you didn't.

Harold nodded. He looked around again and stood up. I reckon we might as well go on home, he said. What else is there to do. He put his old work hat on again.

Raymond still sat as before. You think this here is the one? he said. That give her the baby?

Yes, Maggie said. I think it must be.

Raymond studied her for a moment. Then he said, Oh. He paused. Well. I'm getting old. I'm slow on the uptake. And then he couldn't think what more there might be to say. He stood up beside his brother. He looked past Maggie, out across the room.

I reckon we can go, he said. We thank you for your kindly help, Maggie Jones.

They went out of her house into the cold again and drove off. At home they put on their canvas coveralls and went out in the dark, carrying a lantern to the calf shed where they'd penned up a heifer they'd noticed was showing springy. She was one of the two-year-olds. They'd noticed her bag had begun to show tight too. So they had brought her into the three-sided shed next to the work corrals the day before.

Now when they stepped through the gate, holding the lantern aloft under the pole roof, they could see she wasn't right. She faced them across the bright straw and frozen ground, humped up, her tail lifted straight out, her eyes wide and nervous. She took a couple of quick jittery steps. Then they saw that the calf bed was pushed out of her, hanging against her back legs, high up beneath her tail, and there was one pink hoof protruded from the prolapsed uterus. The heifer stepped away, taking painful little steps, humped up, moving toward the back wall, the hoof of her unborn calf sticking out from behind her as though it were mounted in dirty burlap.

They got a rope around the heifer's neck, made a quick halter of it and snugged her tight to the shed wall. Then Harold took off his mittens and pushed at the hoof for a long time until he was able to move it back inside, and then he went inside with his hand and felt of her and tried to position the calf's head between the two front feet as it was supposed to be, but the head wasn't right and the calf would not come. The little heifer was worn out now. Her head hung down and her back was humped. She stood and moaned. There was nothing to do but use the calf chain. They put the loops inside the heifer over the unborn calf's legs above the hocks, then fit the U-shaped piece against the heifer's hindquarters, and began to jack the calf out. Ratcheting it out of her. The heifer was pulled against the rope around her neck and head and she moaned in harsh pants and once raised her head to bawl, her eyes rolled back to white in terror. Then the calf's head came out with the front legs and suddenly the whole calf dropped heavily, slick and wet, and they caught it and wiped its nose clean and checked its mouth for air passage. They put the calf down in the straw. For the next hour, while the heifer stood panting and groaning they cleaned the prolapsed uterus and pushed it back inside of her and then sewed her up with heavy thread. Afterward they shot her with penicillin and stood the calf up and pointed it toward the heifer's bag. The heifer sniffed at the calf and roused a little and began to lick at it. The calf bumped at her and started to suck.

By now it was after midnight. It was cold and bleak outside the shed and utterly quiet. Overhead, the stars in the unclouded sky looked as cold and arctic as ice.

They came back into the house without yet removing their canvas coveralls and sat spent and bloody at the wood table in the kitchen.

You think she's going to be all right? Raymond said.

She's young. She's strong and healthy. But you don't ever know what might could happen. You can't tell.

No. You can't tell. You don't know how she is. You don't even know where he might of took her for sure.

He might of landed her in Pueblo or Walsenburg. Or some other place besides Denver. You can't never tell.

I'm going to hope she's all right, Raymond said.

I hope it, said Harold.

They went upstairs. They lay down in bed in the dark and could not sleep but lay awake across the hall from each other, thinking about her, and felt how the house was changed now, how it seemed all of a sudden so lonesome and empty.

Guthrie.

Lloyd Crowder called him early in the evening. You better come down here. It looks like they're going to try to blindside you. You better bring your grade book and any papers you have.

Who is? Guthrie said.

The Beckmans.

He went out of the house and got in his pickup and drove across town to the district office next to the high school and when he went in he saw them immediately. They were sitting in the third row of the public chairs off to the far side. Beckman, his wife, and the boy. They turned and looked at him when he entered. He took a seat at the back. The school board members were ranged about the table at the front of the room, each with his name tag facing the public. There were framed pictures of outstanding seniors from the years past on the walls behind them. They had already gotten beyond the minutes of the previous meeting and the approval of the bills and the various items of communication and were now finishing discussion of the budget. The superintendent was taking them through each step. They voted on matters, if that was called for by regulation, and it was going smoothly, all cut and dried since they'd prepared for it earlier in executive session. Then the board chairman called for public concerns.

A thin woman stood up and began to complain about the school buses. I'd like to put a plea out there, she said. My kids used to get on at seven and off at four, now it's six-thirty and four forty-five. The bus driver gets disgusted and starts driving slow, that's what it is. What happens is those kids, all their cussing and getting out of their seats. Well, all their language is cussing. If we took that away from them they wouldn't have a thing to say.

The board chairman said, Safety is the big concern. Isn't that right. That's what we have to think about.

I'll tell you, the woman said, one time the bus finally had to pull over. The driver had to stop and she come back in the row and said to this girl, You been yelling at the top of your lungs all morning, now go ahead and yell. And the girl did too. Can you believe that? Well, my daughter didn't appreciate her yelling at the top of her lungs. I don't think she should have to put up with that.

Riding the bus is a privilege, the board chairman said, till they violate the rules. Isn't that right? He looked at the superintendent.

Yes, the superintendent said. After three misbehaviors they're off.

Then somebody better learn how to count to three, the woman said.

Yes ma'am, the chairman said. You need to come in and talk to the principal about this. About your concern here.

I already did that.

Did you, he said. Maybe you can talk to him again. I appreciate you coming here tonight. He looked around the room. Anything else? he said.

Mrs. Beckman rose up and said, Yes, there's something else. And I can see somebody called him to be here already. She looked at Guthrie. I don't care if he is here, I'm going to say it.

He hates my boy. He flunked him this past semester. Failed him out of American history. You know that can't be right.

Ma'am, what are you talking about? the chairman said. What is this?

I'm telling you. First he fights him in the hall over that little slut. Then he keeps him out of the basketball tournament which might cost him his scholarship to Phillips Junior College, and then he flunks him for the whole semester, that's what I'm talking about. I want to hear what you're going to do about it.

The board chairman looked at the superintendent. The superintendent looked at Lloyd Crowder who was sitting off to the side at another table. The board chairman turned to the principal now. Can you give us some background on this, Lloyd?

He don't need to, Mrs. Beckman said. I just told you.

Yes ma'am, said the chairman. But we'd like to hear from the principal too.

Crowder stood up and explained in some detail what each party in the dispute had done, and remarked on the five-day suspension the boy had been given.

Is Mr. Guthrie here? the chairman said.

That's him sitting back there, Mrs. Beckman said.

I see him now, the chairman said. Mr. Guthrie, would you care to say anything?

You've already heard it, Guthrie said. Russell hasn't done the work required of him. I told him that several times. That he needed to improve or he wouldn't pass the course. He didn't, so I gave him a failing grade.

You hear him? Mrs. Beckman said. That's exactly the lie he keeps telling everybody. Are you going to sit there and have him lie to you like that too?

I have the grade book if you think you have to see it, Guthrie said. But I'd prefer not to show it in public. I'm not even sure it's legal to do that.

Let him show it, Mrs. Beckman cried. I hope he does. Then

everybody can just see what he's been doing to Russell here. He makes it all up anyhow.

The board chairman looked at her for a moment. Now ma'am, he said. I'll tell you something. We don't like to interfere too much with what a teacher does in his own classroom.

Well you better interfere. Guthrie there, is a liar and a son of a bitch.

Ma'am, you can't talk that way in here. You better bring this up with the superintendent if you have a complaint to make, and we'll talk about it in executive session. We can't decide all this in public this a-way.

I see now, she said. You're just like the rest. We voted you in and you turn out like this.

Ma'am, that's my word on it. For now.

Can he graduate then?

Not without American history. I don't believe so.

Can he at least cross the stage and pick up a blank diploma?

Maybe. But I expect he'll have to take the class in the summer for what he failed. For the time being, he better take the rest of American history with somebody else individual. Isn't that right, superintendent?

Yes. That can be arranged.

That's right, the chairman said. That can be arranged. He looked out at them. Mr. Beckman, you haven't said anything. You got something to add to this?

You goddamn right I do, Beckman said. He stood up. We aren't done with this. I'll tell you that right now. You can be goddamn sure of that much. I'll go to the law if I have to. Do you think I won't?

Victoria Roubideaux.

For a while in Denver she took a job. It wasn't much of a job, only working part-time at a gas station convenience store on Wadsworth Boulevard a mile from the apartment, working at night for others when they called in. She had gone in for the interview and the little man with his white shirt, the manager, had walked her through the store and said, Where would you stock the Vienna sausage and the sardines? and she had said, The shelves with the canned foods, and he said, No, next to the crackers. You want them to buy both of them at the same time. There's a reason for what we do here.

He wanted to know when she was due to have the baby and in answer to this question she had told him a lie. She said the baby was coming later than was true, that she was expecting to deliver at the end of May. You still sick a lot? he said.

No, she said. I was at first.

This is just part-time, he said. With little notice. Just when we want you, if we need you to come in. Whenever somebody calls in claiming they're sick. All right. You still want it?

Yes.

All right. We'll train you starting tomorrow.

She went in and trained for parts of three days with the

woman on the afternoon shift and then a night with the woman on the night shift, and then she waited a week and a half for the first call. When it came it was at suppertime on Monday, and Dwayne was tired and didn't want to drive her to work. She said she would walk. She got up from the table to leave, and that shamed him so that he drove her after all and neither one of them said anything to the other on the way. She worked through the night without incident and in the morning when she got off her shift she took the bus home since it was past the time Dwayne was due to start his shift at Gates. Upstairs in the apartment she found a note from him on the table saying, *See you tonight I'm not mad anymore are you*, written like that other note a month ago with a pencil on a scrap of paper in a slanted child's scrawl.

Two weeks later, the third time she was called, she was working behind the counter and a man came in at one-thirty in the morning when she was the only one in the store. He loitered in the aisles picking up different things, putting them back. A skinny man with a badly wrinkled face, with lank brown hair. Then he came up to the counter with nothing in his hand to buy and said, I guess you know Doris, don't you?

Who?

Doris. She works here.

I met her, yes.

What do you think about her?

She's nice.

She's a bitch. She locked me out and called the cops on me.

Oh, the girl said. She watched him, to see what he was going to do.

What do you think I got in the car? he said. Go ahead, think about it.

I don't know.

I got a gun out there, he said, looking straight into her eyes. With three shells loaded in it. Cause there's three of us. Her, me and her goddamn dog. I'd love to kill that son of a bitch. I can't stand that son of a bitch. You think I'm crazy, don't you.

I don't know you.

I am crazy. That fucking dog. I wouldn't hurt you though. When do you get off?

I'm not sure yet.

Sure you are.

No. It may be later. I don't always know.

Here. I'll buy some chewing gum. I got her goddamn dog anyway. I got him out in the car with me right now. She can lock me out but I got her dog. I can start with him if that's what she wants. Okay, don't work too hard, he said. He took his package of gum and went outside.

The girl watched him get into his car and drive away and she made a note of his license plates and gave the numbers to the manager, and in the following days she watched the newspapers for anything about the man, but nothing was ever reported. Doris, when she was told about him, said he was more or less harmless. She didn't know what the girl was talking about, she didn't have a dog. The last dog she'd had was five years ago.

In Denver Dwayne took her to a few parties. They attended one on a Friday night at the apartment of some people he knew from work, Carl and Randy. Randy was a big tall girl with tight jeans and skinny legs, and she wore a little tube top and had fixed breasts. Carl was a talker. By the time they got there he was wound up. There were lots of other people in the apartment too. They were all drinking and smoking and on the coffee table a basket of joints was set out for anybody's use. The walls of the room were covered with tinfoil, with blinking Christmas lights still up, and the room was hot and the music was going so loud she could feel it in her stomach. People were dancing and laughing. One girl was dancing on the sofa, flinging her hair back and forth. A boy was dancing between two girls, in a routine of bumping hips. Randy brought her a drink from the next room and she stood back against the wall and watched, and Dwayne went into the kitchen with Carl. Randy looked at her and said, Hey, enjoy, you know? and smiled brilliantly and spread her arms in a gesture, meaning: You can have all of this, and disappeared. She stood against the wall, watching.

Later she went out to the kitchen to find Dwayne. He was seated at the table playing euchre and drinking with some others and she stood behind him, and once he put his hand on her stomach and said, How's my little man? and patted her and drank from his glass. She watched the game for a while and wandered away to find the bathroom. The door was closed and she knocked and somebody opened it enough that she saw in quickly, and there were two boys sitting on the edge of the bathtub waiting their turn while a girl was taking on another boy on the toilet. The girl was naked from her waist down, her long white legs spread out, and the girl might have been Randy, but she couldn't see her well enough since the door was closed so fast, the boy who opened it only saying, Wrong place. Upstairs.

When Dwayne took her home it was about four in the morning. By that time she had been coaxed into drinking four or five vodka Squirts and taking hits from the joint whenever it came around. She was so out of place and so lonely she couldn't care for a while, she wanted something like everybody else did, and in time she ended up losing herself to the music and the crowd-feeling, and danced and danced, holding herself under her stomach, supporting the baby while she twirled around the room. When she woke the next morning she felt sick immediately, as she had in the first months, except it was for a different reason now. There was a red bruise high up on her leg that she could feel with her fingers though she had no memory of where it had come from. She turned in the bed. Dwayne was still sleeping beside her. She lay for a long time feeling sick and sad. She looked at the bar of sunlight that showed thinly along the edge of the window shade. She didn't even know what the weather was doing anymore. The sun was shining but what else was there? She drifted into a daze of sorrow and disbelief. She didn't want to think what any of the night before might have done to her baby. She could only remember the first of it. She could remember the dancing, but there were other things too. She didn't want to think about them. But it was what she couldn't remember that scared her most.

McPherons.

There came a night at the end of winter when Raymond
McPheron went into town for a meeting of the board of gover-
nors of the Holt County Farmers' Co-op Elevator. He was one
of the seven farmers and ranchers elected to the board. When
the meeting was over he drove out with some of the men for a
drink at the Legion, and he was sitting at a table with them
when the man across from him, not one of the farmers but a
man in town he knew by name only, said:

Too bad that little girl didn't work out.

I think so, Raymond said.

You got some good out of her anyway, I guess.

What do you mean?

You taking turns with her, I mean. Was that how it was? Tell
us the truth now. Was it sweet? The man grinned. He had little
even teeth, well-spaced.

Raymond looked at him for a time, not saying anything.
Then he leaned over the table and took hold of his wrist just
below the shirt cuff and said, You say something like that again
about Victoria Roubideaux and I'll cave your fuckin head in.

Well what in the hell? the man said. He tried to pull back.
Let go of me.

You heard what I said, Raymond told him.

Turn loose. I never meant nothing.

Yeah. You did.

I'm just saying what others have.

I'm not talking to no others.

Turn loose of me. What the hell's a-wrong with you?

You mind me. Don't you even think something like that again about her.

Then Raymond opened his hand and let go. The man stood up. You dumb old son of a bitch, he said. I was joking.

You got some of that right, Raymond said.

The man looked at him, then walked over and stood at the bar and spoke to the bartender and a second man standing there. They had seen what happened. He talked to them, rubbing his wrist, looking back at Raymond.

At the table Raymond finished his beer and got up and went outside to his pickup and drove home in the moonless late-winter night. When he was back inside the house again he walked into the girl's bedroom and switched on the overhead light and stood looking at the old double bed with the quilt on it and the new crib against the wall with the new sheet stretched tight over it and the blanket folded down, all of it in readiness yet for the girl and the baby just as it had been before the girl had left that other morning and not come back. He stood looking around the room for some time. Thinking, remembering, considering different things here and there. Finally he switched the light off and went upstairs and paused in the hall. He stood in the open door to his brother's bedroom. You awake? he said.

I am now, Harold said. I heard you come up the stairs. You must be flat perturbed about something, for the racket you was making. The room was dark, with just the light from the hall shining in. A pale square of window at the back wall gave out onto the yard and barn and corrals. Harold raised up in bed. What's the matter? Something go wrong at the board meeting? Corn prices gone to hell?

No.

What then?

I went out for a drink afterward. At the Legion there with some of em.

Yeah? They haven't made that a crime yet. What about it?

You know they're talking, Raymond said.

Who is?

People in town. They're talking about Victoria. About you and me with her. Saying things about the three of us.

So that's what this is about, is it? Harold said. What did you expect would happen? Two old men take in a girl out here in the country, with nobody else around to look in on em. And the girl is young and good-looking even if she is pregnant, and the two old men that's keeping her are still men even if they are about as old and dried up as some of this calcified horse shit. It's going to happen. People are going to talk.

Maybe they are, Raymond said. He looked at his brother in the dark room with the window squared behind him. Only I don't care for it, he said. They can keep their goddamn mouths off her. I don't care for it even a little bit.

There isn't a whole hell of a lot you can do about it.

Maybe not, Raymond said. He turned to cross the hallway to enter his own room, then he turned back. I might even come to understand that too, he said. But that don't mean I got to like it. That don't mean I'm ever going to get so I got to like it.

Ike and Bobby.

In the early morning they woke in the same bed at almost the same moment, with the stain already visible and distinct above the north windows across the room. Ike got up and began to dress. Then Bobby got up and dressed while his brother stood beneath the water stain, looking out the windows past the well-house toward the barn and fence and windmill. Beyond the fence Elko was doing something to himself. Look at that crazy son of a bitch, Ike said.

Who?

Elko.

Bobby looked at him.

Then he was dressed and they went downstairs where Guthrie was drinking black coffee and smoking cigarettes at the kitchen table, and as usual on a Sunday morning, reading something, a newspaper or magazine opened to the sunlight on the table. Passing through the kitchen they went down off the porch and on across the gravel in a hurry. They opened the gate and stepped into the corral. But the horse wasn't dead then. He was still only kicking himself in the stomach. He was standing off by himself against the barn, away from Easter and the cats, and the sweat was dark along his neck and ribs and flanks. While they watched he dropped down into the dirt and rolled, his feet kicking into the air like a black bug or insect overturned and crawling its legs, his belly exposed while he rolled, lighter colored than the rest of him, brownish, and then he grunted and stood up again and swung his long black head back across his shoulder to look at his stomach. Immediately he began to kick at himself as if he were tormented by flies. But it wasn't flies. They watched him for another minute, until he fell down onto the dirt again beside the barn, then they ran back to the house.

Guthrie was at the stove, stirring eggs. Wait, he said. Can't one of you boys talk at a time?

They told him again.

All right, he said. I'll go look. But you stay here. Eat your breakfast.

He went outside. They could hear his steps on the porch. When the screen door slapped shut they sat down at the bare wooden table against the wall and began to eat, sitting across from each other, chewing quietly and then listening and looking at each other and beginning to chew again, their brown heads and blue eyes almost identical above the crockery plates. When he finished eating, Ike stood up and looked out the window. He's coming back, he said.

I guess he's going to die, Bobby said.

Who is?

Your horse. I guess he's going to die today.

No he isn't. Eat your breakfast.

I already ate my breakfast.

Well eat some more.

Guthrie came back into the house. He crossed to the phone and called Dick Sherman. They talked briefly. Then he hung up and Ike said: What's he going to do to him? He's not going to hurt him, is he?

No. He's already hurt.

But what makes him do that?

I'm not sure.

Was he still kicking himself?

Yes. There's something the matter with him. Something in his stomach, I guess. Dick'll look him over.

I guess he's going to die, Bobby said.

You be quiet, Bobby.

He could die though.

But you don't know that. You don't know anything about it. So keep your mouth shut.

Stop now, Guthrie said.

The two boys looked at each other.

Both of you, he said. And you better go get your papers started. I heard the train half an hour ago. It's time you were leaving.

Can't we do it later?

No. People pay on time and they want their papers on time.

But just this once? Dick Sherman'll be gone already.

He might be. And if he is I'll tell you about it. Go ahead now.

You won't let him hurt him.

No, I won't let him hurt him. But Dick wouldn't anyway.

Anyway, Bobby said. He's hurt already.

They went back outside into that early morning cold sunlight for the second time and walked their bikes out of the yard. They looked toward the barn and corral. Elko was still humped on three legs, still kicking. They mounted the bikes and rode out of the driveway onto the loose gravel on Railroad Street and east a half mile to the Holt depot.

When they were finished with their paper route they met again at Main and Railroad and rode home. It was a little warmer now. It was about eight-thirty and they were sweating a little under the hair on their foreheads. They rode past the old light plant beside the tracks. When they passed Mrs. Frank's house on Railroad Street and then the line of lilac bushes in her side yard, the new little heart-shaped leaves beginning to open along the branches now, they could see the extra pickup was still in the driveway at home, parked beside the corral.

Anyway, Ike said, he's not done with him yet. That's Dick Sherman's pickup.

I bet he's still kicking, Bobby said. Kicking and grunting.

They rode on, pedaling over the loose gravel, past the narrow pasture and the silver poplar and turned in at the drive and left their bikes at the house. They approached the corral but didn't enter; instead they looked through the fence boards. Elko was on the ground now. Their father and Dick Sherman were standing beside him, talking. He was down on his side in the corral dirt with his neck reached out as if he meant to drink at the barn's limestone block foundation. They could see one of his dark eyes. The eye was open, staring, and they wondered if the other eye was open too like that, staring blindly into the dirt under his head, filling with it. His mouth was open and they could see his big teeth, yellow and dirt-coated, and his salmon tongue. Their father saw them through the fence and came over.

How long have you boys been here?

Not very long.

You better go back to the house.

They didn't move. Ike was still looking through the fence into the corral. He's dead. Isn't he? he said.

Yes. He is, son.

What happened to him?

I don't know. But you better go back to the house. Dick's going to try to find out.

What's he going to do to him?

He has to cut him open. It's called an autopsy.

What for? Bobby said. If he's already dead.

Because that's how we find out. But I don't think you want to watch this.

Yes we do, Ike said. We want to watch.

Guthrie studied them for a moment. They stood before him across the fence, blue-eyed, the sweat drying on their foreheads, waiting in silence, a little desperate now but still patient and still waiting.

All right, he said. But you ought to go up to the house. You won't like it.

We know, Ike said.

I don't think you do, son.

Well, said Bobby. We've seen chickens before.

Yes. But this isn't chickens.

They sat on the fence and watched it all. For most of it Dick Sherman used a knife with a steel handle, which was easier to clean up afterward, and there wasn't the problem of a wooden handle's breaking. It was a sharp knife and he began by stabbing it into the horse's stomach and working it sawlike along his length, sawing up through the tough hide and brownish hair and pulling with his other hand to open the cut wider. When the knife grew slippery with blood he wiped it and his red hands on the hair over the ribs. Then the yard-long incision had been made and Dick Sherman and their father began to peel back the hide, their father pulling the upper flap of skin and hair backward while Sherman shaved at it underneath, freeing the hide from the ribs and stomach lining, exposing a thin layer of yellow fat and the fine sheaf of red muscle. Dick Sherman was kneeling at the horse's stomach with the knife and their father was crouched over his back. Both men had begun to sweat. Their shirts showed darker along the back and their faces shone. But they paused only briefly, routinely, to wipe their forearms across their shining foreheads, then fell to work again over the prone horse, whose one visible eye, as far as the boys could determine from the fence, had not changed at all but was still wide open, still staring indifferently into the blank featureless sky above the barn as if he didn't know or didn't care what was being done to him, or as if he had decided at last not to look anywhere else ever again. But Dick Sherman wasn't finished yet.

He drove the knife into the groin inside the top back leg to cut through that big muscle so he could sever the tendon in the joint. Afterward, with their father's help, the leg could be pulled back away, leaving the gut exposed and accessible. It took a while, stabbing and probing, to find the tendon and then to free the joint, but he found it finally.

Try it, Sherman said. See can you pull his leg back, Tom.

Their father took Elko at the back cannon and pulled hard, wrenching it, carrying the long fine-boned leg back and up so that it stood up now into the air almost perpendicular to his body, awful-looking, horrible. Sitting on the fence, watching it, the boys began to understand that Elko was dead.

The rich muscle at his groin where Dick Sherman had opened him lay thick and heavy and raw, exposed to view like steak. The hide had torn some when their father pulled and was bleeding along the tear. But now the gut could be opened. Sherman cut into the stomach lining. Then the yellow bags and the blue knots of stuff spilled out onto the dirt and the wispy manure. There was mucousy blood and fluid, yellow- and amber-colored. The transparent membranes shone silver in the sun.

Sherman said, Have you got a tree trimmer handy, Tom? I could use one.

In the barn, Guthrie said. He stood up stiffly and walked along the side of the barn into the dark center bay and returned with the two-handled double-clawed tool he used to cut tree branches and the spirea bushes around the house. He handed it to Dick Sherman.

Sherman laid his knife down. Pull the hide back again, will you? he said.

Their father crouched over the horse and with both hands pulled the hide back away from his ribs. Then Dick Sherman began to cut through the ribs with the tree trimmer, one rib at a time, making a crack each time like a dry stick breaking; he was exposing the chest cavity. The boys understood then that the horse was dead completely. He couldn't live through that. Watching it, their eyes grew round in their heads and their faces paled. They sat utterly still on the fence.

When enough of the ribs had been cut through, their father pulled the loose flap of the chest wall back so that Dick Sherman could examine the heart and lungs. He lifted them in his hands, turning them, poking and exploring with the knife. There was nothing wrong with the heart. Nor with the lungs. He probed with the knife into the aorta and large veins to look for scar tissue from worms but there wasn't any; the horse had been thoroughly wormed. So he moved back again to the gut and raised the entrails, reaching into the stomach and lifting out more of the moist yellow intestines. He was straining hard now, wrenching the heavy insides out of the horse, and apparently more of it was coming than he wanted because he was discarding some of it, searching and lifting at it while it squirmed and tried to fill in, and then he had some of the bowel and it was too big and too dark entirely and he stopped.

There, he said. See that? That big dark part, kind of bluish-black?

Guthrie nodded.

He had a twisted gut. That's what killed him. Sherman held it up in his hands, displaying it. Below here where it twisted, the gut died. That's why it's so black and bloated and off-color. He released the dead intestine and it folded into place among the rest as though it were alive. Poor bastard, he suffered enough.

The two men stood up. Dick Sherman bent and stretched, unkinked his legs and reached his arms over his head, while Tom Guthrie stood behind the gutted horse, looking at the two boys. They were still sitting as before, on the top board of the fence. You boys all right? he said.

They didn't say anything but merely nodded.

You sure? Maybe you've seen enough.

They shook their heads.

All right. The worst part's over anyway. We're almost through.

It was past midmorning now. The bright sunlight of a Sunday morning toward the end of April. And Dick Sherman was saying, We need some baling wire, Tom. Or twine. Twine'd be better.

So their father left the corral to enter the barn once more and returned again, with twine this time, two or three long yellow strands of it. Sherman took the twine and began to close Elko's stomach. Starting under the chest he knifed a hole into the hide and drew the twine through the hole, knotted it, carved another hole opposite the first and pulled the two flaps of hide together, then moved back six inches and did the same, again and again, moving backward, pulling it tight each time, while their father helped to push the rich organs and slick intestines into place, holding them there until the twine was tight. Soon his hands were as red and slippery as Sherman's. When they had closed Elko's stomach as well as they could they wound the twine around the top back leg and drew it down again, so it no longer stood up above the horse's body, and secured it to his other back leg, then they tied some knots and called it good.

The horse lay in the dirt beside the barn with his eyes and mouth open, his neck reaching out and his long brown stomach crosshatched with yellow twine. From the fence, though, the two boys could still see the dark bloody insides of him through the ragged gap of hide because Dick Sherman and their father hadn't been able to close the cut completely. There was too much of it. It was like a hole in the ground when so much earth has been opened that you can't put all the dirt back in place again. Some of it still shows; the scar is still there. So the two boys could still see into Elko, and even what was no longer visible before them was still there in memory for recollection at night whether they wanted to recall any of it ever again.

But it was late morning now, approaching noon. The two men had risen from their work, stiff and sweaty, and had gone to the horse tank in the corner of the corral to wash their hands and arms under the spill of cold wellwater that ran through a cast-iron pipe from the windmill. Then Dick Sherman cleaned his knife and their father washed the tree trimmer. Finally both men stooped under the trickle of cold water, scrubbed their faces, drank and stood up again, dripping water down their necks, and wiped their mouths and eyes across their sleeves.

Then their father said: It must be getting time to eat. You better let me buy you lunch at the café, Dick.

Sure, Dick Sherman said. I'd like to. But I can't. I promised my boy I'd take him chub fishing over in Chief Creek.

I didn't think you were old enough to have a boy to fish with.

I'm not. But he thinks he wants to try it. When I was leaving this morning he said I'd never get back in time. Then Sherman paused, thinking. I am pretty young though, Tom.

Course you are, Guthrie said. We all are.

Then they walked out of the corral and Dick Sherman started his pickup and drove home. The two boys got down from the fence and stood beside their father. He put his hands on their brown heads, dry and hot from the sun, and studied their faces. The boys weren't so pale now. He brushed the hair back off their foreheads.

I've got one more thing to do, he said. Then we're finished with this. Can you stand it?

What is it? Ike said.

I've got to drag him out into the pasture. We can't leave him here.

I guess so, Ike said.

You can open the gates for me.

All right.

Open that corral gate first. And Bobby.

Yes.

You watch Easter. Don't let her get out while the gate's open. Keep her back.

So Guthrie backed his pickup into the corral, and while he was hooking a log chain around Elko's neck Ike closed the gate and then both boys got up into the back of the pickup and watched over the tailgate. When the pickup moved, Elko swung around and followed headfirst, dragging heavily across the dirt, the dirt pushing up in front of him a little and the dust rising to hang momentarily in the bright air, the horse still coming behind them, his legs loose and bumping, bouncing some when they hit something, and on around the barn toward the pasture, leaving behind them a wide dirt-scraped trail on the ground. For fifty yards or more Easter followed, trotting and interested, then she stopped and dropped her head and bucked and stood still, watching the pickup and Elko disappear. They pulled him across that first small pasture north of the barn. At the gate to the big pasture to the west, Guthrie stopped while Ike jumped down and opened the gate for the pickup to go through.

You can leave it open, Guthrie said. We're coming right back.

Ike got back into the pickup and they went on. The horse was dirty now, dust-coated. The twine at his stomach had broken in one place and they could see a dirty ropelike piece of him trailing out behind as they moved out across the pasture and sagebrush, and then the piece caught on something and was torn away.

Their father drove the pickup down into the gravel wash at the far side of the pasture and stopped. He got out and unhooked the chain from Elko's neck. They were finished now.

One of you boys want to drive back? he said.

They shook their heads.

No? You can take turns.

They were still looking at the horse.

Why don't you get up front with me anyway?

We'll stay back here, Ike said.

What?

We want to stay back here.

All right. But I'll let you practice driving if you want to.

They went home then. Guthrie took them out to eat lunch at the Holt Café on Main Street though they weren't very hungry. In the afternoon they disappeared into the hayloft. After a couple of hours, when they hadn't returned to the house or made any noise, Guthrie went to the barn to see what they were doing. He climbed the ladder and found them sitting on hay bales, looking out the loft window toward town.

What's going on? he said.

Nothing.

Are you all right?

What will happen to him now? Ike said.

You mean Elko?

Yes.

Well. After a while he won't be there. It'll just be bones that's left. I think you've seen that before, haven't you? Why don't you come back to the house now.

I don't want to, Bobby said. You can.

I don't want to either, Ike said.

Pretty soon though, Guthrie said. Okay?

In the evening they ate supper at the kitchen table and afterward the boys watched tv while their father read. Then it was nighttime. The boys lay in bed together upstairs in the old sleeping porch, with one of the windows opened slightly to the quiet air, and once in the night while their father slept they were quite certain that out in the big pasture northwest of the house they could hear dogs fighting and howling. They got up and looked out the windows. There wasn't anything to see though. There were just the familiar high white stars and the dark trees and space.

Maggie Jones.

In the night, while they were dancing slow, she said, Do you want to come over afterward?

Do you think I should?

I think so.

Then maybe I better.

They'd been dancing and drinking for two hours in the Legion on the highway in Holt, and sitting between dances with some of the other teachers from the high school at a table in the side room with a view of the band and the dance floor through the big sliding doors that were pushed back for Saturday night.

Ike and Bobby were in Denver with their mother for the weekend, and Guthrie had come in by himself about ten o'clock. The Legion was already smoky and loud when he'd come down the stairs and paid the cover to the woman sitting on a stool at the doorway and gone past her toward the crowd standing at the bar. The band was on a break, and people were standing close together in front of the bar, talking and ordering more drinks. He bought a beer and moved over to the edge of the dance floor, surveying the tables and booths along the wall. That was when he'd noticed some of the teachers sitting at a table over to the left in the other room, and that Maggie Jones was among them. When she saw him and waved him over, he raised his glass to her and walked across the empty dance floor. Care to join us? she said.

Doesn't look like you have any chairs left.

There'll be one in a minute.

He looked around. There must have been a hundred people crowded into the booths and tables and standing around the dance floor and massed in front of the bar, all drinking and talking, telling stories, with every now and then somebody shouting in laughter or hollering, a big loud smoky racket of a place. He looked down toward the teachers' table. Maggie Jones looked very good. She had on black jeans and a black blouse; the drawstring of her blouse was loosened considerably, affording a good view of her, and she wore hoop earrings fashioned from silver. In the dim light of the Legion her dark eyes were as black as coal. After a while, when nobody left a chair free, she stood up and leaned beside him against the wall. I thought you might just decide to come tonight, she said.

I'm here, he said.

The band came back and stepped onto the riser and took up their instruments. As they made warm-up riffs and runs, Maggie said, You better ask me to dance.

You'd be taking a hell of a risk, Guthrie said.

I know what I'm asking. I've seen you dance before.

I can't imagine where that would've been.

Here.

Guthrie shook his head. That would've been a long time ago.

It was. I've been watching you for a long time. Longer than you have any idea about.

You're going to scare me now.

I'm not scary, Maggie said. But I'm not a little girl either.

I never thought you were, Guthrie said.

Good. Then keep that in mind. Now ask me to dance.

You're pretty sure of this?

I'm very sure.

All right, said Guthrie. Would you care to dance, Mrs. Maggie Jones?

That's not very goddamn gallant, she said. But I guess it'll have to do.

He took her hand and led her out onto the floor. A fast song, he swung her out and she danced back to him and he twirled her around and she swung out again and came back and he spun her around once more and when she came back up to him she said, Damn you, Tom Guthrie, I'm doing all the work.

But Guthrie could see she was smiling in her eyes.

Then it was late. The lights had come up and the band had played its last song for the night. The crowd wanted more but the band was tired and wanted to go home. More lights came on and suddenly it was very bright all over the hall and more so over the bar, and people began to rise from the booths and tables as if from some manner of sleep or dream and began to stretch themselves and look around and to pull their coats on and move slowly toward the doors.

You know where I live, Maggie Jones said.

Unless you moved lately, Guthrie said.

I'm still in the same place, she said. I'll see you there. She went out ahead of him and he came up the stairs and stopped in the rest room off the main hall. They were two deep at the urinals and he waited his turn. Over on the right an old man in a blue shirt was talking to the man next to him, both of them holding themselves, finishing up. How long you been married, Larry?

Twelve years.

Goddamn, boy. You got a long way to go.

Larry turned to look at him, then zipped up and went out. Guthrie moved forward into his place.

Once he was outside, the midnight air was cold and frosty. Little pretty glittering flecks of ice were falling under the streetlights. People were calling and yelling across the parking lot. Through the breaking clouds overhead the myriad flickering stars showed fresh and pure. He cranked the old pickup and went out of the gravel drive onto the highway and over a couple of blocks and turned south another block to her house. The porch light was on and a low lamp burned in the front room. He went up to the door and didn't know whether to knock or not, but decided to go on in. Inside it was quiet. Then she came toward him from the kitchen. She was barefoot when she stopped in front of him. Are you going to kiss me?

Who's here? he said.

My father. I've just checked on him. He's settled for the night. He's deeply asleep.

Well, he said. I might try it once.

She leaned toward him and he kissed her. Even without shoes she was still nearly as tall as he was. He stepped forward a little and took her in his arms and they kissed harder.

Why don't we go back to the bedroom, she said.

When her clothes were off Maggie was soft and creamy, as rich as if she were painted. She had large full breasts and wide hips and long muscular legs. He was sitting on a chair next to the bed looking at her. For the first time since he'd known her, she seemed almost reticent and tentative. I'm just a big old girl, she said. I'm not like what you're used to. She stood with one hand covering her stomach.

Why, Maggie, you look beautiful, Guthrie said. Don't you know that? You take the breath out of me.

Do you think so?

God, yes. Don't you know that? I thought you knew everything.

I know a lot, she said. But that's very nice to hear. I thank you. She got into bed. Now hurry up, she said. What are you doing?

I'm trying to get my boots to come off my feet. They've

swelled up so bad I can't get them off, from all that dancing you made me do. It's like I been walking in river water or something, they're soaking wet.

You pitiful thing.

You damn right.

You want me to get out of bed to help you?

Just give me a minute, he said.

Finally he succeeded in hauling both boots off and he stood up and got out of his clothes and stood naked, shivering, looking down at her, and she opened the bed covers to him and he crawled in. Lord, you're just freezing, Maggie said. Come closer here. In bed she felt unbelievably warm and smooth and she was the most generous woman he'd ever known. He could feel her like satin all along his body.

But listen to me, she said.

What.

You don't actually think I'm scary, do you?

Yeah, I do.

Tell me the truth. I'm serious now.

That is the truth. At times I can't say I know what to make of you.

Can't you?

No.

What do you mean? Why not?

Because you're different than everybody else, he said. You don't seem to ever get defeated or scared by life. You stay clear in yourself, no matter what.

She kissed him. Her dark eyes were watching him in the dim light. I get defeated sometimes, she said. I've been scared. But I'm just crazy about you. She reached down and touched him. Here's one part of you that seems to know what to make of me.

You do make a person feel interested, said Guthrie.

Afterward they slept. The stars wheeled west in the night and the wind blew only a little. About four-thirty she woke him and asked if he wanted to go home before daylight.

Does it matter to you?

Not to me, she said.

They went back to sleep and then at gray dawn she got up when they heard the old man moving about in the kitchen. I need to get up and fix his cereal, Maggie said.

Guthrie watched her get out of bed and put a robe on and leave the room. He lay in bed for a while, listening to them talk, then got dressed and went into the bathroom. When he came out into the kitchen, Maggie's father was sitting at the table with a dish towel tied around his neck and a bowl of oatmeal before him. The old man looked at him. And who do you think you are? he said.

Dad, you know Tom Guthrie. You've met him before.

What's he want? We don't need another car. Is he trying to sell you a car?

Guthrie told her goodbye and went home and traded his boots for gym shoes and went back out and drove over to the depot where a ragged stack of Sunday *Denver News* lay sprawled out beside the tracks, wrapped in twine. He sat down at the edge of the cobblestone platform with his feet out in the ballast and rolled the papers, and then rose and loaded them into the pickup cab and drove through Holt along early morning streets almost empty yet of traffic or any commotion at all, and hurled the papers from the pickup window in the approximate direction of the front doors and porches. He climbed the stairs over Main Street to the dark apartments above the places of business, and about midmorning he finished the boys' paper routes and returned home and went out to the barn and fed the one horse and the cats and the dog. At the house he fixed himself some eggs and toast and drank two cups of black coffee, sitting in the kitchen with the sunlight slanted across his plate. He sat smoking for a while. Then he lay down on the davenport to read the paper. Three hours later he woke with the newspaper folded across his chest like a bum's blanket. He lay still for a while, alone in the silent house, remembering the night before, what that had been like, wondering what might be starting. Thinking did he want it to start, and what if he did. Late in the afternoon he called her. You doing all right? he said.

Yes, aren't you?

Yes, I am.

Good.

I enjoyed myself, he said. You think you'd like to get together again sometime?

You're not suggesting an actual date, are you? Maggie said. In broad daylight?

I don't know what you'd call it, Guthrie said. I'm just saying I'd be willing to take you out for supper at Shattuck's and invest in a hamburger. To see how that would go down.

When were you thinking of doing that?

Right now. This evening.

Give me fifteen minutes to get ready, she said.

He hung up and went upstairs and put on a clean shirt and entered the bathroom and brushed his teeth and combed his hair. He looked at himself in the mirror. You don't deserve it, he said aloud. Don't ever even begin to think that you do.

Victoria Roubideaux.

The next week he came home and informed her that he wanted to go to another party. But she wouldn't go again. She was afraid of what would happen and how she'd feel afterward, because of the threat to the baby. She knew she shouldn't take anything bad into herself, and she didn't want to go anyway. She wasn't happy with him. It wasn't what she had expected or thought of, dreaming about it. They seemed to have gone straight into the problems and middle years of marriage, missing, passing the honeymoon, the fun and youthful times.

When she wouldn't go to the party he got mad and went out alone, slamming the door. After he was gone she watched television for a while and retired to bed early. In the middle of the night, about three in the morning, she heard him knock over something in the kitchen and it broke, a jar or glass, and he cursed viciously and kicked the pieces away, and afterward she heard him in the bathroom next door, then he was in the bedroom taking off his clothes. When he got into bed beside her he smelled of smoke and beer, and even with her eyes shut she could feel him looking at her. You awake? he said.

Yes.

You missed a good time.

What happened?

You missed it. I'm not going to tell you.

He slid closer and began to touch her hip and thigh, feeling under her nightgown. He was breathing close to her face now, his breath coming hot on her cheek, moving her hair.

No, she said. I'm too sleepy.

I'm not.

He lifted the gown, passed his hand over her swollen stomach, and felt of her sore breasts.

Don't, she said. She turned to move away.

He kissed her, pulling close again, he smelled strong and hot, then he drew down her pants.

I can't, she said. It's not good for the baby.

Since when.

Since now.

What about what's good for me?

He was already hard against her. He pushed her hand so she felt him, pressing her hand over it, that live feel of muscle.

Then you can do something else, he said.

It's too late.

Tomorrow's Sunday. Come on.

He lay back. She hadn't moved yet. Come on, he said. She pushed her nightgown down over her heavy stomach and past her hips and then she kneeled up in bed next to him with the blanket around her like a shawl and took him in her hand and began to move it.

Not that, he said.

So she had to bend over him, leaning over her stomach. Her long hair swung forward and she collected it and lifted it to one side. He lay back, his legs stiffened out and his toes turned up, and because he was drunk it seemed to her that it took a very long time. While she bent over him she made her mind go blank. She wasn't thinking about him, she wasn't even thinking about the baby. Finally he groaned and throbbed. Afterward she rose and went into the bathroom, brushed her teeth and looked at her eyes in the mirror and scrubbed her face, taking time, wanting him to be asleep now, and he was, when she went back into the room. She lay down beside him again in the bed but she didn't sleep herself. She lay awake for two hours thinking and wondering, watching the dim presence of light in the room move gradually to faint gray on the high blank ceiling, and all the time she was deciding what she should do. Around six-thirty she slowly got out of bed and eased the door shut and went out to the front room. She called for information and got the number in Holt. Maggie Jones sounded sleepy.

Mrs. Jones?

Victoria, is that you? Where in the world are you?

Mrs. Jones, can I come back? Do you think they would let me come back?

Honey, where are you?

I'm in Denver.

Are you all right?

Yes. Can I come back though?

Of course you can come back.

Out there, I mean. With them.

I can't say about that. We'll have to ask them.

Yes, she said. All right.

She hung up and went into the bathroom and gathered the few things she'd purchased since she'd been in Denver, and put them in a little zippered bag and returned to the bedroom and silently sorted out from the closet the few clothes he'd bought her, and she had them folded over her arm ready to walk out of the room when he turned over and opened his eyes.

What are you doing? he said.

Nothing.

What are you doing with those clothes?

I want to do some laundry, she told him.

He looked at her for a moment. What time is it?

It's early.

He stared at her. Then he closed his eyes and almost immediately drifted back to sleep. She returned to the front room.
His wallet and keys were on the kitchen table inside his upturned
cap, and she took money from his wallet and folded her meager
belongings into a cardboard box together with her few toilet-
ries, and tied a string around it, then left the apartment, wearing
her new maternity pants but the same shirt she'd come in, with
the same winter coat and red purse she'd had all along, and carrying the box by the string she went down the hall and stepped
outside into the cold air. She walked fast to the bus stop and sat
waiting there for more than an hour. Cars went by, people going
to work or going early to church. A woman walking a white lap-
dog on a piece of ribbon. The air was chill and crisp, and west-
ward above the city the foothills rose up stark and close, all red
rocks now in the early morning sun, but the high dark snowy
mountain ranges beyond were hidden from view. Finally the
city bus came and she got on and sat looking at Sunday morning
in Denver.

At the bus station she waited for three hours for one going
east out across the high plains of Colorado and from there
eastward toward Omaha and still farther to Des Moines and
Chicago. When they finally called her bus, she carried her box
of clothes and stood in line with the others, moving forward
toward the black driver who stood at the door, checking tickets.
When she reached the front she discovered that Dwayne had
come looking for her, and she felt suddenly frightened of him.
Standing in the station exit, looking around, he saw her and
came over, hurrying in a kind of stiff-legged trot, looking uncombed and angry in the dark interior of the bus bay.

Where do you think you're going? he said. He took her by
the arm and pulled her out of line.

Dwayne, don't. Let me go.

Where you running off to?

What's this here? the driver said.

Was I talking to you? Dwayne said.

The driver looked at him, then turned to the girl. Do you have a ticket? he said.

Yes.

Can I see it?

She showed it to him. He looked at her closely, taking in the fact of her pregnancy, then inspected her face and looked once again at Dwayne. He took the cardboard box from her. It was labeled simply *Victoria Roubideaux Holt Colorado*. This belong to you? he said.

Yes, she said, it's mine.

You go ahead and get on then. I'll stow it underneath. That what you want?

Stay out of this, Dwayne said. This don't pertain to you.

No sir. I'm going to tell you something. I believe this girl here wants to get on this bus. He moved between them. He was a medium-sized man with a gray shirt and tie. So that's what she's going to do.

Goddamn it, Vicky, Dwayne said. He grabbed at her and got hold of her red purse and jerked it. The strap broke.

Oh, don't, she said. Let me have that.

Come and get it. He held it away from her.

Here now, the bus driver said. That don't belong to you.

I don't give a shit. He stepped back. Let her come and get it if she wants it.

The girl looked at him and immediately there was nothing else to think about. She turned away and when the driver held out his hand to steady her, she took it and stepped up carefully into the bus. The people sitting in seats on both sides looked at her as she faced them, and she moved slowly up the aisle and they watched her pass, and afterward they looked at what was happening outside. Dwayne was moving now along the length of the bus, following her from outside until she found a seat and sat down, then he stood with one hand in a back pocket of his pants and the other hand brandishing the red purse, and he stared at her, talking, not even yelling. You'll be back, he was saying. You don't even have any idea how much you're going to miss me. You'll be back.

Though she couldn't hear, she could read from his lips what he was saying. He said it all again. She shook her head. No, she whispered against the glass. I won't. I won't ever. She turned away from the window and looked forward toward the front of the bus, her face shiny with the tears she wasn't even conscious of, and soon the driver swung up into his seat and pulled the door shut and they rolled away from the curb in the dark underground departure bay of the station. When the bus turned up the ramp out into the bright street, she looked once more at him, standing where he had stood before, looking after her, watching the bus as it left, and she thought she might have been sorry for him, she felt she could be sorry, he looked so lonesome and forlorn now.

She slept part of the way. Then she woke when the bus stopped at Fort Morgan. It stopped again at Brush. Out on the high plains the country was turning green once more, she felt a little cheered by that, and the weather was starting to warm up again and she sat looking out the window at the sagebrush and soap-weed scattered in dark clumps in the pastures, and there were the first faint starts of blue grama and timothy.

They stopped again in the town of Norka where his mother was. She had never seen his mother. She had only talked to her that one time, from the public phone booth beside the highway when she had tried to find out where Dwayne was, and now she would never meet the woman or even see her, and it didn't matter anymore. His mother would never know about a baby being born in a town just forty miles away.

The bus went on and they crossed into Holt County, the country all flat and sandy again, the stunted stands of trees at the isolated farmhouses, the gravel section roads running exactly north and south like lines drawn in a child's picture book and the four-strand fences rimming the bar ditches, and now there were cows with fresh calves in the pastures behind the barbed-wire fences and here and there a red mare with a new-foaled colt, and far away on the horizon to the south the low sandhills that looked as blue as plums. The winter wheat was the only real green.

It was dusk when they turned the last curve west of town and drove under the railroad overpass and slowed down coming into Holt, passing Shattuck's Café and the Legion. The street-lamps were just coming on. The bus stopped at the Gas and Go at the intersection of Highway 34 and Main Street. She got up from her seat and came slowly down the steps. The evening air was chilly and sharp.

The driver removed the girl's box from underneath the bus and set it down on the pavement, then he nodded to her and she thanked him, and he stepped into the gas station to buy a paper cup of coffee and he came back holding it out in front of himself so he wouldn't spill it, then the bus went on.

The girl carried her box over to the side of the building where a telephone was bracketed to the wall under a little hood. She called Maggie Jones again.

Victoria? Is that you? Where are you now?

Here. I'm back here in Holt.

Where?

At the Gas and Go. Do you think they'll take me back?

Honey, nothing's changed since this morning. Maybe they will. I don't know. I can't speak for them.

Should I call them?

I'll drive you out there. I think you should do this in person.

You haven't told them I'm coming, have you? That I was coming back?

No. I leave that for you to do.

McPherons.

Once more, as on that other Sunday in the fall, she drove her out into the country seventeen miles south of Holt and the girl was frightened again as she was on that previous day, yet she looked at everything closely now as they passed along on the road because it had become familiar to her, and after twenty minutes they pulled up the track to the old country house off the county road and the car stopped at the wire gate. The girl sat for a long moment looking at the weathered house. Inside, the kitchen light came on. Then the porch light above the door and Raymond stepped out onto the little screened porch.

Go on, Maggie Jones said. You may as well find out.

I'm afraid what they're going to say, the girl said.

They're not going to say anything if you just sit here in the car.

She opened the door and got out, still looking at the house and at the old man standing on the porch. Then Harold appeared beside his brother. The two of them stood unmoving, watching her. She walked slowly, heavily up to the porch, leaning back a little to balance her weight. In the cool darkening evening she stopped at the bottom step to look up at them. The wind gusted up. The winter coat she wore was too tight now, it was unbuttoned over her stomach and the coatskirts flapped against her hips and thighs.

It's me, she said. I've come back.

They looked at her. We can see that, one of them said.

She looked up at them. I've come back to ask you, she said . . . I wanted to ask if you'd let me come back here to live with you.

They watched her, the two old brothers in their work clothes, their iron gray hair short and stiff on their uncombed heads, the knees of their pants baggy. They said nothing.

She looked around. It all looks the same, she said. I'm glad of that. She turned back toward them once more. She waited, then went on: Anyway I wanted to thank you. For what you did for me. And I wanted to say I'm sorry for the trouble I caused. You were good to me.

The old brothers stood regarding her without speaking, without moving. It was as though they didn't know her or didn't want to remember what they knew about her. She couldn't say what they were thinking. I hope you're both well, she said. I won't be bothering you anymore. She turned to go back to the car.

She was halfway to the gate when Harold spoke. We couldn't have you leaving like that again, he said.

She stopped. She turned around to face them. I know, she said. I wouldn't.

We wouldn't want that again. Not ever.

No.

That has to be understood.

Yes, I understand. She stood and waited. The wind blew her coat.

Are you all right? Raymond said. Did they hurt you?

No. I'm all right.

Who's that out in the car?

Mrs. Jones.

Is it?

Yes.

I thought it would be.

You better come in, Harold said. It's cold out here, outside here in this weather.

Let me get my box, she said.

You come in, Harold said. We'll get the box.

She approached the house and climbed up the steps and Raymond went out past her to the car. Maggie Jones got out and removed the box from the backseat and handed it over to him while Harold and the girl stood waiting on the porch.

Do you think she's okay? Raymond said softly to Maggie.

I think so, she said. So far as I can tell. But are you sure you want to try this again?

That girl needs a place.

I know, but . . .

Raymond turned abruptly, peering out into the dark where the night was collecting beyond the horse barn and the holding pens. That girl never meant us no harm, he said. That girl made a difference out here for us and we missed her when she was gone. Anyhow, what was we suppose to do with that baby crib of hers?

He turned back and looked once directly at Maggie Jones and carried the girl's box of clothes up to the house. Maggie called, I'll be in touch, and then got back in the car and drove away.

Inside the old house, the two brothers and the pregnant girl sat at the kitchen table. Looking around, she could see that the room had fallen into disorder again. The McPheron brothers had let it go. There were heel-bolts and clevises and screwed-down Vise-Grips and blackened springs loaded onto the extra chairs and stacks of magazines and newspapers piled against the back wall. The counters held days of dirty dishes.

Harold got up to make her some coffee and canned soup at the gas stove. You want to tell us about it? he said.

Could I wait till tomorrow? she asked.

Yes. We'd like to hear it when you're ready.

Thank you, she said.

The old house was quiet, just the wind and the sound of the food beginning to heat on the stove.

You had us worried, Raymond said. He was looking at her, sitting beside her at the table. We got worried about it. We didn't know where you was. We didn't know what we might of done to cause you to want to leave here like that.

But you didn't do anything, the girl said. It wasn't you.

Well. We didn't know what it was.

It wasn't you at all, she said. Oh, I'm sorry. I'm so sorry. She began to cry then. The tears ran down her cheeks and she tried to wipe them away, but she couldn't keep up. She didn't make any sound at all while she was crying.

The two old brothers watched her uncomfortably. Here now, Raymond said. It's all right. We won't have any of that now. We're glad if you come back.

I didn't mean to cause you any trouble, she said.

Well no, he said. We know. That's all right. Don't you mind it now. It's all right now. He reached across the table and tapped the back of her hand. It was a clumsy act. He didn't know how to manage it. Don't you mind it, he said to her. If you come back here we're glad. Don't you mind it now anymore.

Ike and Bobby.

They sat down front in the first row at the movie theater with the other boys, watching up at the faces turned three-quarters to each other, their outsized mouths talking back and forth while the patrol car was taking the third one away, the red lights rotating flickering light across the faces as the car passed, and behind it all the country gliding past on the screen like it was some manner of dream country that was being blown away by an unaccountable wind. Then the music came up and the house-lights came on and they came back up the aisle into the lobby among the movie crowd and emptied with it out onto the side-walk in the night. Above the streetlamps the sky was filled with bright hard stars like a scatter of white stones in a river. Cars were waiting double-parked at the curb to pick up kids, fathers waiting and mothers with younger children, while the high school boys and girls broke away and got into their own loud cars and began immediately to drive up and down Main Street, honking at one another as they passed as if they hadn't seen the passengers in the other cars for weeks and months.

The two boys turned northward on the wide sidewalk. They crossed Third Street and looked in the furniture store window at the velvet couches and the wood rockers, and the *Holt*

Mercury offices and the hardware store, both dark inside, and crossed Second Street and passed the café whose lunch tables were all set in place and the chairs turned up, and the Coast to Coast and the sports store and the sewing shop, and then they stepped over the shiny railroad tracks at the crossing, the grain elevator down the way looming up white and shadowy, as massive and terrific as a church, before turning homeward onto Railroad Street. They went along the empty street under the trees that were beginning to swell though the air was still sharply cold at night, and they were not yet as far as Mrs. Lynch's house when a car suddenly pulled up in front of them. They recognized the three people inside at once: the big red-headed boy and the blond girl and the second boy, from the room with flickering candles at the end of Railroad Street five months ago in the fall.

You little girls want a ride? the redheaded boy said from behind the wheel.

They looked at him. The side of his face was yellow, lit up by the dashlights.

Bobby, Ike said. Come on.

They tried to walk across the street, but the car rolled ahead in their way.

You never answered my question.

They looked at him. We don't want a ride, Ike said.

He turned and spoke to the other high school boy. He says they don't want a ride.

Tell him it's tough shit. They're going to get one anyway. Tell him that.

The red-haired boy turned back. He says you'll get one anyway. So what do you want to do? Want to call your daddy? Does that asshole know where you are?

Russ, the girl said. Let them go. Somebody's going to see us. Leaning forward, watching what was happening, she sat in the front seat between the two boys, her hair framed like cotton candy about her face. Russ, come on, let's go.

Not yet.

Let's go, Russ.

Not yet, goddamn it.

You want me to get em in? the other boy said.

They don't act like they want to get in by their own selves. I'll get em.

The other boy got out of the car on the far side. He stood out in the street and came around, and they began to back up. But now the red-haired boy was out of the car too. He was strong and as tall as their father. He was wearing his high school jacket.

Bobby, come on, Ike said.

They turned to run but the red-haired boy grabbed them by their coats.

Where you think you're going?

Leave us alone, Ike said.

He held them by their coats and they kicked and swung at him, hollering, trying to turn around, but he held them away at arm's length and the other boy grabbed Bobby and twisted his arms up behind him and Ike was lifted off his feet, and together they were shoved into the backseat. The big boys got in the car again. Ike and Bobby sat behind them waiting.

You better let us go. You better quit this. We didn't do anything to you.

Maybe you didn't, you little shits. But somebody did.

Russ, the girl said, what are you going to do? She was half-turned in the seat, watching them.

Nothing. Take em for a little ride.

She faced forward again, looking at him. Where to?

Just shut up. You'll find out when they do.

One of them little fuckers kicked me, the other boy said.

Did he get your nuts?

He'd like to.

The redheaded boy put the car in gear and it jumped forward, leaning over as it spun gravel and turned completely around, the wheels squealing, and rushed back up Railroad Street, then squealed again, onto Ash Street and north onto a dirt road heading into flat open country.

Outside through the car windows it was just blue-black. The flare of the headlights pointed forward on the road, fanned out along the ditches on both sides, picking up brush and weeds and fence posts, and beyond, only the blue farmlights in the dark country. In the front seat they were drinking beer. The one boy drank, then turned the window down and flung the can out, hollered and turned the window up again. Ike and Bobby sat in back watching them, as still as country rabbits, waiting, and pretty soon the girl turned around once more and peered at them, then she turned back.

They're scared, she said. They're just little boys, Russ. They're afraid. Whyn't you let them go?

Whyn't you just shut up like I told you, he said. He looked at her. Fuck's wrong with you tonight anyway?

He drove on. The gravel pounded up under the car. They topped a little rise and abruptly he slid the car to a stop. This is far enough, he said.

He got out as the other boy did on his side, and they bent into the back and pulled them from the car onto a low hill in the night. The snow was gone but the wind was blowing, and they were out on a dirt road with sagebrush and last year's dry bluestem sticking up from the new grass behind the barbed-wire fences on both sides, all of it pale and cold-looking, showing dim and shadowy in the blue light of the high white stars.

Russ, the girl said.

What?

Russ, you won't make them walk from here.

I'm going to, he said. It's not even five miles. Now shut your mouth like I told you. Or maybe you want to walk back with em yourself. Do you?

No.

Then keep out of this.

He looked at the two boys standing next to each other against the car, waiting for what was going to happen, their eyes like outsized coins in the night. The car was still idling and the headlights were pointed forward along the dirt road, showing the washboards and the uneven grading.

You little girls know where you are?

They looked around.

That's town back there, he said. Where you see those lights. Look where I'm pointing at, goddamn it. Don't look at me. See em? All you got to do is walk back on this road. But you better not cry to nobody about this. I don't even want to think what I'll do the next time, if somebody finds out.

They looked toward the lights of town. Then they looked at the girl still in the car. The door was open and the dome light was shining and she was watching them, but her face was blank. There wouldn't be any help from her. They stood in their mackinaw coats, bareheaded, waiting, their faces ashen and frightened.

You hear what I said?

We heard you.

All right. Take off.

They pushed away from the car, moving in the direction of town.

Wait a minute, the other boy said. I mean, hell. That's all you're going to do?

You got something else in mind?

I can think of something.

He looked at the two boys, who started to back away from him, then he grabbed Bobby by the coat arm. This here's the little fucker that kicked me. He dragged him out into the middle of the road, Bobby was yelling and swinging his arms, trying to kick at him, until the high school boy wheeled him around and upended him facedown in the dirt.

Quit it, Ike cried. Leave him alone, goddamn you.

The red-haired boy grabbed Ike and forced him back against the hood of the car. The other boy bent over Bobby and pulled off his shoes and flung them backward into the darkness, then hauled his jeans down and threw them spinning into the barrow ditch. Afterward he jerked Bobby's underwear down, disentangled them from his feet and sent them sailing away. Bobby's naked white legs flailed in the dirt.

Ike pulled loose from the first boy and ran at the other one holding Bobby and hit him in the neck and kicked him before he was grabbed from behind.

You got him now? the other boy said.

Yeah, the red-haired boy said. I got him.

Well hang on to him, goddamn it.

He ain't going nowhere.

I still got this other one.

He stood up and lifted Bobby into the air, holding him aloft like some specimen for them to consider. He turned him toward the girl in the car.

How'd you like to suck his little dick, Sharlene?

The girl was looking at Bobby, she looked at each of them, but she didn't say anything.

Below his mackinaw Bobby was white-legged and naked, shriveled up and podlike, as though he'd been skinned. He was crying now.

Leave him alone, Ike cried. Leave him alone. He fought against the red-haired boy. You son of a bitch. He didn't do anything to you. Why don't you leave him alone. You dirty sons of bitches.

I want you to listen to that little fucker's mouth? the boy said. Can't you shut him up?

I'll shut him up, the redheaded boy said. He held Ike by the arms and suddenly tripped him forward onto the road, kneeling on him. He hauled Ike's shoes off one at a time and jerked his pants down, threw them away, and hauled off his underwear and flung them backward over his shoulder. Finally he stood up and pulled Ike to his feet, holding him forward in front of the others.

He don't have any fuzz yet either, the other boy said. You reckon anybody in that family's got any? You figure their daddy's sprouted his feathers yet?

I'm not even talking about that son of a bitch, the red-haired boy said. He shoved Ike forward. Ike was crying now too. He moved over to Bobby and together they crouched in the road. Stretching their coats over their knees, they looked like forlorn and misshapen dwarfs caught by some great misfortune out in the night on a dirt road, a long way from any help.

Let's go, the other boy said. I've had enough of this.

We're going, the redhead said, looking at Ike and Bobby. But you remember what I told you. Nobody better hear about this shit tonight.

They watched him, looking up at him from where they squatted in the road. They said nothing.

You hear me? You just remember what I said.

He and the other boy got back in the car which then roared away in the night with the dust boiling up behind it and the dim taillights fading to nothing above the narrow road.

Afterward they could hear it without seeing it. Then it was just quiet. Overhead the stars flickered, white and hard-edged, myriad and distant. The wind still blew.

Are you all right, Bobby? Did he hurt you?

Bobby shivered and wiped his eyes and nose on his coat sleeve. I can't find where my shoes are, he said. He stepped barefoot in the cold dirt, looking. That girl never even tried to help us, he said.

He wouldn't let her.

She didn't try hard enough, Bobby said.

.   .   .

It was thirty minutes before they found their shoes and both pairs of their jeans and their underwear in the dark. The clothes felt cold and stiff when they pulled them on, and then they started south toward the clustered lights of Holt. The lights seemed far away.

We should stop at one of the farmhouses, Bobby said.

You want them to know? Tell them what happened?

We wouldn't have to say.

We'd have to tell them something.

They walked on, staying close together. The road showed dimly before them, paler than the bar ditches to the sides.

They all keep dogs anyhow, Ike said. You know that.

It was after midnight by the time they walked once more onto Railroad Street and then turned in at the familiar gravel drive at home. A while before, when they were still out on the quiet dirt road in the country, they'd seen the lights of a car coming toward them and thought it was the redhaired boy and the other one coming back, and they'd dropped down into the ditch and then the car had gone rattling past, peppering their backs with dirt and gravel and the ground had been icy cold and smelled rank of dust and weeds, but when the car passed they saw that it wasn't driven by the high school boys. It was somebody else. A different car, just somebody going home. So they might've waved it down and gotten a ride, but afterward it was too late. They climbed up to the road and went on. They didn't talk very much. They kept walking. A couple of times they heard a coyote yapping and howling, crying out somewhere in the country, and they knew there were cattle somewhere out to the west, they heard them moving about in the corn stubble across the dark. Ahead, the lights of Holt seemed to stay far away, and they were foot-weary and tired by the time they finally passed into the town limits and walked under the first of the corner streetlamps.

When they walked inside the house, their father wasn't

there. They called out but there was no answer. It made them scared again. They locked the door, dropped their coats on the floor in the front hall and went upstairs and began to wash themselves at the bathroom sink. In the cabinet mirror their faces were dirty and tear-streaked with little runnels along their noses, and their eyes looked shadowy and strange. They were bent over the sink when their father came home. They heard him call as soon as he came in.

Ike? Bobby? Are you here?

They didn't answer.

He noticed their coats and came rushing upstairs and found them in the bathroom, the rinse water clinging to their faces, both turned toward the door, looking at him as though he'd walked in on them in some shameful ritual act.

He entered the room. Why didn't you answer me? he said. Where'd you go? When you didn't come home after the show I went out looking for you. I was about to call Bud Sealy.

They stood looking at him.

What is it? he said. One of you better tell me what's going on.

They wouldn't say anything. Yet Bobby's eyes had welled up and the tears ran unchecked on his cheeks and he began to sob terrifically as though he couldn't breathe, crying but uttering no words at all.

What's wrong? Guthrie said. Here now. What is it? He took a towel and dried Bobby's face, then his brother's. Is it that bad? he said. He led them down the hall to their bedroom in the old sleeping porch at the back of the house, sitting between them on the bed and encircling them with his arms. Tell me what's wrong here. What happened?

Bobby was still crying. Now and then he shuddered. Both boys were turned away from him, facing the windows to the north.

Ike, Guthrie said, tell me what's wrong.

The boy shook his head.

Something is. You've gotten dirty. Look at your pants. What is it?

Ike shook his head again. He and his brother looked at the window.

Ike? Guthrie said.

At last the boy turned to him. His face appeared desperate, pent-up, as though it would burst. Leave us alone, he cried. You have to leave us alone.

I'm not going to leave you alone, Guthrie said. Tell me what happened.

We aren't suppose to say anything. He said we can't tell anybody.

Who said you can't tell anybody? Guthrie said. What's this about?

That big one with the red hair, Ike said. He said . . . We can't talk about it. Don't you understand?

Guthrie watched him, the boy's eyes were red and flaring, but he had stopped talking. He would not say anything more. Not now. He was ready to cry again and he turned back toward the window.

Guthrie.

He sat with them that night in their bedroom until they slept, and did not want to think what they would be dreaming. The next morning, Sunday morning, after breakfast and after they'd talked about the night before in the cold dark, the boys were able to tell more because in the daylight they were no longer so afraid. Then he drove to Gum Street on the south side of Holt, the old, the best part of town. A pleasant neighborhood with box elder trees and elm and hackberry, with lilac bushes along the side yards and kept lawns, though everything was still only faintly green at this earliest start of spring. A block or two to the west church bells were starting up from the tower at the Methodist church. Then the Catholic bells started up a block east.

He got out of the pickup and walked up to the white clapboard house, stepped onto the porch and knocked on the door. After a time the door swung open. Mrs. Beckman looked out. Squat and blocklike, she appeared to be rancorous already. She wore a housedress and toeless slippers, her hair sprayed up stiffly onto her head. You, she said. What do you want?

Tell Russell to come out here, Guthrie said.

What for?

I want to talk to him.

He don't have to talk to you. She held on to the doorknob in her thick hand. This isn't the school. You don't have no say here. Why don't you just get the hell out.

Tell him to come here. I'm going to talk to him.

Doris, a man's voice came from inside the house. Shut the damn door. You're letting the cold in.

You better come out here, she called. She didn't even turn her head to speak. Instead, she watched Guthrie steadily. Come out here, she called.

Who is it?

Him.

There were footsteps, then her husband appeared in the door. What's he want?

He's after Russell again.

What about?

He hasn't said what about.

Guthrie looked at the couple framed in the door, Beckman tall and thin above the short heavy woman, Beckman in a white shirt and dark shiny trousers, carrying a section of newspaper in his hand.

What's this about, Guthrie?

Your son hurt my boys last night. I intend to talk to him about it.

What the hell are you talking about now? This is Sunday morning. Can't you even leave him alone on a Sunday morning?

You tell him to come out here, Guthrie said.

Beckman studied Guthrie. All right, by God, he said. We'll see about this. He turned to his wife. Go get him.

He's still sleeping.

Get him up.

He don't have no right coming here, she said. What right does he have?

Don't you think I know that? Do what I say.

She left and after a moment Beckman stepped backward

into the house and shut the door. Guthrie waited on the porch. He looked out toward the street and curb, the trees budding along the parkway, the big houses standing quiet and peaceful across the street. Next door, Fraiser came out of his white house in his Sunday clothes and stood for a moment on the front steps and took a cigarette out and lit it. He looked about and saw Guthrie and nodded to him and Guthrie nodded back. Mrs. Fraiser came out and her husband pointed to something in the flower bed at the front of their house. They moved off the step and Mrs. Fraiser bent over to look at it. She lifted her head and said something and he answered. They were still talking quietly back and forth when Beckman stepped out on the porch. The big boy was following him, and Mrs. Beckman came out behind him. They stood out on the railed porch in the bright fresh air. Guthrie faced them. The boy was in his jeans and tee-shirt and wore no shoes. He was just awake.

Now, Beckman said, talking to Guthrie. Tell him in front of us what this is about. What do you say happened?

Guthrie spoke directly to the boy. His voice sounded strained and tight. You finally went too far, didn't you. You've hurt my two boys now. You and that Murphy kid. Last night you took them out in the country and scared them and then you figured it would be smart to pull their pants off and leave them out there to walk home. They're just little boys. They're just nine and ten years old. They didn't do anything to you. They told me about it. You're just a coward, aren't you. You have something against me, then you come see me about it. But you leave my boys out of it.

What's all this? Beckman said. What's he talking about? Do you know anything about this?

I don't know what he's talking about, the boy said. I don't have any idea what the hell he's saying. He's full of shit, as usual. I don't even know his little kids.

Yeah you do, Guthrie said. He was barely able to speak now. His voice sounded tight even to himself, scarcely within his control. You're lying again. You know exactly what I'm talking about.

I don't know his kids! the boy said. I wouldn't know em if they was standing right here in front of me. He's always making trouble for me. Get him out of here.

Goddamn you, Guthrie said. You're lying again. Then it was past talking. Guthrie rushed the boy and grabbed his shirt at the neck. You sorry son of a bitch. You leave my boys alone. He slammed the boy back against the front wall of the house, his fists up under his chin. If you ever touch my kids again . . .

But Beckman was in it now too. He grabbed Guthrie's arms. Let him go, he was hollering. Let him go.

I'm warning you, Guthrie said, shouting, his voice still awkward and strained, his face inches away from the boy's. Goddamn you. He rocked the boy's head back against the house wall, the boy's eyes flaring in alarm and surprise and anger, his chin tilted up above Guthrie's fist, his head canted back; he was pulled up onto his toes, his hands scrabbling at Guthrie's wrists.

Let go, goddamn it! Beckman yelled. His wife was slapping at Guthrie from the back, clawing at his jacket, screeching something unintelligible, not even words, just a high-pitched furious noise. Beckman was still jerking at Guthrie's arms, then he stopped and drew back and hit Guthrie at the side of the face and Guthrie went over sideways, pulling the boy with him. Guthrie's glasses hung crookedly from his face. Beckman bent over and swung again, hitting him above the ear.

Next door the Fraisers were watching. Mrs. Fraiser went running into the house to call the police, and her husband came hurrying across the yard between the two houses. Here now, he called. Here, you men, stop this.

Guthrie rose up and shoved the boy away, and Beckman came at him again, swinging wildly, and Guthrie ducked under his arm and hit him in the throat at the open neck of his white shirt. Beckman fell back choking. His wife screamed and tried to help him but he pushed her away. The boy rushed Guthrie from the side, his head lowered, and tackled him backward. They hit the porch rail and Guthrie felt something pop in his side, then they dropped down, the boy on top of him.

Guthrie fought with the boy on the floorboards and Beckman, recovered now, came once more and leaned over his son and found an opening and hit Guthrie in the face. Guthrie released the boy, then father and son worked on him together, punishing him, while he tried to roll over. When they stopped, Mrs. Beckman rushed forward and kicked him in the back. Guthrie rolled toward her and when she drew back to kick again he caught her foot, and she sat down violently on the porch boards, her dress flung up onto her thighs, and she sat just screaming until her husband lifted under her arms and raised her to her feet and told her to shut up. She sobered and straightened her dress. Guthrie got onto his knees, then stood. His face was smeared with the blood that ran from his nose and there was a cut over his eye. The chest pocket of his jacket was torn open, flapping like a tongue. He stood panting. One eye was already swelling shut and his side hurt where he'd hit the rail. He looked around for his glasses but couldn't find them.

You men, Fraiser said. Here now. This isn't the way.

Guthrie, you better get out of here, Beckman said. I'm telling you.

You son of a bitch, Guthrie panted.

You better go on. We'll take you again.

You tell that boy . . .

I'm not telling him a goddamn thing. You leave him alone.

Guthrie looked at him. You tell him he better never touch my boys again. I'm telling all of you that now.

Wait, Fraiser said. Listen, you men.

Out in the street Bud Sealy suddenly pulled up in the blue sheriff's car and got out in a hurry, the door swinging open, and he came hustling toward the house. He was a heavy red-faced man with a hard stomach. What's going on here? he said. This don't look like no Sunday school church meeting to me. He stepped onto the porch and looked at them. What's all this? Who's going to tell me?

Guthrie here attacked my boy, Beckman said. Come right to the house this morning raising hell, claiming some bullshit story about his kids. He called my boy outside and attacked him. But we fixed him.

That right, Tom? Is that what happened?

Guthrie didn't answer. He was still looking at the Beckmans. Don't you ever touch them again, he said. This is the one time I'm going to tell you.

Do I have to listen to this? Beckman said to the sheriff. This is my house. I don't have to listen to this shit on my own front porch.

I'll tell you what, Bud Sealy said. You all three better come down to the station with me. We're going to talk this out. Tom, you better ride with me. And Beckman, you and the boy there follow us in your car.

What about me? Mrs. Beckman said. He attacked me too.

You come too, the sheriff said. With them in the car.

McPherons.

She told them about it that morning. About Dwayne coming to the school to get her and about climbing in his car and driving to Denver without even knowing why, and how she hoped for it to be one way but how it was another, and how it was generally in his little apartment on the second floor in Denver. The McPheron brothers listened to her, watching her face all the time she talked. And after breakfast they went outside and fed out and then came back to the house and cleaned up and put on their good Bailey hats and took her into town to see Dr. Martin.

On the way she told them what she hadn't said two hours earlier while they were still seated at the kitchen table. She said she'd gone to a party with him and had let herself go and had gotten to drinking too much, and then she stopped talking and was just quiet, riding between the two old men in the pickup, her hands cupped in her lap under her stomach as though she were holding it up, supporting it.

Did you? they said.

Yes, she said, I did. Then without warning her eyes filled and tears ran down her cheeks and she looked straight ahead over the dashboard at the highway.

Is there something else? Raymond said. You seem like there is, Victoria.

Yes, she said.

What is it?

I got high smoking pot.

Is that marijuana?

Yes, and I don't know what all I did. I couldn't remember the next day and I had bruises and cuts on me and didn't know where I got them.

Did you do it again? Go out to them parties with him?

No. That one time. But I'm scared. I'm afraid I might have done something to my baby.

Oh. Well. Do you think so?

Well, I don't know. That's just it.

I wouldn't guess so, Raymond said. I knew of this heifer we had one time that was carrying a calf, and she got a length of fencewire down her some way and it never hurt her or the calf.

It didn't?

No. Never bothered either one.

The girl looked at him, examining his face under the brim of his hat. They were okay?

Yes ma'am.

They were? You're telling the truth?

That's right. They were no worse for it.

She looked at him for a time and Raymond met her gaze, simply looking back at her and nodding once or twice.

Thank you. She swiped at her cheeks and eyes. Thank you for telling me that.

A heifer calf, as I remember, Raymond said. Good-sized.

They went on. They drove on into Holt to the clinic beside the hospital, on this bright clear day, the sky as pure and blue as the inside of a bowl from China. At the clinic the girl told the middle-aged woman behind the window at the front counter who she was and what she was there for.

We haven't seen you for months, the woman said.

I've been out of town.

Take a seat, the woman said.

She sat down in the waiting room with the McPheron brothers and they waited and would not talk very much even to one another because there were other people in the room, and about an hour later they were still waiting.

Harold turned and looked at the girl and abruptly he got up and crossed to the counter and spoke to the woman through the window. I guess you don't know what we're here for.

What? the woman said.

This girl right over here come in to see the doctor.

I know.

We been here a hour, Harold said. Tell him that.

You'll have to wait your turn.

No. I aim to wait right here. For you to tell him. Tell him we been here a hour. Go ahead now.

The woman stared at him in outrage and disbelief and he stared back, then she got up and went back into the hallway to the examination rooms and in a short while she returned. She said, He'll see her next.

That'll be better, Harold said. It's not what a man might hope for. But it'll do.

He sat down. Presently they called the girl and the two brothers watched her leave. They sat and waited for her to come back. After she'd been gone for five minutes Harold leaned sideways toward his brother and spoke to him in a loud whisper. You going to tell me now what in hell all that was, back there in the pickup?

All which? Raymond said.

That about that heifer taking fencewire. Where in hell'd you come up with that? I don't remember any such thing.

I made it up.

You made it up, Harold said. He regarded his brother, who was staring out into the room. What else you going to make up?

Whatever I have to.

The hell you say.

I'm going to talk to this doctor too, when Victoria comes out.

About what?

I aim to put some questions to him.

Then I'm coming with you, Harold said.

Come or stay back, Raymond said. I know what I'm doing.

They waited. They sat upright in their chairs without reading or talking to anyone, simply looking across the room toward the windows and working their hands, their good hats still squared on their heads, as if they were outside in a day without wind. Other people came and went in the room. The sunlight on the floor, showing in through the window, moved unaccounted. Half an hour later the girl came out by herself and walked over to them, a tentative little smile on her face. They stood up.

It's due in about two weeks, she said.

Is that so?

Yes.

What else did he say?

He says I'm all right. Both of us seem to be fine, he says.

That's good, Raymond said. That's just fine. Now you go on out to the pickup.

Why? Aren't you coming?

Go ahead, if you would. It won't be long.

She went outside and the McPheron brothers walked back, one after the other, past the middle-aged woman who was seated as before at the window. She stood up at once when they started unannounced down the hall and she rushed after them, calling to them, asking what they meant by this, they weren't allowed back there, didn't they know that much, and they went on regardless, as though they couldn't hear her or else didn't care even a little what she was saying, sticking their heads in any doors that were open along the way and opening two or three closed ones upon unsuspecting waiting patients who afterward came out into the hallway too, watching after them in shock and amazement. At the end of the hall the McPherons came upon a closed door behind which they could hear old Dr. Martin consulting with a female patient. They listened briefly, their heads cocked in an attitude of concentration under their silver-belly hats. Then Raymond knocked one time and shoved the door open.

Come out, he said. We got to talk with you.

What in the name of God! the old doctor cried. Get the hell out of here.

The woman whose heart he'd been listening to hurriedly pulled her paper shirt together and looked over at them, her pendulous breasts pressing against the thin material.

Come on out here, Raymond said again. Harold stood behind him, looking over his shoulder. The woman from the front counter stood back of Harold now, still objecting and remonstrating, talking quite loudly. They paid her no attention whatsoever. The doctor stepped out of the room and shut the door. His eyes were fiery glints behind his rimless glasses, above his good blue suit and immaculate white shirt and his neat hand-tied bow tie.

Just what is it you think you're doing? he said.

We're going to talk to you, Raymond said.

It won't wait?

No sir, it won't.

All right then. Talk. What's this about?

This don't concern her, Raymond said, indicating the woman from the front desk.

The old doctor turned to her and said, You can go back, Mrs. Barnes. I'll take care of this.

It's not my fault, she said. They came barging back here by themselves. I didn't let them back here.

I know. You can return to the front desk now.

She wheeled and marched away, and the doctor led the McPheron brothers into the vacant examination room next door.

I don't suppose you want to take the time to do anything so civil as to sit down, he said.

No.

No. I didn't think so. Very well. What did you want to talk about?

Is she all right? Raymond said.

Who?

Victoria Roubideaux.

Yes, she is, the doctor said.

That boy didn't do her any good.

You're talking about the boy in Denver, I take it.

Yes. That miserable son of a bitch.

She told me about him. She said what happened there. But she seems all right.

He better not of hurt her permanent, Raymond said. You better be sure.

There's no use threatening me, the old doctor said.

I'm telling you. You better make this come out right. That girl's had enough trouble.

I'll do everything I can. But it isn't all up to me.

Some of it is.

And you better not get so wrought up, the doctor said.

I am wrought up, Raymond said, and I'm going to stay that way till this baby is born good and healthy and that girl is okay. Now you tell us what you told her.

Ike and Bobby.

Of an afternoon, a Sunday, when Guthrie was out for a drive riding in the pickup with Maggie Jones along the empty country roads, they wandered about the house, room to room, thinking what they wanted to do. They went into Guthrie's and their mother's bedroom upstairs at the front of the house and inspected the things that belonged to their parents, the minute examination of the various items that had been accumulated over the years, most of them bought and collected before the boys' own time—pictures, clothes, drawers of underwear, a box containing necktie pins and old pocket watches and an obsidian arrowhead and rattles cut from a snake and a track medal—and put the box back and drifted out of the room down the hall to the guest room where some of their mother's possessions were still located and picked them up and smelled and felt of them and tried on one of her silver bracelets, and lastly they went into their own room at the back of the house and looked out and saw the old man's house next door and the abandoned place to the west at the end of Railroad Street and all the land open beyond, with the fairgrounds to the north across the pasture behind the barn, the grandstands white-painted and empty, and then they left and went downstairs to the outside and mounted their bikes.

They went up once more to the apartment above Main Street, passing along the dim corridor and stopping at the last door. She had taken in the *Denver News* they'd dropped off on the mat early that morning, but when they knocked there was no answer. They used the key she'd given them months ago when they'd gone to the grocery store, when she'd said: *I am going to trust you with that.* They used the key now and went in. She, the old woman, Iva Stearns, was sitting across the room in the stuffed chair against the wall. Her head was lapsed sideways onto the shoulder of her blue housedress. As usual the room was too hot, as stifling as a sickroom, and as always it was crowded with the stores of her accumulation.

From the doorway Ike said, Mrs. Stearns.

She didn't respond. They approached, moving closer. A cigarette had burned out in the ashtray placed on the wide arm of the chair. It was a long white cold ash.

Mrs. Stearns. It's us.

They stood still in front of her. Ike reached forward to touch her thin arm to wake her and then he drew his hand back as suddenly as if he'd been struck or burnt. Her arm was cold and rigid. It was as though the chill skin of her arm had been drawn over sticks of wood or some manner of iron rods in a winter basement, to make her feel so hard and cold.

Feel her, Ike said.

Why?

Go ahead.

Bobby reached forward and touched her arm. Immediately he put his hand in his pants pocket.

The two boys looked at Iva Stearns for a long time, standing before her slumped and silent motionless figure in the quiet overheated room, the smell of smoke and dust still present in the close air, with the faint vague muffled noise of the street coming up to the room as if from a great distance. In the hours since she had stopped breathing, before they found her, the old woman's face had collapsed and now her nose seemed to have risen, thin and high-ridged, shiny and waxy in the middle of her face, while her eyes seemed to have fallen away altogether behind her glasses. In her lap the old blue-veined freckled hands still clasped each other fiercely in a kind of mute and terrific stasis, as hard and silent as dug-up tree roots.

I want to touch her again, Ike said.

He did so. He felt her arm, touching her longer this time. Then Bobby touched her again.

All right, Ike said. You ready?

Bobby nodded.

They went out of her apartment and locked the door, then pedaled home and left their bikes at the house and went on to the barn, where they saddled Easter.

And so, in the middle of the afternoon in the spring of the year, mounted up like sojourners in the great world, Bobby in the saddle, Ike behind, they rode out.

By sundown they were eleven miles south of Holt.

They still had not found the right crossroad. When they left the house they'd skirted the town, and then had followed the two-lane blacktop, riding south along the barrow ditches and fencelines, the horse all the time making steady progress in the dry weeds and the new spring grass, her head up, nervous and antsy with the traffic on the highway. As they rode in the lowering sun the cars raced by, honking at them sometimes and the people inside hollering and waving, and three times big trucks roared down on them, blowing them up against the barbed-wire fences, making the mare want to squat and take off, but they held her back and she only danced sideways, sidling, throwing her head a little, and afterward they went on.

By dark they knew they'd gone too far, had somehow passed the turnoff. They believed they would recognize the road they were looking for, but the roads all looked so much alike that they hadn't. At last they stopped at a ranch house next to the highway and Ike got off and went up to the door and asked for directions.

The man at the door was wearing slippers and dark trousers and a white Sunday shirt, and holding a newspaper. Don't you want to come in, son? he said.

We're suppose to go over there.

Over to their house?

Yes sir.

Well.

Could you tell us how to find their place? We missed their road.

You come too far, he said. You got to go back two miles and take that one. Not the first mile road, but the next one. He told Ike what they should look for when they got there. Can you remember that? he said.

Ike nodded.

You're sure you don't want to come in?

No. We got to go on.

All right. But you be careful out there on that highway.

He went back out to his brother, who still sat the horse in the yard under the new-leafed trees, and Bobby kicked his foot out of the stirrup and he climbed up and they turned back out of the drive. They traveled back northward along the highway with the headlights of the onrushing cars coming at them now out of the increasing darkness, the lights growing bigger and brighter and then blinding them, after which the cars and their lights would rush past like some kind of runaway train racing to hell, while down in the ditch the horse would start to hop and dance and collect herself as if she were going to jump, and it was all they could do to hold her back. Finally they rode her up onto the hard blacktop and clattered down the highway, making time between the approaching cars, galloping, letting her out, and they passed the first county road that way and then turned east off the highway onto the second one. At the gravel road they slowed down and let her breathe.

He said about seven miles from here, Ike said. Turn off at the track, next to the mailbox. We'll see a cedar tree and the house sitting back from the road with outbuildings down below. A horse barn and loafing shed and corrals.

It was completely dark now, and turning cold again since the sun had gone down. They rode on, the land all flat and starlit around them. They could hear cattle over to the south. When they found the mailbox and track leading off the gravel it was about ten-thirty.

I don't see any cedar, Bobby said. Didn't he say a cedar tree?

Down by the outbuildings he said, by the garage.

I can't read the mailbox.

But that's the track like he said leading off to that place back there. To that farmlight that's shining.

What do you want to do?

We got to try it. We don't have any choice. It's late.

They put the horse forward again and turned up the old track. She had sweated and dried and sweated again and they let her take her time moving back toward the house where it was all dark except for that single yardlight, shining from a high lightpole. When they rode into the drive the old dog came barking out of the garage, standing on stiff legs in the gravel. They dismounted and tied Easter to one of the hogfencing posts, and as they did this the dog came up and sniffed at them and seemed to recognize them and licked their hands, and then they went in through the wire gate up to the house and climbed the steps to the porch and stood knocking. After a while a light came on in the kitchen. Then somebody was at the door: a girl in her nightgown. They didn't know who she was. They thought they must in some way have come to the wrong house. The girl looked heavy and misshapen, like there was something wrong with her; she was holding herself under the front, the soft material of her gown pulled tight over her enormous stomach. They realized that they had seen her before in town, but had no idea what her name might be, and they were about to turn and leave without saying anything at all to her, when the McPheron brothers appeared behind her in the door.

Well, what in the goddamn? Harold said. What's this?

What have we got here? Raymond said. Guthrie boys?

The two old men were wearing their flannel striped pajamas, their short stiff hair standing up like wire brushes. They had already been asleep.

Yes sir, Ike said.

Well goddamn, boys, Harold said, come in, come in. What are you doing? Is that your horse out there?

Yes sir.

You rode out here?

Yes sir.

Who else you got with you? Is your dad with you?

Nobody. Just us.

Well damn, boys, that's a pretty good ride. Are you boys lost?

No sir.

You just decided to take yourself a horseback ride of a Sunday evening. Is that it?

We thought we'd come out here to see you, Bobby said.

You did? he said. Well. He looked at them, studying their quiet serious faces. But is there something in particular you had in mind you wanted to see us about?

No.

Nothing in particular. Is that so? Well then. That'll have to do, I reckon. I guess you better come on in, what do you think?

Is our horse going to be all right out there? Ike said.

Is she tied up pretty good, so she won't run off?

Yes sir.

She'll be all right then, I expect. We'll look at her in a little bit.

She got sweaty coming on the highway and again on the road.

I see that. We'll wipe her down after a while. You come on in here now.

So they entered and immediately the kitchen seemed very warm and brightly lighted after being out in the dark. They stood beside the table, not knowing what to do now that they had arrived.

Now for the first time the girl said something. Would you like to sit down? she said. Her voice sounded kindly. They looked at her, and in the light they could see that she was a high school girl, not so much older than themselves, but she was so big in front. They knew enough to know that she was carrying a baby, though it made them uncomfortable to look at her. Wordlessly they pulled out two chairs and sat down.

You must be tired, she said. Have you eaten anything? I bet you're hungry, aren't you.

We had something to eat a while ago, Ike said.

When was that?

A while earlier, he said. We had something at lunch.

Then you must be starving, she said. I'll get you something to eat.

She seemed very efficient at what she was doing. They sat at the table and watched her moving about in the kitchen, this black-haired girl with the tremendously swollen stomach, and avoided her eyes so much that whenever she turned toward them they seemed to be looking elsewhere. She moved back and forth familiarly, from the refrigerator to the stove, warming their food. When it was ready she set it out before them on the wood table: meat and potatoes, warmed-up canned corn, with glasses of milk and a plate of bread with butter. Go ahead, she said. Help yourselves.

Aren't you going to eat? Ike said.

We ate hours ago. I'll sit down with you, if you like. Maybe I'll have a glass of milk, she said.

While the boys ate, Harold went out to see to their horse. He walked the mare over to the corral and let her drink at the stock tank, then he led her into the barn, hauled off her saddle and wiped her down with a gunnysack and afterward grained her and left the half-door open so she could move back to the water if she wanted to.

Meanwhile Raymond went into the other room to the phone and carried it on its long cord into the parlor and made a call. He spoke in a quiet low voice. Tom? he said.

Yes.

We got em out here with us.

Ike and Bobby?

By God, Tom, they come out here ahorseback. All this way.

I knew they had the horse. I had the police out looking for them, Guthrie said. I didn't know where they were. I've been worried sick.

Well. But they're here now.

Are they all right?

It appears like it. I reckon they are. They seem kind of upset, though. Pretty quiet.

I'll be right out.

Tom, the old man said. He looked out into the kitchen where the two boys were seated at the table with the girl. She was talking to them, and both were watching her intently. I just wonder if you don't want to leave em to stay out here tonight.

Out there?

That's right.

What for?

I think it'd be better.

What do you mean, better?

Well. Like I say, they seem kind of upset.

There was quiet on the other end of the line.

You could come out in the morning and get em, Raymond said. You'll want to bring along a horse trailer when you come.

I got to think about this, Guthrie said. Would you hold a minute?

He could hear Guthrie talking to somebody in the background. After a time he came back.

I guess it's all right, Guthrie said. I have Maggie Jones here with me and she thinks you're right. I'll come out in the morning.

Right. We'll see you then.

But you tell them you talked to me, Guthrie said, and that I'll be there the first thing in the morning.

I'll tell em. Raymond hung up and went back to the kitchen.

When the boys were finished eating, the girl made them a bed with blankets in the parlor. The McPheron brothers shoved the old recliner chairs out of the way and she spread the thick blankets down on the wood floor in the middle of the room and found them a pair of old pillows and said, I'll be right in here.

You boys going to be all right? Harold said.

Yes sir.

Just holler if you need anything.

Holler loud, Raymond said. We don't hear too good.

You need anything else right now? Harold said.

No, sir.

That's it then. I guess we better go to bed. It's getting pretty late. I'm going to say we had enough excitement for one night.

The girl went back to her room off the dining room and the McPheron brothers went upstairs. When they were gone the two boys removed their shoes and set them in place on the floor in front of the old television console and removed their pants, and then they lay down in their shirts and underwear in the thick blankets on the floor in the old room at the far end of the house, and lying on the floor they looked up into the room where the yardlight shone in on the wallpaper and the ceiling.

She looks like she's going to have two babies, Bobby said.

Maybe she is.

Is she married to them?

Who?

Them. Those old men.

No, Ike said.

What's she doing out here then?

I don't know. What are we doing out here?

They both looked at the pale light showing in onto the ceiling and studied the faded pattern in the old wallpaper. It went all the way around the room and there were stains on it in places and water spots. After a while they closed their eyes. And then they breathed deeply and were asleep.

The next day Guthrie was at the McPherons' place very early in the morning and he had already loaded the horse into the trailer by the time the two boys had finished the big breakfast of ham and eggs the girl had made for them.

On the way back into town Guthrie said, I missed you. I was worried when I couldn't find you.

They didn't say anything.

Are you all right this morning?

They nodded.

Are you?

Yes.

All right. But I don't want you to do that again. He looked at them seated beside him in the pickup. Their faces were pale and quiet. He changed his tone. I ask you not to do that again, he said. I ask you not to leave like that again.

Dad, Ike said. Mrs. Stearns died.

Who?

The lady over on Main Street. In her apartment.

How do you know that?

We saw her yesterday. She was dead then.

Did you tell anybody?

No. We're telling you.

But somebody better do something about her, Bobby said. Somebody better take care of her.

I'll call somebody when we get back to town, Guthrie said.

They drove on down the road. After a while Ike said, But Dad?

Yes.

Isn't Mother ever going to come back home again?

No, Guthrie said. He thought for a moment. I don't think she is.

But she left her clothes and jewelry here.

That's right, Guthrie said. We'll have to take them to her.

She'll want them, Bobby said.

Victoria Roubideaux.

They started about noon. That was on a Tuesday. Then she delivered about noon on Wednesday, so it was still a good twelve hours longer than the old doctor had told her it would likely take. But on that Tuesday noon when they started they were not very heavy at first and she wasn't even sure what they were in the beginning, only that she had had the predictable cramps in her back which moved around to the front, and then in the next few hours they had come on more purposefully and she began to feel more certain then, and then she was both scared and proud, and she was pleased too.

But she didn't want to make any fuss. She wanted to do this right. She didn't want to be cheated by alarm or false emotion. So she didn't tell them right away, the old McPheron brothers, who were outside all afternoon with the cattle in the work corrals, checking the new cow-calf pairs in the bright warm late-spring afternoon. In the last two weeks the brothers had taken to staying in close to the house, ever since they'd driven her to the doctor, locating work for themselves to do in the barn or the corrals, and on those occasions when they both couldn't be nearby they had begun to take precautions so at least one of them was always close to the house, near enough to hear any call that the girl might make.

So on this Tuesday she had been in and out of her small bedroom throughout the afternoon, during those first few uncertain hours, busying herself with the new crib and the sheet and the blankets, and moving about in the neat little room, tidying up what wasn't untidy, straightening what wasn't out of order, dusting where no accumulation of dust had been allowed at any time since she had come back from Denver. And as a result she had everything about two times more than ready, and she had already packed and repacked at least twice whatever it was she would need to take with her to the hospital in the travel bag, including a nightgown and pads and baby clothes, all that the books said she would need, all that Maggie Jones had told her to take as well. Earlier she had thought that she would call Maggie on the day that the pains started, but she had decided against it now. She had decided she would call her later from the hospital when she had something certain to call about. She had a feeling about wanting this to happen just for herself. And just for them too, the old brothers, without others being involved. She thought they had earned that. So she busied herself about the house and about the little room and waited until they got harder and more definite, and then late in the afternoon, about five o'clock, she went out to the corrals where they were working and stood waiting at the board fence until they should look up from the cow and calf they were inspecting and see her. And then they did look up and she called to them:

It's started. I'm just telling you. But I don't want to go into town yet. It's too soon. He said it would be a while after they started, about twelve hours or so, he said, so there isn't any rush yet. I'm just telling you.

They were holding on to a big red calf, holding it down in the corral dirt on its side so they could check it, while its excited mother eyed them balefully from a distance of about ten feet. The McPheron brothers looked up at the girl. Then it was as if they had all at once, and both at the same moment, understood what it was that she was trying to tell them. They released the rope on the calf and it bawled and jumped up and trotted over to its mother, hiding behind her where the old cow had already begun to lick it into calmness and quiet, while the two men came hustling over to the fence across from where the girl stood and said, What's this? Are you sure?

Yes, she said.

And you're feeling all right? Raymond said.

I feel fine.

But you shouldn't even be out here, Harold said. You ought to be back there in the house.

I just came out to tell you, she said. That they started.

Yes but, he said—well damn it, Victoria, you shouldn't even be on your feet. You need to go back to the house. This ain't no place for you.

I'm all right, she said. I just wanted to tell you. I'll go back now.

She turned and started back. They stood together at the fence, watching her, this slight young heavy-laden girl with the long black hair fallen down her back, walking carefully, picking her steps slowly across the rutted gravel drive under the late afternoon sun. Then she stopped once out in the open before she got up to the house. She stood still, her head bowed, holding herself, waiting for it to pass, then after a time she raised her head again and she went on. Five minutes later the McPheron brothers, without saying anything to each other about it, without ever having to make any apparent decision whatsoever, turned all the mother cows and calves back out into the pasture, quit the work corral together and followed the girl, one after the other, directly into the house.

They found her lying on the old soft double bed in her room. They hovered over her. They let her know that they thought she should get up, they wanted to take her into town now, not to wait, that they thought that such would be better, safer, they didn't want to take any chances, they told her to take care and get up cautiously and they would drive her in right now, and that in effect altogether she should hurry up and do it in a slow way. But she simply looked at them and said again, Not yet. I don't want to be a bother and make a fool of myself.

So they waited the rest of the afternoon. They waited through the remainder of daylight. Then the sun started down and the air darkened. The brothers turned the lights on in the house. Raymond went out into the kitchen and made some supper for the three of them at the stove. Yet when it was ready the girl would not eat; she came out and sat with them for a while at the table and drank a little warm tea, but that was all. Once while she sat with them a pain came to her and she stared straight ahead, breathing, and when it was over she looked up and smiled at them and waved a little dismissively with her hand. They watched her from across the table, stricken. Presently she rose and went back into her room and lay down. The brothers looked at each other. After some time they got up and went in and sat down in the parlor under the single floor lamp and made a pretense at reading the *Holt Mercury*. It was very quiet. Every twenty minutes or so one or the other of them would rise and go in and stand at the doorway to look at her in the old bed.

Then about nine o'clock the girl came out of her little room into the dining room carrying her bag. She stopped beside the walnut table. I think we should go now, she said. I think it's time.

At the hospital the nurses asked her all the questions. Name, and expected date of confinement, and blood type, if the membranes had ruptured, and when, what the contractions were, how often, how long, where she felt them, what bleeding, the amount and color of it, movement of the baby, last food taken, what and when, what allergies, what medications. She answered these all with patience and thoroughness while the McPheron brothers stood in a kind of mute panic and intolerable outrage, waiting beside her at the counter, waiting for them to be done with this exasperation and waste of time and remove her to safety. Then the nurses wheeled her away into the labor room while the brothers waited behind in the hall, and she got out of her clothes into a loose hospital gown and the one nurse examined her and afterward said she was only three centimeters dilated, that was all. She asked if she could say again how long she had been feeling the pains. The girl told her. Then yes, she would very likely be a good while yet since she was no more dilated than that. Still, that was something no one could ever tell about, how long it would be, because she herself had seen cases where the babies came very fast once they had decided to start coming, and they could hope.

After an hour, when nothing was changed, the nurses allowed the McPheron brothers to come in and stay with the girl in the labor room. The girl had asked the nurses to let them. They came in very quietly and circumspectly, carrying their hats in their hands, as if they were attending some formal occasion or entering upon some religious service for which they were late due to circumstances beyond their control even though their best intentions had been otherwise, and sat down against the wall beside the bed and seemed reluctant at first even to look at her. It was a double room with a ceiling rail for a curtain to be drawn close around the bed, and the bed was raised so that the girl was sitting up in it. The nurses had started an i.v. and there was a monitor on a stand at the head of the bed. When they did look at her, her face appeared flushed and a little puffy. Her eyes had a dark look in them.

Did they tell you it may be a while yet? she said.

They nodded.

I should have waited, she said. I came in too soon.

No, now, Raymond said. You come just right. We come too late, if anything. This is a considerable lot better for you here, instead of out at the house.

I didn't want to be such a bother, she said. I thought I was closer.

No, Harold said. You done us a favor. We was going to get a little antsy waiting like that, miles out of town that way. We was pure ready to come in about five hours earlier, if you want to know.

I just wanted to have it right away and not for you to have to wait around. Now that's not going to happen.

Well, you can just stop concerning yourself about that, Raymond said. Don't you even think about us. You just take care of your own business there and you do what you need to do. And if there's something else we can do, you got to let us know. We don't know a thing about this. We don't know how to help you.

Well, Harold said, I guess we could go get the calf-puller. I reckon we know that much about getting new things born into this world.

She looked at him. There was a kind of blank look on her face.

Oh, hell, he said. You got to excuse me. I was trying for a joke. I didn't mean nothing, Victoria.

She shook her head a little and smiled. Her face was quite flushed and her teeth looked very white. I know that, she said. You can joke if you want to. I want you to. You're both so good to me. Then another pain came and they watched her tighten into herself in the bed, breathing and panting, her eyes closed. After a little while, when it was finished, she opened her eyes again but it was clear that her concentration was still focused on what was going on inside herself and nowhere else except there, and the McPheron brothers sat in the chairs against the wall near her bed and worried about her more than they had ever worried about anything in the last fifty years and watched it all and stayed with her into the night.

At midnight old Dr. Martin came in and said they might as well go home for a while. He had come in to check on the girl for himself and had found that she was still far from delivery. It wasn't that unusual, he said, since it was her first baby. He said he would be staying all night himself, sleeping at the hospital, and that the nurses would call him if she got closer, and the nurses could call them too, if that's what they wanted. But the McPheron brothers wouldn't leave. They stayed in the room and the girl managed to sleep a little between the contractions, taking little bits of naps occasionally, while beside the bed they sat up awake, silently, in a kind of daze, waiting with her. The nurses came in and out several times every hour to check on her and the brothers would have to step outside in the hall then, and then they would come back after the nurses were satisfied. It went on in that way through the night. By daybreak the McPheron brothers looked bad. Their faces looked as haggard and colorless as chalk, their eyes gone scratchy and red. The girl was relatively calm, though, and determined to do it right. She was very tired but she was all right. She was still concentrated and working hard. She begged them to go home and rest, but they would not leave at her request any more than they had at the doctor's.

Finally, at about nine o'clock in the morning, during one of the brief periods when they were waiting in the hallway, Harold said to his brother, At least one of us has got to go home and feed. You know that.

I'm not leaving, Raymond said.

I didn't think so. I figured as much. I'll be back, then. You stay here. You stay in here for both of us. I'll be back as soon as I can.

When they were allowed into the room again Harold told the girl what he was doing and she said, Yes, he should please do that, and he touched her on the arm and walked out. Raymond sat down again on the chair near her bed. When the contractions came he offered what encouragement he could think of to give her and she worked hard, and time continued to pass.

Then sometime later they told Raymond to step out into the hall again. He stood and waited for them to finish examining her but it took longer than usual, and then they came out, wheeling the girl on the bed and he saw her and she looked at him and smiled a little, and they took her on down the hallway before he could think to say anything to her at all or even to make some gesture of hope for her sake. One of the nurses informed him that Dr. Martin was giving her oxytocin by i.v. drip to accelerate the labor and they were moving to delivery now. The nurse said he should go outside and get some air, he looked like he needed it. One of them would find him afterward.

Is she going to be okay?

Yes. You mustn't worry.

He stood outside at the back entrance to the hospital in the fresh air and stood just breathing and waiting, not leaning against anything but simply standing away from the wall and the porch support as if he had been located there by some happenstance and told not to move or to lean against anything that might hold him up or support him until somebody should come and tell him he could do otherwise. No one else was out there. He stared toward the alley and the back parking lot. He stood, and didn't move. His arms dangled at his sides. An hour later Dr. Martin found him that way, still standing in a kind of rigid isolation on the back step.

McPheron?

Raymond slowly looked at him.

You can see her now.

Victoria?

Yes.

Is she alive?

What? Of course she is.

She's all right?

She's awake and she's talking. But she's tired. Don't you want to know about the baby?

What is it?

It's a girl.

And you say Victoria Roubideaux is all right.

Yes.

Raymond studied him.

And what you say, that's the truth.

Yes. I tell you, she's all right.

I didn't know, Raymond said. I was afraid . . . Then roughly he stooped forward and took hold of old Dr. Martin's hand and pumped it hard, two times, and let it go, and then he started back inside.

She still had the baby with her in the bed lying on her chest when he entered the room in the maternity ward, and she was gazing at the baby, holding it close. She looked up when he came in, her eyes shining.

He says you're okay, Raymond said.

Yes. Isn't she beautiful? She turned the baby toward him.

He looked at it. The baby had a full thatch of crow-black hair and its red face was misshapen a little, pushed out of its true shape, and there was a scratch on its cheek, and he thought in his inexperience that the baby looked like an old man, that it resembled nothing so much as some old wrinkled grandpa, but he said, Yes, she's a beautiful little thing.

You want to hold her?

Oh, I don't know about that.

You can.

I don't want to harm her.

You won't. Here. You've got to support her head.

He took the baby in her white hospital blankets and looked at her, holding her fearfully out in front of his old face as though she were a piece of rigid but delicate kitchen crockery.

My goodness, he said after a minute. The baby's eyes looked up at him without blinking. Well, my my. My lord almighty.

While he was holding the baby, Harold came into the room. They said I'd find you in here now, he said. You're all right?

Yes, the girl said. It's a little girl. You can hold her too.

Harold was still dressed in his work clothes, with hay dust on the shoulders of his canvas chore jacket, bringing with him the smell of the outdoors and of cattle and of sweat. I better not get over-close, he told her. I'm not tidy.

You can just wrap the blanket around her tighter, she said. She's got to get used to you sometime.

So he took the baby in his turn too, and Raymond sat down and patted the girl's arm. She was tired and ashen and blurry.

Well then, Harold said, well then, looking at the baby girl. He held her before him and she looked back at him unblinking just as she had looked at his brother, as though she were studying the make of his character. I'm going to tell you what, Harold said. I believe we have just doubled our womenfolk. But I reckon it's something we can get used to.

Then a different nurse came in and she was angry and said they were not even supposed to be in there, didn't they know that, not in the maternity room when the baby was in the room, because they were not the husband, were they, they were not the father, and she told them they would have to leave at once, and besides the girl needed to sleep, couldn't they see she was exhausted, and then she complained bitterly about the baby needing to stay clean and sterile and she took the baby away. But neither the McPheron brothers nor the girl objected to the nurse, because things were all right now; the girl had had the baby satisfactorily after all, and the baby she had delivered was a healthy little clear-eyed girl with her mother's own black hair, and that was everything anybody in the town of Holt or anywhere else in the world had any right to hope for, and so it was all right.

The next morning, an hour after sunrise, the man at the Holt County frozen food locker on Main Street called Dr. Martin at his home about the half-steer. He wanted to know what the doctor wanted him to do with it.

With what? the old doctor said.

This meat here.

What meat?

McPherons'. They showed up about an hour ago this morning and made me open before I was anywhere near ready, before I even had my morning coffee. With two whole butchered-out hindquarters of prime young black baldy steer. What do you want me to do with it, is what I'm calling about. They said it was yours.

Mine?

They said you'd know why.

The hell they did.

That's what they said.

All right, the old doctor said. I suppose I do then. I expect I might even have earned it too. Then his voice rose in pitch. Well, hold on to it, for christsake. Don't give it away. I'll be down there just as soon as I can get dressed.

Ike and Bobby.

Eight days school had been let out. But the town swimming pool was not yet opened in the park. The summer baseball program had not yet taken up. The fair and carnival rides would not be starting until the first week of August.

In the mornings the two boys delivered the paper and came home and did the chores at the barn, fed Easter and the dog and the cats, then went up to the house to breakfast. Three afternoons a week Guthrie was teaching a summer class for the community college in Phillips. And their mother was still living in Denver. They were to understand that their mother was going to stay living there in Denver from now on. Often in the mornings they rode out along the tracks on Easter and took their lunch and once rode as far as the little cemetery halfway to Norka where there was a stand of cottonwood trees with their leaves washing and turning in the wind, and they ate a lunch there in the freckled shade of the trees and came back in the late afternoon with the sun sliding down behind them, making a single shadow of them and the horse together, the shadow out in front like a thin dark antic precursor of what they were about to become. School had been let out eight days already, and they were alone much of the time.

On an afternoon when Guthrie was in Phillips, teaching, they walked out on the railroad tracks on the creosoted cross ties between the rails going west and walked out past the old man's house and then on past the abandoned house at the end of Railroad Street and it was hot and dry. Walking a mile and more farther west on the black ties between the shining twin rails along the red ballast. Then they stopped at a railroad cutout gouged through a low sandhill, and they got out the coins and the glue bottle from their pockets.

So the four bright coins lay stuck now on the hot rail, glued and waiting, the four denominations in a row, penny, nickel, dime, and quarter, while the high afternoon sun glinted on them, copper and silver alike, and shone on her bracelet too from the chest of drawers where they had taken it from the guest room where she had left it months ago, the one they had tried on their own wrists that once, before they had climbed up to the apartment and discovered Mrs. Iva Stearns already dead five hours in her chair. At first they hadn't seen how to rest the bracelet on the rail with the four coins since it would not lie down flat, since on its side it would most likely flip off when the first big driving wheel of the engine hit it, to go spinning off in the air like some piece of glittering ice or glass to land in the cheetweed and redroot where they'd have to look for it and maybe not even find it again, because they had lost pennies and quarters that way before, before they had learned to use the single little drop of glue. Then they hit on the expedient of fitting it over the rail as though it were fitting over an arm and tried it, and it worked satisfactorily like that. So it was hooked over the rail below the coins now, waiting too. And the train would be coming soon.

They waited. They were squatted back fifteen feet from the raised railbed in the cutout, their backs against the high embankment, shaded by the sheered red dirt. No one out on the

high plain could have seen them, had anybody been looking at this hour late in May in the middle of the afternoon. Ike
got out two of Guthrie's cigarettes from his shirt pocket and
handed Bobby one. He took out a box of matches from his
pocket and struck one and lit their cigarettes, first his then his
brother's, and poked the burning match head into the dirt. It
made a little white puff when the flame was extinguished. They
smoked and waited. After a little while they spat, one after the
other, between their feet on the dirt. There wasn't any train
coming yet. They smoked and held the cigarettes out in front to
see and then drew on them and blew smoke and looked at each
other, and smoked again. It wasn't coming yet. Ike spat in a
looping arc toward the rail. Bobby spat likewise, railward. They
smoked the cigarettes down and put them out. Then Ike stood
up and looked up the track. He couldn't see it yet, not its light
nor its black shimmering bulk, and he stepped up to the trackbed and lay along the track holding his ear to the rail. After a
while his eyes changed. It's coming, he said. Here it comes.

You can't tell from that, Bobby said.

It's coming, Ike said. His head was next to the rail. I hear it.

Bobby got up and listened too. Okay, he said. So once more
they crouched together against the dirt embankment within
its shade, waiting for the train. There was a grasshopper on the
weeds, watching them, chewing its mouth. Ike threw a piece of
dirt at it and it hopped onto the track. The train came on from a
distance, whistling sudden and long at a mile crossing. They
waited. The coins and her bracelet were out on the track. After
a time they could see the train, dark-looming in the haze. It
came on and got louder, bigger, and appeared as terrific as if it
were dreamed, shaking the ground, the grasshopper still watching the two boys, and then the train was on them. They looked
at the man standing high above inside the roaring locomotive
and dirt was flying everywhere in the air in a white gale so sudden and violent that they had to protect their eyes, then its long
string of freight cars was rushing past, clattering and squealing,

whistling, a loose rattling clacking noise, the joint in the iron rail before them dipping as the wheels passed, carrying the weight, and then it was gone and the man in the caboose looked back at them and they stared back, not waving. When the train was far down the tracks they rose and picked up the coins and her bracelet.

In the shade of the cutbank they squatted and inspected what they had now. The coins were misshapen oval disks, the profiled heads of the presidents like ghostly shadows, bright, shiny, out-of-round. The faces in outline only, no depth or texture, no dimension. Her bracelet was flattened the same, thin as paper, they could break it. They turned the coins over in their hands and regarded the bracelet, and after a while they poked a hole in the dirt and buried the four coins together with their mother's bracelet in the dirt under the sheered bank and put a rock over the place.

You going to want to smoke again? Ike said.

Yes.

All right.

He got out two more of the cigarettes from his shirt pocket and together they sat smoking fifteen feet back from the tracks in the shade. They watched out into the sun on the trackbed and neither talked nor moved for some time.

McPherons.

When they came up to the house from the horse barn in the afternoon near the end of the month they saw there was a black car parked at the gate in front of the house. They didn't recognize it.

Who's that?

Nobody I know, Harold said.

The car had a Denver license plate. They went on around it and up the walk onto the porch. Inside the house they found him sitting at the walnut table in the dining room seated across from the girl. She was holding the baby. He was a tall thin young man and he didn't get up when they came in.

I come back to take her with me, he said. And the baby too. My daughter.

So that's who you are, Harold said.

He and the old McPheron brothers looked at one another.

You don't stand up when somebody enters the room in his own house, Harold said.

Not usually, no, the boy said.

This is Dwayne, the girl said.

I reckoned it must be. What do you want here?

I told you, he said. I come back for what belongs to me. Her and the baby too.

I'm not going though, the girl said.

Yeah, he said. You are.

Do you want to go, Victoria? Raymond said.

No. I'm not going. I told him. I'm not leaving here.

Oh yeah, she's coming. She's just playing hard to get. She just wants to be coaxed.

No, I don't. That's not it.

Son, Harold said. I reckon you better leave. Nobody wants you here. Victoria's made that pretty clear. And Raymond and me damn sure don't have any use for you.

I'll leave when she gets ready, the boy said. Go on, he said to the girl. Go get your stuff together.

No.

Go on, like I told you.

I'm not going.

Son. Are you kind of hard of hearing? You heard her and now you heard me.

And you heard me, the boy said. Goddamn it, he said to the girl, go on now. Get your things. Hurry up.

No.

The boy jumped up and started around the table and grabbed her by the arm. He pulled her up out of the chair.

Goddamn it, do it. Like I been telling you. Now move.

The two brothers came around the table toward him.

Son. Now you leave her alone. Let go of her.

The boy jerked her arm. The baby fell to the floor and was shocked and began to wail. And she jerked loose and squatted to pick her up. The baby was crying wildly.

I'm sorry, he said. I didn't mean that. Just come on. She's mine too.

No, the girl cried. I'm not going. We're not going.

That's enough, Harold said. That'll do. The brothers took

him by the arms and he started to fight them, and they lifted him off his feet, squirming and twisting and caterwauling, and carried him out the door, and they were hard and determined and stronger than he was, and they took him outside down the steps through the yard gate.

Let go of me.

On the gravel drive they released him.

The boy looked at them. All right, he said. I'm going, for now.

Don't come back.

You haven't heard the last of me, he said.

Don't you ever come back bothering her again.

He turned and went on to the car and got in and started it and turned around, spraying up gravel behind him, and roared out past the house into the lane and onto the county road. The McPheron brothers went back into the house. The girl had the baby in her arms, sitting at the old table again. The baby was quieted to a whimper now.

You all right, Victoria? Raymond said.

Yes.

Did he hurt you?

No. But he scared me. I tried to hold him here, talking till you came up to the house, hoping you would. I packed some things, taking my time, hoping you'd come up to the house as soon as you could.

Do you reckon he'll come back? Harold said.

No.

But he might. Is that what you think?

I don't know. Maybe he will. But I think he just wanted to make a show.

You didn't want to go with him, did you? Raymond said.

No. I want to be here. This is where I want to be now.

All right. That's what's going to happen then.

The girl turned and unbuttoned her blouse and began

to nurse the baby and it stopped whimpering, and the old McPheron brothers looked away from the girl out into the room.

Holt.

Memorial Day. The two women came out onto the steps of the porch in the evening with the light behind them burning in the kitchen, visible through the open door, backlighting them. Except for the discrepancy in their sizes, they might have been mother and daughter. Their dark hair was damp about their faces and their quiet faces were flushed from the hot kitchen, from the cooking. Behind them in the dining room the table had been pulled open and the leaves put in and the white table-cloth laid on, and afterward the table had been laid with tall candles and with the old china the girl had discovered in the high shelves of the kitchen, the old dishes that had been unused for decades, that were chipped and faded but still serviceable.

Alone at the table the old white-haired man, Maggie Jones's old father, sat facing the windows, waiting without words or complaint, a dish towel already tied about his neck. He stared across at the uncurtained windows in some thought of his own that was long familiar to him. Absently he took up the silver from beside his plate and held it in his hands, waiting. Suddenly he spoke into the air. Hello. Is anybody there?

On the porch the women looked out into the yard where the two boys were seated in the swing with the baby and farther out toward the barn lot and the work corral where the three men stood at the fence, each with a booted foot crooked on the bottom rail, an elbow slung over the top rail, comfortable, talking.

The boys had the baby in a glider swing, rocking her a little in the evening, this little thatch-haired black-eyed girl. Guthrie had said an hour earlier, I don't know about this. They might be careless with her, forget her for a moment. But the girl had said, No they won't. I know they'll take good care of her. And Maggie Jones had said, Yes. To which Guthrie had said, But you boys be careful with her.

So they had the little girl in the glider under one of the stunted elm trees inside the old hogfencing wire, rocking her by turns on their laps in the cool evening, while the blue farmlight played over her face.

Meanwhile out at the work corrals the McPheron brothers and Guthrie looked over the fence at the cattle and calves. The red-legged cow was among them. Guthrie noticed her. The old cow eyed him with rancor. Is that her? he said. That same one I'm thinking of.

That's her.

Didn't she have a calf? I don't see one with her.

No sir. She was open all along, Raymond said.

She never threw a calf this spring?

No.

What do you plan to do with her?

We aim to take her to town, to the sale barn.

Harold looked out past the red cow toward the darkening horizon. We heard in town the Beckmans got theirselves a lawyer now, he said.

Yes, Guthrie said. I've been hearing that.

What'll you do?

I don't know yet. I haven't made up my mind. It depends on what comes of it. But I'll be all right. I'll do something else if I have to.

Not farming, Harold said.

No. Guthrie grinned. Not farming, he said. I can see what that leads to. He nodded back toward the house. What about her now?

We want to hope she'll be here for a good while yet, Raymond said. She has another year of school. Besides this last term she missed. She'll be here a while still, we believe. We sure hope she will.

She might want to go to college, Guthrie said.

We'd favor that. But there's time enough to think about that later. We don't have to think about that just yet, I don't guess we do.

Now the wind started up in the trees, high up, moving the high branches.

The barn swallows came out and began to hunt leaf-bugs and lacewinged flies in the dusk.

The air grew soft.

The old dog came out from its rug in the garage and wandered into the fenced yard and sniffed the boys' pantslegs and sniffed the baby and licked its hot red tongue across the baby's forehead, and then it scuttled up to the women on the porch and looked up at them, and looked all around and turned in a circle and lay down, flopping its matted tail in the dirt.

The two women stood letting the breeze blow coolly on their faces, and they opened the fronts of their blouses a little to let it play on their breasts and under their arms.

And soon, very soon now, they would call them in to supper. But not just yet. They stood on the porch a while longer in the evening air seventeen miles out south of Holt at the very end of May.

KENT HARUF

The Tie That Binds

PICADOR

In his critically acclaimed first novel, Kent Haruf delivers the sweeping tale of eighty-year-old Edith Goodnough. Narrated by her neighbour, Edith's tragedies unfold: a tough childhood, a mother's death, a violence that leaves a father dependent on his children, forever enraged. She is a woman who sacrifices everything in the name of family – until she is forced to reclaim her freedom in one dramatic and unexpected gesture. Breathtaking and truthful, *The Tie That Binds* is a powerful tribute to the demands of rural life, and to the tenacity of the human spirit.

'A novel which dramatically and accurately explores the lives of people who work the land in the stark American Middle West'
New York Times Book Review

KENT HARUF

Where You Once Belonged

PICADOR

Heavy-built Jack Burdette is quite literally too big for his boots – and too big, certainly for the small-town attitudes of Holt, Colorado. But when he fails to make the grade as a college footballer, and takes a job with the local farmers' co-operative, it seems he has finally settled into the rhythm and routine of everyday life. Outward appearances can be deceptive, however, as Jack proves: returning from a weekend conference with a new wife in tow, then leaving her behind and skipping town with a bundle of other folks' money.

Nearly a decade later, no one has forgiven or forgotten, and when Jack reappears, resentment runs high. Once again though, it is Jack whose presence – even more than his eight-year absence – proves the most devastating.

'Each phrase is spare and straightforward, yet out of all of them together, an extraordinary poetry emerges'
Los Angeles Times

KENT HARUF

Eventide

PICADOR

Welcome to Holt County, Colorado. Home to Victoria Roubideaux, the McPheron brothers, Tom Guthrie and Maggie Jones.

Eloquent and evocative, *Eventide* continues the story begun in *Plainsong*, introducing new characters alongside familiar faces: Betty and Luther, struggling to keep their heads above water and their children out of care; eleven-year-old DJ and his cantankerous grandfather Walter; DJ's friend Dena, her mother and sister, all of whom are adjusting to a home without the girls' father.

'This is a novel that succeeds in affirming life without ducking its hardships. A rural soap opera written by a poet'
Mail on Sunday

'*Eventide* is imbued with an unspoken affection that transforms the commonplace into specific, intimate and moving reality'
Times Literary Supplement